ADVANCE PRAISE FOR
CITY OF GRUDGES

"*City of Grudges* captures my hometown of Pensacola, Florida, much the same way *Midnight in the Garden of Good and Evil* immortalized Savannah. Rick Outzen's Southern thriller moves his colorful characters through the corruption of small town politics under the piercing gaze of Walker Holmes—a newspaper publisher that his friends either want to drink with or punch out. Readers get a gripping front row seat of Walker's wild ride."

—JOE SCARBOROUGH
Host of MSNBC's *Morning Joe*, former congressman (R-FL)

"Outzen's twenty-year experience as a newspaper journalist has shaped him into an innovative and skilled storyteller. His first novel captures the voice of the Deep South in a way that would make Flannery O'Connor proud. I hope *City of Grudges* is only the beginning of a long series of books we see from this writer."

—MIKE PAPANTONIO
Bestselling author of *Law and Disorder* and *Law and Vengeance*

"With *City of Grudges*, Rick Outzen directs the Florida glare onto his adopted city of Pensacola as brilliantly as Carl Hiaasen has done for so many years for South Florida. Corruption, dead bodies, and smooth, wise-cracking dialogue pile up as quickly as cars in a I-10 fender-bender. The newspaperman-as-hero is in safe, entertaining hands with this experienced journalist, so move over all you Florida crime novelists—there's a new pen in town!"

—W. HODDING CARTER
Author of *Stolen Water: Saving the Everglades from Its Friends, Foes, and Florida* and five other critically acclaimed books of nonfiction

CITY OF
GRUDGES

CITY OF GRUDGES

RICK OUTZEN

SelectBooks, Inc.
New York

This edition published by SelectBooks, Inc.

For information address SelectBooks, Inc., New York, New York.

First Edition

ISBN 978-1-59079-443-2

Library of Congress Cataloging-in-Publication Data

Names: Outzen, Rick, author.
Title: City of grudges / Rick Outzen.
Description: First edition. | New York : SelectBooks, Inc., 2018.
Identifiers: LCCN 2017020722 | ISBN 9781590794432 (pbk. book : alk. paper)
Subjects: LCSH: Newspaper publishing--Fiction. | City and town
life--Fiction.
| Secrecy--Fiction. | Corruption--Fiction. | Homicide--Fiction. |
Malicious accusation--Fiction. | Pensacola (Fla.)--Fiction. | GSAFD:
Mystery fiction.
Classification: LCC PS3615.U98 C58 2018 | DDC 813/.6--dc23 LC record
available at https://lccn.loc.gov/2017020722

Manufactured in the United States of America

10 9 8 7 6 5 4 3 2 1

"I have stood with my elders and betters and dared the ill-doers to do their worst.

I have read and glorified in the defiant paeans of editors who are obscure save in the hushed lodges of their homelands.

This is America. I thank God that I have contributed something to its story."

—Hodding Carter, II, the late publisher and editor of the *Delta Democrat Times*, Quotation is from *Their Words Were Bullets: The Southern Press in War, Reconstruction, and Peace*

1

begged for a hint of a breeze. The early morning humidity in Pensacola made it difficult to clear my head and focus on the problems that needed to be solved by afternoon. The late night drinking at Intermission hadn't helped.

I contemplated this as Big Boy, my seven-year-old chocolate Labrador/beagle/who-knows-what mix, tugged me down Jefferson Street for a daily jog, our only regular exercise before the blazing sun moved across the sky.

To be clear, no one would ever mistake me, Walker Holmes, for a runner. My wardrobe didn't include any bright orange or lime green shorts that matched a tight tank top or the stripes of expensive running shoes. I hated coordinated outfits.

My shoes were five-year-old Reebok tennis shoes that I found at a yard sale. I wore wrinkled khaki shorts speckled with white paint from when I painted an old dresser that was bought at the same sale and a Sandshaker Lounge T-shirt that I won when an Alabama redneck bet he could knock me off my bar stool with one punch.

Though not a fighter, I knew how to take a punch. Growing up Roman Catholic in the Protestant-dominated Mississippi Delta had taught me that. The trick was to move ever so slightly so that the blow only glanced off me. In this instance, the sunburned would-be pugilist sat on the stool next to me and was so drunk he was barely upright. When he launched his roundhouse, I leaned inside his punch and swayed for a few seconds as his blow struck the back of my shoulder. But I remained on my stool.

The last part of my ensemble, which was not an ensemble, was my Los Angeles Dodgers baseball cap that the damn dog had chewed out of spite one morning when I was too hungover to get out of bed.

Big Boy stretched his leash to the point of choking. He pulled me south, down the street past Seville Quarter's parking lot where a couple of taxis were dropping off their disheveled, half-dressed customers so the young professionals could recover their cars and drive home for a shower and change of clothes before reporting to work.

My dog ignored them and jerked me towards Pensacola Bay, forcing me into a run several times. Well, sort of. It was more like a series of lurches punctuated by the dog stopping at irregular intervals to sniff a weed in the sidewalk or whiz on a tree. He was smart enough—or maybe just taking mercy on me—to not cross my path too closely. Otherwise I would have fallen on my face. I tended to walk with my eyes closed for the first few minutes of every morning outing to let myself acclimate to the sun as it peeked over the horizon.

The downtown streets were quiet, with no traffic. A gaggle of slim, half-dressed men sprinted by as they did every morning, snickering at my ratty attire as they passed. They wore matching neon shorts and no shirts. Big Boy growled. I imagined him taking bites out of their color-coordinated butts.

A bald, large black man named Tiny greeted us as we passed the Bodacious Brew. "When you gonna put my pretty face on the cover of your newspaper?" he said, smiling and tossing Big Boy a piece of his cinnamon bun.

Tiny was an Iraq War veteran with no visible means of support. I wasn't sure where he slept at night, but he bussed tables at the coffee shop in exchange for breakfast and lunch. He refused to go on their payroll.

He wore a Pensacola Marathon T-Shirt that someone had given to him, and his shorts and shoes were better than mine. He was on a break sitting at a table on the sidewalk outside the Bodacious Brew watching *Fox & Friends* on the flat-screen TV above the door.

"Well, Mayor, not this week," I said, "but maybe next month. When can we set up the photo shoot?"

"It's about time you write about me, the mayor of Palafox," he said, as he petted the dog. "I have a lot to say."

"I'm sure you do, but I'm not sure we're the right medium for your story," I said, pointing to the television. "Have you heard from your friends at Fox News?"

Tiny shook his head. "No, but I'll write them again today."

I gave the man a dollar as I did most mornings to contribute to the postage. Big Boy and I crossed Main Street and continued toward the bay.

The humidity soaked the Sandshaker Lounge T-shirt. No breeze came off the water. Both the dog and I panted. Thirty-five minutes. That's how long I had to endure this torture to work off Tuesday night's beer.

Wednesday morning usually was my favorite day of the week. We had gotten the week's issue of the *Pensacola Insider*, the newspaper I owned, to the printer, and we shifted to planning mode. We caught our breath and talked about what worked or didn't work with last week's issue. Our next press deadline was six days away.

This Wednesday was different. I had to testify against my friend, Bowman Hines, a man I thought I knew, but who had played me and Pensacola as a bunch of fools. The town's golden boy would stand trial for embezzlement because of my reporting.

However, Pensacola didn't want to see Bo Hines disgraced. I had become the town's pariah. The trial would be my opportunity to save my reputation, validate my reporting, and avert the demise of my newspaper.

The dog and I jogged, walked, and stumbled past the Trillium property, thirty acres of vacant land on Pensacola Bay that sat across from Pensacola City Hall. The property was once the site of a gasoline terminal where barges offloaded fuel from Louisiana and Texas refineries. The fuel was stored in huge tanks and shipped by trucks to gas stations along the Florida panhandle.

In the early 1980s, Phillips 66 closed the facility after the Florida Department of Environmental Protection discovered the soil was contaminated. The oil company determined the terminal wasn't profitable enough for them to pay for a massive cleanup and left Pensacola.

A few years later, the city bought the property for $3.5 million.

Our paper supported the public-private partnership that had won the city's approval to build a maritime park. This would include a baseball stadium, maritime museum, and commercial development with a huge public space on the waterfront.

Just as the project was to about to begin, Jace Wittman, a former city councilman and Bo Hines' brother-in-law, notified the City of Pensacola that he planned to lead a petition drive to halt the construction. Wittman had opposed the project when he served on the council and had already forced one referendum on the park. He lost both the vote on the park and his reelection bid. His new angle was to claim the construction plan was not what the voters had approved.

Why did Wittman oppose the maritime park? He said it was because the city government had not allowed for enough time for citizens to voice their opinions on how the land should be developed, but the real reason, I learned, was that it was because Stan Daniels supported it. In high school, Daniels had beaten him out for the quarterback position at Pensacola Catholic High School. It was rumored that Wittman never forgave him for this.

"Grudges—" my late mentor Roger Fairley had told me over dirty martinis at Global Grill, "Pensacola runs on them."

I could still see my old friend stirring the drink and plucking the green olive off the toothpick. He said, "When you can't figure out the grudge, go back to high school. It will be some slight over a girl, sport, or class honor—or maybe even something much deeper."

Apparently Wittman would fight Daniels' park project for the rest of his life because of a grudge over not making quarterback on the high school football team.

Progress be damned. Forget the plan to revitalize downtown Pensacola after the ravaging by Hurricane Ivan. The hell with the jobs the development would generate. Wittman had to humiliate and defeat Daniels, and he could care less about the negative impact on the City of Pensacola.

"Grudges are the lifeblood of Pensacola," Roger told me. "Remember, we are the site of the first European settlement in North America. Before St. Augustine, Jamestown, and Plymouth, Don Tristan de Luna landed on Pensacola Beach. Within days of celebrating the first Mass in America, a hurricane wiped out the settlement. The settlers wanted to lynch Luna and almost did."

Roger and I had often enjoyed a few cocktails on Tuesday night before he headed off for choir practice. I had no idea what his singing voice was like but knew he had a crush on the female choir director. She was half his age, which meant she was in her forties.

"She doesn't know that I'm not as harmless as I look," he said with a smile. Roger had always dressed up for choir practice. He often wore a seersucker suit with a bow tie and white buck shoes. His thinning gray hair was combed over to hide some new bandage on his scalp or ear.

Roger battled cancer but never complained. I rarely mentioned the bandages or the fedora he had worn the last few months before he died.

"For the next four hundred and fifty years after the hurricane, Pensacola has repeatedly tried to recapture the excitement of the Conquistadors and the first settlers when they entered Pensacola Bay and achieve its potential," said Roger, before paying our tab as he always did.

"What has held it back?" he continued. "Grudges."

When the dog and I got back to our loft, I stripped off the damp T-shirt as we climbed the three floors past the back entrance of the restaurant on the first floor and the *Insider's* offices on the second to our apartment on the third floor. I put on the coffee, filled Big Boy's bowl with water, and jumped into the shower. As I toweled off, I glanced into the mirror and saw a six-foot-tall Mississippi Delta boy with brown hair that was starting to gray on the temples and what some called "piercing" blue eyes. My forty-one-year-old face still seemed youthful enough, even with a few faint distinguishing scars on both cheeks, nose, and a corner of the mouth from fights long forgotten. The belly had thickened some, but I could still see my feet.

I turned on the television to watch a few minutes of the local morning news before I walked downstairs to our offices. Everyone else owned flat screens, but my TV still had a booty and occasionally lost its color.

Bo Hines was on the screen. A local hero and the symbol of what made Pensacola great, people always tried to curry his and his wife Sue's favor. His smile made everyone feel that all was right in the world. If he chaired a charity event, the donations poured in, especially when he served as the master of ceremonies and auctioneer. He coaxed thousands of dollars out of the wallets and purses of those sipping fine wines and bourbon. Yes, everyone loved him.

And I was responsible for his arrest

I turned up the volume. The morning host, who showed none of the aftereffects of celebrating her promotion to the anchor spot on the ten o'clock news with her buddies at Intermission the previous night, said, "Mr. Hines, what prompted you to write a $25,000 check to help the Warrington Middle School buy new band instruments?"

Hines smiled. "When my wife Sue heard of the fire that destroyed the school's band room, she insisted we do something."

The station showed video of the smoldering blaze that was caused by lightning. He said, "Sue and I have always been committed to children, public education, and the arts."

The host said, "Earlier this year, the governor bestowed upon you the prestigious Patron of Florida Culture in recognition of your long history of supporting arts and culture—"

Hines cut her off, "Yes, but we don't do what we do for any recognition. It's about giving back to a community that helped raise me." The only thing missing was applause from the station crew.

Reluctantly the TV host brought up his pending trial. Bo acted like nothing was wrong in his world.

"Mr. Hines, your trial for embezzlement and organized fraud starts today. Would you like to comment?"

Hines smiled, even broader. "I'm guilty of nothing but placing too much trust in an executive director of a nonprofit—who still hasn't been located, I might add. I was a volunteer who signed the checks and raised funds, nothing more. My attorneys and I are confident my name will be cleared of all charges. The trial might not even last beyond tomorrow."

I felt like bashing my head against a wall. The man was a fake. Why was I the only one who saw it?

The trouble with being a publisher of a small town weekly paper is that you can't control the facts or where they may lead you. The path can be surprising and appalling. The facts can destroy lives and shatter dreams forever. But they remain the facts, immutable and damning.

I had spent days agonizing over the story about Hines. People don't like to see their heroes disgraced, not ones that they have known all their lives. What made this especially hard for me was that the man was my friend.

The first time I met Bowman Hines was three years earlier when he asked for my help with the Surfer's Ball, a fundraiser to help victims of domestic violence.

Bo stood six foot two inches tall and was tanned and lean with a dazzling smile. His blonde hair blended with a little gray was still unusually full for someone in his mid-fifties and always stayed in place, defying all laws of physics. The *Pensacola Insider* had facilitated the formation of the Pensacola Young Professionals to give those under forty, like me at the time, a more organized voice to weigh in on issues like the maritime park, and I had served on its board until my fortieth birthday. PYP also helped potential *Insider* advertisers visualize our paper's readership. Bo wanted to tap into PYP for his fundraiser and needed my help to make the event cool enough to bring fresh dollars into the kitty.

Eighty thousand dollars later we became friends, or as good friends as an alt-weekly publisher who was focused on battling injustices and challenging the status quo can be with someone like Bo. Over countless mugs of beers and baskets of spicy buffalo wings, we brainstormed on how to pull Pensacola into the twenty-first century. The conversations were deep enough to put Bo on my very short Christmas card list—if I ever got around to sending Christmas cards.

Bowman Hines grew up in Pensacola. His grandparents, Dr. Louis Bowman and his wife, Sarah, raised him. Bo's parents had died in a car accident on Interstate 10 when they were driving home from a Florida State University football game, back when head coach Bill Peterson finally had the team winning games. The Florida Highway Patrol found nine-year-old Bo strapped in the back by his seat belt, unharmed. "A miracle"—that's how Dr. Lou described it on the front page of the *Pensacola Herald*.

Pensacolans watched young Bo grow up and were filled with admiration as he became an Eagle Scout, won the Optimist Speech contest, and was the star quarterback the year that Pensacola's Booker T. Washington High Wildcats were state champions. Scholarship offers poured in. Of course, Bo chose Florida State. He was redshirted his freshman year and sat on the bench during the 1974 and 1975 seasons. In 1976,

Coach Bobby Bowden was hired and switched Bo to linebacker. His senior year, FSU won ten games, lost two, and beat Texas Tech University in the Tangerine Bowl. Bo made second team All-American. The Pensacola Sports Association honored him as its college athlete of the year.

After graduating, Bo passed on the NFL draft and got an MBA while working as a graduate assistant for Coach Bowden. He came home to Pensacola and married Sue Eaton, another Pensacola native. Bishop Roberto Garcia presided over the wedding that rivaled Prince Charles and Princess Diana's ceremony. Both weddings took place in July 1981. The wedding dress—designed and dreamed up by the French fashion designers who made spare money in New Orleans and Mobile during Mardi Gras—created a sensation.

When the couple returned from their Bali honeymoon, Bo bought a dump truck with a loan from his grandfather and began his road construction company, hauling gravel at first. He eventually built his own asphalt plant, which led to his dominance of much of the state, county, and city road work in Northwest Florida and South Alabama. Pensacola's golden boy could do no wrong.

For years Bo chaired the Florida Panhandle Arts Council, a nonprofit organization that supported many of the cultural groups in the area, including the Pensacola Opera, Pensacola Little Theatre, Pensacola Symphony, and dozens of art galleries.

He and his wife Sue put on huge galas and auctions at the Saenger Theatre that raised thousands for the arts. These affairs always had elaborate silent auctions and lasted until two in the morning. Everyone came, and everyone enjoyed themselves—even old Phyllis Longfellow, the *Pensacola Herald's* society columnist, who liked to tell people that Sue was tacky and Bo was nothing more than an overgrown fraternity boy.

The governor of Florida put Bo on the state arts commission. He honored Bo with the coveted Patron of Florida Culture Award, which got his handsome, smiling face on *Florida Trend* magazine.

In March 2010, I had decided to write a personal profile of my friend Bo for the *Insider* and maybe tease him a little, but also show how much his efforts meant to the arts and culture in Pensacola. However, I found I had a problem. Some of the executive directors of the cultural groups gave me less than glowing reviews of my friend. They replied to my questions with stilted answers, and a few board members didn't even return my phone calls.

I finally tracked down a former art gallery director who had moved to St. Louis. He told me the reason few wanted to talk about Bo Hines and the Florida Panhandle Arts Council. He said Bo's Arts Council was a sham.

Apparently little of the money ever made it to the art galleries, opera, symphony, or community theater. When the arts groups received their grant checks from the Arts Council, they were dated months earlier, as if they had sat in a desk drawer somewhere before being mailed. The amounts were often much less than promised. But since this was Bo Hines, the millionaire road contractor, they assumed there was some mistake.

When the executive directors and board chairs of the cultural groups called him, Bo always had an excuse about the delay. And for the first year or so, the checks kept coming, even if they were late and less than expected. Then the payments stopped altogether. Payroll checks bounced. Rent and utility bills fell behind. My source still had paychecks that he couldn't cash.

When I asked about it, Bo tried to bluff his way through my questions. When I told him that this wasn't a smart move, my normally affable friend suddenly became guarded and evasive. Then he quit taking my calls. I felt like he was daring me to write the article.

Bo would understand my predicament. I had friends and, more critically, advertisers, who wouldn't appreciate this story, even if I proved every allegation. The easiest course of action would have been to walk away and hope the *Pensacola Herald* picked up the story.

My closest friend in Pensacola, Dare Evans, begged me to put off publishing the article. She and I had known each other since our freshman year at Ole Miss. I had a few high school pals that I occasionally called to catch up with, mostly on birthdays and during the Christmas holidays, but Dare was a constant in my life. Dare was my sounding board, my fiercest defender, and one of the few people who really knew me.

Dare felt I needed to find the Arts Council executive director and interview her. She had two valid reasons. The first was that no matter how well I wrote it, Dare knew the article was going to cost me advertisers, something I really couldn't afford.

"Walker, why are you so hell bent on self-destruction?" Dare said over glasses of wine at Blazzues after she had read my first draft. "I don't understand your death wish mentality. Do you want the town to hate you? Take the time to get it right."

"Dammit, I do have it right," I said. "Bo stole that money and the executive director bolted because she is afraid to testify."

"You don't know that for sure," she said.

"I'm convinced I have this right. You're letting your friendship with Sue color your analysis."

And that was her second reason. Sue and Dare had been nearly inseparable since Dare's husband died. They played tennis regularly, dined at Jackson's or Pensacola Yacht Club at least twice a week, and took vacations together. Because of Dare, Sue had become my friend before I ever met Bo.

"That's not fair, Walker," Dare said. "You're too stubborn to admit I'm right. You want the glory of breaking this story."

I shook my head, "No . . ."

"It's always the story. Well, this one will have no glory. You will be vilified, and I can't, I won't rescue you."

Dare stood, grabbed a twenty-dollar bill out of her purse, and threw it on the table. "I won't. You will hurt people that I care about."

Even though Dare might have been right, I couldn't back down. I had already gone through all the stages of grief—denial, anger, and finally acceptance. The man I thought I knew, the man that Pensacola loved, was a phony. Even worse, he was a crook.

I had no choice but to expose him.

So, I did. I reported the financial woes of the Arts Council. The next week the City of Pensacola and Escambia Board of County Commissioners, which each gave the nonprofit organization half a million dollars annually, called for an audit. They found nearly $200,000 was missing. The money had been stolen through a variety of schemes. Several checks had no supporting documentation. Some vendors appeared to have charged substantial markups for their goods and services. They claimed to have rebated part of the surcharge to the Arts Council, but the funds were deposited in a bank account that didn't show on the nonprofit's financial reports. Bank records showed a series of ATM withdrawals that gradually drained the mystery account.

Hines had signed the checks, the vendors' contracts, and the bank documents setting up the off-the-books account. Adding to the confusion, the paid executive director of the Arts Council had vanished.

The state attorney's office reviewed the audit and my article and indicted Bo Hines. He pled not guilty and refused to waive his right to a speedy trial, which placed the case on the June docket.

The public reacted as Dare predicted, not to defrock its favorite son but to attack me. The *Pensacola Herald* jumped immediately and ferociously to his defense and gave me, the accuser, a severe beating. They cast doubts over my reporting and alluded that the real culprit was the sloppy bookkeeping of the missing executive director. Hines was merely the victim of his soft heart that had kept him from firing the director. He wasn't aware of how bad the money and bookkeeping issues were.

Readers began to distrust my facts. They wanted to believe anything that maintained Hines' hero status. They reasoned that a guilty man wouldn't want to go to trial so quickly. Bo knew he was innocent, they thought, and he didn't want to waste any time in clearing his name. At the downtown restaurants and bars I frequented, longtime acquaintances turned their backs on me. But love, support, and comfort poured out for Hines.

Grudges fueled the public attacks on me. Hines' arrest and pending trial put blood in the water—not Bo's, but mine. And the sharks were swarming. They believed this could be the time to settle old scores with me, like the former assistant city manager who lost his job after we reported his golf junkets were financed by city vendors, the contractor who saw his string of no-bid contracts broken when we revealed the numerous cost overruns, and the county commissioner whose reelection and congressional aspirations evaporated after we disclosed how his hunting buddy's son wound up with a county job and six-figure salary. And those were only a few of my enemies that had waited years for the right opportunity to pounce.

I became the target of Pensacola's scorn. This would pass after the trial concluded, I hoped. Until then, I had little choice but to endure the disdain directed my way.

2

Dressed in my work clothes—starched white button-down, khaki slacks, and Chuck Taylors—I descended to the *Pensacola Insider* offices on the second floor. My work area was nestled between two windows in the southwest corner overlooking Palafox Street, Pensacola's main downtown street.

The neighborhood of Palafox had a New Orleans French Quarter feel to it. City leaders with the help of the banks created a grant program during the seventies to encourage owners to build balconies with wrought iron railing above the retail shops, restaurants, bars, and offices on the avenue. Red brick sidewalks lined the street, and history permeated the area.

From my southern window I looked down on Blazzues, a jazz club located on the site that had been Andrew Jackson's house when he was the first governor of the Florida Territory in 1821. One block further south Plaza Ferdinand marked where the Tennessee general was sworn in as the military governor. Winos toasted his bust daily.

A fire destroyed the Jackson residence in 1839 and robbed the city of a possible tourist attraction. Only a bronze plaque erected in 1935 by the Pensacola Historical Society near Blazzues's outdoor seating marked the town's one connection to the White House.

Jackson, the patron saint of grudges, fought thirteen duels, many over his wife Rachel's honor. Biographers claimed he was wounded so frequently in the gunfights that he "rattled like a bag of marbles." One bullet from an 1806 duel was lodged so close to his heart that it could never be removed, causing him pain for the rest of his life. It probably fed his ill temper, but he won the duel and killed the man who shot him. Roger told me that was very apropos of Pensacola to win the duel but carry the victim's bullet for the rest of his life.

The bartenders at Blazzues often talked about the bar being haunted. Doors locked when they took out the garbage. Beer taps suddenly started flowing. Glasses fell off the bar with no one near them. No one went into the big cooler without a fellow worker standing guard. Probably the ghosts had been court-martialed or shot by Jackson. They had grudges for good reasons.

Big Boy and I would have the office to ourselves for a couple of hours before the staff arrived. It was our quiet time. The dog jumped up on the couch next to my desk. His gray snout gave away his age, although he was so boisterous many mistook him for a puppy. He never barked but moved among the work areas and watched over the office. Whenever a visitor arrived, Big Boy perked up and joined the guest on the couch, hoping for some petting. If the guest ignored him, he would reach out a paw and tap him on the leg or arm and flash his adorable brown eyes. Big Boy was the star of the office, and he knew it.

Up until last Thanksgiving, Big Boy had been Roger Fairley's dog. Fairley was an outstanding citizen who built a nice fortune opening temporary employment and day labor agencies along the Gulf Coast. He once owned the Pensacola Conquistadors of the defunct Continental Basketball Association. The voters had elected Roger to several terms on the Pensacola City Council and Escambia Board of County Commissioners. He taught me how Pensacola politics worked and where the bodies were buried.

We enjoyed each other's company. He explained to me the mysteries and intricacies of Pensacola politics. When he died, he bequeathed Big Boy to me. He also had owned the three-story building that housed our offices and me. His widow told me that Roger left instructions that she could sell the building only to me—that is if I ever pulled together enough money to buy it. Until then, we didn't pay rent as long as we ran ads for the Pensacola Symphony and Pensacola Opera.

When I sat down at my desk, constructed from an old door on top of two sawhorses, I cranked up Cowboy Mouth's *Voodoo Shoppe* on the computer, took a sip of my coffee, and began surfing the web. I perused the top Florida papers: *Miami Herald, Tampa Bay Times, South Florida Sun-Sentinel, Florida Times Union, Orlando Sentinel,* and *Tallahassee Democrat.* Like some evil troll under the bridge of my life, my blog had to be fed.

A web journal that I created about the same time as the maritime park initiative, the blog was my mistress, demanding constant attention. I fed it news, viewpoints, and political buzz constantly. And the public loved it, making it one of the most popular political blogs in the state.

On the blog, I honed my writing skills, pushed ideas, battled the naysayers, and made my paper relevant daily. It required—no, it demanded—perpetual attention. Readers wanted more and more. And I gave it to them.

After scanning the state newspapers, I looked online at the *Pensacola Herald,* our town's Barnett Press-owned daily newspaper. Barnett USA ran the largest newspaper chain in North America with more than two hundred newspapers in the United States and Canada. It specialized in medium-sized markets like Pensacola that could only support one daily paper. Without competition, the paper set the ad rates and drained the community dry. Very little real news was reported, especially if the article would impact ad sales.

A cash cow for Barnett Press, the *Herald* gobbled up all the ad dollars and continually developed new websites and faux publications to saturate the market and satisfy their corporation's insatiable hunger for more profits.

I hated them. In our paper's early years, I read the daily newspapers obsessively to see if they reported one of our stories before our weekly issue came out, but they seemed to have adopted a policy of ignoring anything we published or else going in the complete opposite direction. They loved defending Bo Hines and not too subtly attacking my journalism. Their ad reps used it to poach our customer list, and we were seeing our ad revenue slip.

An alt-weekly in a small market had no chance to beat a Barnett daily. They had all the money, resources, and staff. If they made the decision to go after the *Pensacola Insider*, Barnett would crush us. Until then, we danced on the razor's edge. Taunting and weaving through the decades-old grudges as we pushed the ancient, self-important city ahead.

Ultimately, we would fail. I had no exit strategy with a big payoff. The only uncertainty was when the executioner's ax would fall. Would it be today? Next Week? Or in five years?

I woke up every day knowing this. No amount of jogging, drinking, or writing could change that fact or erase it from my thoughts when I sat at my desk drinking coffee and watching downtown Pensacola wake up.

Morbid? No, realistic.

Pensacola's current narrative had me as the bastard who tried to ruin their hero, Bowman Hines. An unprofessional tabloid journalist, or worse a blogger, set on building his reputation by destroying the man who had selflessly helped Pensacola all his life. Bo Hines was one of their own; I was not.

At eight o'clock, I donned my blue blazer and walked two blocks to the M. C. Blanchard Judicial Building and sat outside Courtroom B waiting for the prosecutors to arrive. Television crews were already there. The *Herald* had a photographer and two reporters ready to cover every nuance of the trial.

As we waited, all their phones suddenly began to vibrate at the same time. A sheriff's deputy approached us. Mrs. Bowman Hines had been found dead at her residence. The judge had postponed the start of the trial.

A few of the reporters looked to me for a comment. I brushed them off and found a corner of the judicial center to call Bo. Though dreading the conversation, I had to call. He didn't answer. Thank God.

"Bo, I am so sorry to hear about Sue," was all I thought to say in the message I left on his voice mail. Brilliant. But I meant it. That was all I could summon. And like everything else, it was the truth, alone and naked and standing there.

Maybe I should disappear for a few days. I hadn't taken a vacation in years. However, I didn't have the cash to leave town and my credit cards had maxed out.

I had friends in Cajun country, deep in the swamps near Thibodaux in south Louisana. Those weird places in the bayou where nobody knew or gave a crap about your name. I could go there and eat gumbo and jambalaya and wash it down with a six-pack of Dixie beer.

My phone vibrated. It was a text message from Bo: "Leave me alone." I was so screwed.

I texted Jim Harden to call me. A private investigator and a somewhat reliable source that had helped me in the past, Harden spent most of his life on the fringes, having lunch meetings at convenience stores and roadside food trucks with people who contacted him via notes shoved under the mat of his office, which was sandwiched between a tattoo parlor and Domino's Pizza in a bad part of town. He might know what had happened to Sue.

I needed to call Dare. No, I would visit her offices. This conversation needed to be face-to-face.

Dare was the president of the Evans Timber & Land Company, the largest landowner in Northwest Florida after the US military, and the widow of Rory Evans. Rory had leveraged his family name, wealth, and superior intelligence to become the Florida Senate president by age 36. He had died nine years earlier of a massive heart attack while giving a speech on the Senate floor.

The Evans dynasty didn't skip a beat after Rory's death. Dare took his place in Florida politics and the Northwest Florida business community. No one trifled with Dare Evans.

As a wealthy widow, Dare was never criticized too harshly, either. She expressed her opinions and asserted her influence without fearing pushback from the country club wives. The whole of Pensacola society found no reason not to take her seriously—or if they did, they were too afraid to say it.

Rory and Bo had grown up in the same neighborhood. Because the Hines and Evans families were close, he had been an usher in Hines' weddings. Dare loved Sue, who 'adopted' her when she moved to Pensacola in 1991 to marry Rory, but she never liked Bo.

"Too cocky," Dare once told me. Still, Sue was her friend, and Dare cherished her friendships.

My phone vibrated as I began to leave the Blanchard building. I needed another cup of coffee. The caller ID said "Dare Evans."

"Do . . . do you know what happened?" she asked. "I've tried to call the house and Jace. Nobody would pick up the phone."

"A deputy told me about it just as we were about to go into the courtroom," I said. "How did you find out so quickly?"

"I subscribe to the *Herald's* web alerts. Walker, this is horrible."

"I'm so sorry, Dare. I know you two were close."

"She was a good friend." Dare paused, and I didn't rush to fill the silence. I did note it however. "The online article on the *Herald's* website makes it sound like it could be suicide."

I said, "I haven't had time to do anything. The daily rushed to break the story. But you need to prepare for the worse."

"Sue wouldn't take her life, not Sue," she shouted, her temper flaring. "She was upset about the trial, but she was convinced Bo would be found innocent. We had an unspoken rule not to talk about you, but she was fine when we had lunch on Monday."

"Dare, you never know what's in someone's mind, what's happening behind closed doors—"

"I knew Sue. She wasn't suicidal, dammit." After Dare interrupted me, she hung up.

I should have consoled her, but my mind had jumped far past that. Like a dropped needle skipping over vinyl . . . scratch, thump . . . sheesh, I had already moved on to trying to figure out this puzzle and its impact on the trial.

I tried to pull up the *Herald* website on my cell phone but couldn't get service.

It vibrated. Harden texted: "@ Breaktime."

The Breaktime Café was one block north of my office. It was 8:48 a.m. The runners had already pranced home or to their offices, but the bums were out rummaging through the trashcans. They nodded as I passed. They knew I was about as broke as they were.

The heat was beginning to surpass the humidity. I perspired heavily as I walked into the cafe. A line of customers stood in front of the long counter that dominated the narrow space and waited for their lattes, mochas, and espressos. Many turned away as I called out to Bree, who manned the cash register. It would only get worse once they learned of Sue's death

Bree smiled and handed me a large cup of house coffee. I didn't know if she was happy to see me or only wanted to get me away from her other patrons.

Bree wore an unbuttoned blue blouse over a stretched-to-its-limits yellow tube top. The shirt covered tattoos that the owner frowned upon, but the flowers and birds peeked out now and then. A devoted runner, Bree ran Palafox Street every afternoon at three. Men timed their afternoon breaks to see her bounce by their offices. She almost made me want to take running seriously and buy trendier athletic gear. Almost, but not quite.

Jim Harden peeked around the corner from the back room when he heard my voice and waved me back. Bree winked and let me through. She and Jim had already figured out how to hide me away from the regular customers.

Harden was Pensacola's version of the Invisible Man. He was so nondescript and blended so well into any crowd that you had difficulty remembering where you last saw him. He was five foot ten, not too skinny or too fat, and odorless. Sometimes he wore wire-rimmed glasses. He was dressed in a light brown T-shirt and black slacks. Your eyes naturally passed over him when you scanned a room.

A retired FBI agent, former Navy SEAL, and one of the more sought-after private investigators in Pensacola, Harden could dig up dirt on anybody. We hadn't been on the same side of every issue, election, or referendum. You never quite knew who Harden was working for on any given day. Most of the information he shared was accurate, but you still needed to verify his tips.

Harden had saved my ass a few times, and I had helped him disrupt the plans of a few mutual enemies. Though he denied it, I thought he had been paid a few times to follow and report on me. Trust was not part of our relationship, but it always paid to listen to Jim Harden.

"You on top of Sue Hines' death?" I asked as we sat down out of earshot of Bree and her customers.

Harden nodded, "I listened to dispatch route the officers and EMS to the home and was on the scene when they hauled the body off. I thought you might want someone there, and I knew your staff probably hadn't gotten out of bed yet."

"What did you learn?"

"It was most likely a drug overdose," Harden said. I always liked his directness, but this time I would have appreciated a warning.

"Her husband called 9-1-1 after finding her on the floor of the bathroom off the master bedroom this morning at 7:25 a.m.," said Harden leaning over a notepad next to his coffee cup to read the words written in tight, perfect cursive. "She was putting on her makeup and getting dressed for the trial."

Bo must have just gotten home from his television interview.

"She died before the ambulance arrived."

"Damn," I said. "Was there a note?"

"The cops didn't find one," Harden said, still reviewing his notes. "Holmes, Mrs. Hines may have overdosed on Phenobarbital. The police found open prescription bottles in the bathroom. We will need to wait for the ME's report."

"Sue took the drug for her epilepsy," I said when Harden paused to see my reaction to his news. Sue had chaired the local epilepsy board of directors and openly talked about her seizures.

I continued, "She has—had—been afflicted since eighth grade. It would be just like Sue to forget she had taken one dose and down another. Maybe it was accidental."

Harden looked down and sipped his coffee. He didn't believe it was an accident but didn't care enough to argue with me. He let me hold on to that ray of hope but only for a few sips.

"The media will blame you, Holmes," he said. "The state attorney might even ask for a delay in Hines' trial. They are worried about finding open-minded jurors. Her death will be all over the media for the next two weeks. You forced their hand on this case. Hines pushed to get in court as quickly as possible, which has hampered the prosecutors who wanted more time to prepare for the trial. Some in the state attorney's office would like to see it and you go away."

I didn't say a word, just continued drinking my coffee. I felt every-thing slipping away—my newspaper, my friends, and my life.

"I'm not going anywhere," I said and stared into Harden's eyes. "Maybe Bo will change his plea to guilty."

Harden half smiled. "You have always been a hard-ass."

I looked back at Harden as I left a tip on the table for Bree and walked toward the front door. "You let me know if you hear anything else."

As I turned the corner from the backroom, I ran into Jace Wittman, Sue Hines' stepbrother. His face looked weary and his blue dress shirt was untucked and wrinkled. His hair needed to be brushed. His goatee was unkempt.

Before I could offer any condolences, Wittman hurled his vanilla latte at my head.

"You son of a bitch," he shouted. "You killed my sister."

I shielded my face, and most of the hot liquid scalded my arm. I smelled the vanilla and imagined my skin blistering.

Wittman doubled me over with a punch to my exposed gut. Bree screamed for him to stop. I slipped and hit my head on the corner of a table. Harden blocked Wittman's path and pushed him as he tried to deliver a kick to my ribs. They had been cracked one time too many and wouldn't have taken the kick well.

Even though he had twenty pounds on Harden, Wittman knew he was overmatched. He turned angrily and walked out of the cafe. Harden stayed with me. "You okay?" he asked. "We need to get that shirt off and see how much damage Wittman did. Want to call the cops?"

I shook my head imagining that I felt my brain rattle around in my skull. I struggled to catch my breath and not show any emotion. Bree, Harden, and the customers stared down at me.

"He must have come looking for you," said Bree. "His eyes were glazed over when he walked in until he saw you. I thought he was going to kill you."

"I have that effect on people," I said.

She handed me a ziplock bag filled with ice for my head. When they got my shirt off, my left arm was pink, but the starched sleeve had repelled most of the coffee. There were no blisters. Funny how my writer's imagination had gotten carried away. I also had a knot on the back of my head from the fall, but no other injuries.

Bree gave me a kiss on the forehead and a green, red, yellow, and blue tie-dyed Breaktime T-shirt to wear. Harden walked with me back to the *Insider* office.

It was a little after nine o'clock in the morning, and I'd already had my ass kicked and seen my chance for redemption possibly evaporate. Perfect.

3

The *Insider* staff would not be in the office until after ten. We had worked late into the night to get the issue finished. I had taken them out for beer and pizza afterwards and told them the staff meeting would be at 11:00 a.m.

I went online to read the *Herald's* article on Sue's death, which had already been updated twice while I was at Breaktime. The Hines residence showed no sign of forced entry. Bo had come home from the television station and found Sue unresponsive in their master bathroom. Her stepbrother, Wittman, and his daughter lived with the Hineses. They were asleep in their rooms and had heard nothing. The police said they did not suspect foul play.

Sue's death was either health-related or a suicide. Neither possibility fit the Sue Hines I knew.

Sue Eaton Hines had stood a full six feet tall—or "five foot twelve," as she liked to say. She possessed such a radiant presence that when she walked into a room, conversation left it. You couldn't take your eyes off her. Men, even the most confident players, forgot their names when she smiled at them.

If she shook your hand, your knuckles popped. If she knew you well enough, she called you "sweetie" and might haul you off kayaking or sailing. Sue exuded health and vitality, looking thirty-five instead of fifty. When she laughed, it came out with a roar, filled with delightful, childlike innocence.

Her curly red hair, green eyes, and light array of freckles on her nose and cheeks gave away her Irish heritage. But instead of a fiery temper,

Sue had a warm way of scolding you that made you so ashamed you would instantly vow never to repeat the offense. She had scolded me often.

Beautiful enough to live a step beyond convention, other women might comment about Sue that she spent too much time talking with their husbands and boyfriends at dinner parties, but they could do nothing about it. Men loved her because she liked to talk football, hunting and politics, but she wasn't a flirt. You savored a conversation with her like a fine whiskey.

Sue worshiped Bo. She had fallen in love with him when she was a sophomore at Pensacola Junior College and working in Dr. Lou Bowman's office during summer break. Bo had been accepted into Florida State's masters program and spent time that summer in Pensacola helping his grandparents. He also spent a lot of time with Sue. When she graduated from PJC, Sue enrolled in Florida State. Bo hung around Tallahassee an additional year and delayed his MBA so that he and Sue could both graduate in the spring of 1981.

Up until my article about Bo appeared, she had called me "sweetie." When the cops came to their North Hill home to arrest her husband in early April, she called my cell phone crying, "All Bo ever did was stand up for you when the rest of this town wanted you drummed out of Pensacola, and this is how you reward his friendship?"

Before she hung up, Sue screamed, "He was your friend! Doesn't that mean anything to you?"

I didn't say a word, and the phone went dead. That was the last time I heard her voice. And for weeks her words lingered, like cigarette smoke in my blazer after I had spent the night closing Intermission.

The *Pensacola Herald* gave few other details of how Sue died. While the police told the reporter they didn't suspect foul play, the officers also didn't say natural causes. In other words, the wife of my one-time friend may have committed suicide. The article stated that friends said she had been distraught over her husband's arrest, which the reporter added was caused by an audit prompted by allegations made by *Insider* publisher Walker Holmes. It also mentioned the trial was set to begin that morning and that I had refused to comment on her death.

In other words, I pushed Pensacola's most unlikely candidate for suicide to take her life.

I knew all the public information officers at the Pensacola Police Department and the Escambia County Sheriff's Office and they hated commenting on possible suicides. If a victim took his or her own life, the PIOs would file it away as such and tell the press off the record, "We don't comment on suicides but, of course, that is up to the medical examiner to decide."

The official statement would be that law enforcement did not suspect any foul play and would wait for the medical examiner to perform the autopsy. The ME usually took four to five weeks before she issued a report, long enough for the suicide to be a nonstory.

The *Herald* allowed readers to comment on articles. The first few posted below the article on Sue's death offered condolences to Bo, his grandparents, and Sue's stepbrother, Jace Wittman. The next thirty-five anonymous comments attacked me:

WallyTaxesRanger: "Does Walker Holmes have an alibi?"

JollyRoy: "Holmes is the one who needs to be arrested. He killed her, even if he didn't pull a trigger."

SallyBeach: "The so-called reporter is a backstabbing jerk. Hines should sue him for everything he has. Hines will own his tabloid."

And those were the kindest comments about me. The *Herald* didn't moderate its website. More comments meant more hits and more ad revenue. They could have at least given me a commission.

I put on a new button-down shirt and headed to Dare's offices at Jackson Tower. The one block walk was one of the most difficult I had traveled in quite some time. She was expecting me to tell her more about Sue's death. I wouldn't do it in an email or over the phone.

Evans Timber & Land Company owned Jackson Tower, which loomed at the end of Palafox Street and overlooked Pensacola Bay. In 1903 it was the tallest building in Florida, the state's first twelve-story skyscraper. Only two taller buildings had been built in Pensacola since then.

When I got off the elevator, I nodded at the young receptionist and walked through a maze of cubicles filled with real estate agents and back to the corner office.

Dare's office had a spectacular view of Pensacola Bay. One could see Pensacola Beach, the Gulf of Mexico, and the Naval Air Station in the distance. An enormous Oriental rug covered the floor. One wall had mahogany bookcases filled with books, many of them first editions signed by Robert Penn Warren, Eudora Welty, Truman Capote, Harper Lee, Margaret Mitchell, and other Southern writers. Dare liked to tease me that she had a spot for my first novel.

Behind her massive desk hung a portrait of Rory, smiling like he owned the Gulf Coast—which he did. Under the portrait was a silver tray with bottles of Jack Daniels and Cutty Sark and a set of crystal glasses. Next to the tray was Rory's most prized possession, the football from Ole Miss's 1969 Sugar Bowl victory over Arkansas, autographed by Coach Johnny Vaught and Archie Manning.

The three of us had met for the first time at the University of Mississippi. Rory had been a first-year law student. Dare and I were freshmen.

I was the first in my family to attended college, hailing from the Mississippi Delta town of Belzoni, the "Catfish Capital of the World." I would have gone to Mississippi Delta Junior College in nearby Moorhead or Delta State University like my classmates who didn't immediately enlist in the military or work on their parents' farm out of high school, but Ole Miss had offered me an academic scholarship. My parents drove me to Oxford in the family station wagon and told me they would return to pick me up at Thanksgiving break.

Dare had graduated from St. Agnes Academy, a private Roman Catholic, all-girls high school in Memphis, the same school that Priscilla Presley attended while Elvis Presley courted her. Dare's father was a corporate attorney for Holiday Inn and a running back on Johnny Vaught's undefeated 1962 football team, and her mother was a former Ole Miss homecoming queen.

We met at a Pi Kappa Alpha pledge swap. Somehow I had ended up the pledge class president of the fraternity. Dare held the same position with the Chi Omegas. We launched the pledge toga party and ducked out to drink beer at the Gin, one of the few bars in Oxford that kept its kitchen open past nine o'clock on Monday nights. Over burgers and fried mushrooms, we talked for hours about William Faulkner, Ronald Reagan, Jimmy Carter, and how we were going to change the South.

We stayed until closing time, and Dare drove me back to the dorm in her convertible Spyder. We didn't kiss. No, we hugged, knowing that we would always have each other's backs.

Rory came on the scene later. For some odd reason, he was jealous of me, but Dare refused to end our friendship. I served as an usher in their wedding in Pensacola in 1991. I found that I liked the town and made a pledge to myself that I would find a way to relocate to a coastal town.

The opportunity came three years after I had written an exposé for the *Commercial Appeal* on how Ole Miss boosters were taking football recruits to strip clubs in Memphis. Head football coach Billy Brewer lost his job and athletic director Warner Alford resigned. The football program was put on probation for four years and lost twenty-five scholarships. Ole Miss fans called me a "traitor." Advertisers pressured the paper's publisher and editor to terminate my employment. I was reassigned to cover the court beat and promptly turned in my resignation.

I moved to Pensacola, rented a cinderblock house on Pensacola Beach, and wrote for several local papers along the Gulf Coast for the next seven years until I got fed up with the revolving door of editors, layoffs, and unpaid leaves. I cashed in my 401(k), convinced a couple of investors to take the chance on a 33-year-old, and started the *Pensacola Insider* in 2002.

Dare was the only one in Pensacola who had known Mari, my fiancée. She had helped me deal with Mari's death and got me through graduation. These days, I didn't mention Rory, and she never brought up Mari.

As I walked into her office, Dare looked up from her desk as if she had been waiting for me to appear. I leaned over to place a kiss on her cheek, but she pulled away. She wasn't ready to completely forgive me for setting the Hines trial in motion. We had barely spoken since Bo's arrest. I sat in a leather chair by the bookcase, thinking that maybe a swallow of the Cutty Sark would relieve my headache.

Dressed in a black Armani suit with a white blouse and pearls, Dare's blonde hair, flawless, luminous skin, and brilliant blue eyes captivated me as they did everyone who met her. Her speech had only a hint of a Southern accent, which became more pronounced when she was tired. I had missed hearing that accent.

She sat quietly as I relayed what Harden had told me. When I finished, Dare turned her chair away from me and stared out the window at sailboats in the bay. I sat and waited.

When she turned back to face me, Dare wiped her cheeks with the back of her right hand, held back her head, and shook off the remaining tears. She didn't wear a lot of makeup, didn't need it.

"Do you think it was an accidental overdose?" she asked, twisting her strand of pearls.

I shrugged. "It's possible, and maybe the medical examiner will even say that happened. I don't know."

"She was the old Sue when we were at Jackson's on Monday. We didn't talk about you, but she believed Bo would be acquitted."

The girls frequently met at Jackson's, the town's only five-star restaurant that had long windows opening out onto Ferdinand Plaza. Jackson's was where you went if you could afford it and didn't mind being seen.

"So do you and much of this town," I said.

"No, no, no, that's not my point," said Dare. "I'm talking about someone who was like a big sister to me. Sue had no reason to kill herself."

"Maybe something changed since Monday . . ."

"No, dammit, Walker! Sue wouldn't kill herself!" Dare yelled.

She started to tear up again and turned her chair away from me. Dare was tough. Rory had two brothers, but they had both let her run the family empire.

I addressed the back of her leather chair. "How about her health? Was she having seizures?"

Dare stayed facing the window. One of the sailboats had tacked wrong, and its sail flapped, begging for the captain to recapture the breeze.

She said, "She hadn't had a seizure in over a year. She may have had one martini too many at our lunch, but that wasn't unusual for Sue, especially since your article."

I said nothing, ordering myself not to get defensive.

She continued, "Sue and I were planning a long weekend to the Keys. We would stay at my house on Duck Key. She wanted to do some deep-sea fishing, and I wanted to catch up on my reading. Sue couldn't wait to try the new tapas at Santiago's Bodega."

The sailboat caught a breeze and headed toward the Pensacola Naval Air Station.

I said, "People are going to blame me for her death."

Dare swung her chair around to face me. "Dammit, Walker, everything isn't about you and your goddamn newspaper. You always want to make it about you."

I said, "Because this is about me and my paper. Bo Hines stole that money. If Sue killed herself because of the trial, her death is on him, not me."

Dare clenched her fists. Her jaw tightened. She said, "I sure as hell hope you find out what happened."

Then she turned her chair away from me again. I had been dismissed.

"You are killing us with this Bo Hines crap," Roxie Hendricks said as she slapped her sales reports onto the conference table. "Three more ad cancellations this morning since Sue Hines' death hit social media. I'm losing more advertisers than I'm signing up."

Our sales director and part-time copy editor on Mondays and Tuesdays, Roxie helped the paper survive hurricanes, recessions, and an assortment of protests, all without a hair out of place. Bright, determined, and opinionated, she spoke her mind on the paper's news coverage and fought for themed issues to help her clients and attract new ones.

Her boyfriend had proposed last Christmas. I had approved her trading advertising in the *Insider* in exchange for a venue, DJ, photographer, and caterer for her wedding reception in two months. Roxie needed to maintain her sales commissions to pay for their upcoming honeymoon.

Roxie and I had more invested in the wedding than the boyfriend did. The bargains kept her motivated, and she didn't mind playing the devil's advocate in our staff meetings.

An *Insider* staff meeting was always a battle—few casualties, but lots of alliances, attacks, retreats, and regroupings of forces. My staff was younger than me, and the age difference gave them a safe distance from whatever trouble I caused. They lobbed flaming arrows at me from behind a nice, neat, generational barrier.

Well, they never played Atari, saw The Clash, or marched in an apartheid protest, so whatever I did was my own thing.

"It's your paper," Roxie added as she sat down with Teddy and Mal Taulbert, the married couple who were my art director and production manager respectively, A&E writer Jeremy Holt, and news reporter Doug

Yoste. "I hope you know what you're doing because it won't be long before my church bulletin has more ads than this paper."

Our resident pessimist, Mal smiled while she looked down at her notes that listed the problems encountered publishing that week's issue, which she would run down with the group during the meeting. Smart enough to wait before she interjected herself into office battles, Mal hadn't picked a side yet.

Most of the kids who applied to work at the *Insider* came from the University of West Florida where they studied things like communications theory while munching on bagels, drinking expressos, and playing hacky sack. Mal and Teddy were notable exceptions.

Mal had gone away to Loyola University in New Orleans where she studied political science and philosophy, fought for AIDS research, campaigned for Al Gore and John Kerry, and saw some decent bands. Her approval meant a little more because it was worth a little more.

She met her husband Teddy when he joined the newspaper in 2005 after Hurricane Dennis, which was our second storm in less than a year. The other was Hurricane Ivan.

My art director at the time had walked into the office and told me he was tired of cleaning up after storms and was moving to Atlanta. He introduced Teddy and said that the Air Force veteran, who had an associate degree in graphic design and deejayed at local clubs, would be his replacement.

During his one-month probationary period, Teddy learned how to lay out the newspaper. His skills as a photographer and artist took the paper's look to a new level. Within six months, Teddy and Mal moved in together.

Teddy seldom voiced his opinion. He never talked about his tours in Iraq and Afghanistan. But he had great cover design ideas that he worked out with Mal. Teddy drank his coffee in an Incredible Hulk mug, played with the ring that pierced his bottom lip, and waited to hear the story ideas for the next issue.

A cab had dropped Jeremy off at the office at nine-thirty. He had been slamming down Starbucks between cigarette breaks and was on such a caffeine high that he could barely contain himself. He had to jump into the discussion about the paper's future, and he took Roxie's side. He always did, bravely going where she had gone before.

"I can't get anyone to return my calls," he said. "Even the art galleries don't seem interested in getting a story in our paper. They all worry about their donors pulling funding if they appear in the *Insider*. Now this news of Sue Hines' death— ."

I cut him off. "This whole thing started because Bo Hines stole grant money intended to help the art galleries. They are why we did the story in the first place."

Roxie interjected, "Yeah, but they and, more importantly, their board members and benefactors aren't so sure that Hines stole anything. The buzz is you jumped the gun on this story."

I held back my temper. Dare had told me the same thing when we published the news story. I didn't have time for this mutiny.

"The audit backed up our reporting," I said. "The state attorney charged him, and Hines will be convicted."

"If there is ever a trial," Roxie said as she took a long sip from her water bottle. She didn't drink coffee. Mal snickered.

"We push ahead," I said. "We did the right thing reporting on Hines. We all discussed the possible fallout. There will be a trial and it will validate everything we wrote."

I sounded more confident than I felt and continued, "It would help if we could locate Pandora Childs. As the Arts Council director, she knows better than anyone what Hines did. Even if she had some part in the embezzlement, the state attorney would cut her a deal in exchange for her testimony. Anyone got any leads about where to find her?"

I asked this question every week.

Roxie and Jeremy shook their heads.

Teddy said, "I asked around again. She dated a bartender at Seville Quarter for a couple months when she first moved to Pensacola but hasn't been seen for a while."

"She was friends with one of our freelancers," said Mal. "But all Tish would tell me was Childs liked to smoke pot and had started hanging out with some older man, but she didn't know who."

Doug Yoste finally woke up. He had been in a daze drinking coffee and staring out the conference room window. He needed three cups of coffee before he could form words into sentences. Wearing a vintage NBA Denver Nuggets T-shirt over jeans that looked like they had been worn five days in a row, Doug hadn't shaved and needed to run a brush through his mop of brown hair.

He said, "I've had several people tell me her family had a condo in Destin. I've called her parents several times, as have the state attorney's investigators. Childs didn't have the best relationship with her parents. They had stopped talking with her since she moved to Pensacola. They didn't text or email each other."

"Keep asking," I said. "I've got Harden working on it, too."

Mal left the room and brought back the coffee carafe. She refilled everyone's mugs.

"What can you tell us about Sue Hines' death?" she asked me as she settled down and drank from her pink Hello Kitty mug.

I filled them in on the details Harden had shared without telling them about the confrontation with Wittman. Then we moved into the editorial portion of the meeting.

The cover story for next week was on Escambia County Sheriff Ron Frost's request for more funds from the county commission for pay raises for his employees. Since it involved Frost, I took lead on the investigation, but I needed the sheriff's office to release a few more public records.

"Do we need a backup plan if you don't get the records?" asked Mal.

"If I don't hear back by this afternoon, I'll get the state attorney's office involved," I said. "Plan on thirty-five hundred words and two charts. Teddy, find us a current photo of Frost and his deputies working some crime scene."

Teddy jotted down a few notes. He said, "We will have the online database ready to go live once we get the salary spreadsheets."

Teddy and Mal had a friend who offered to design a searchable online database that would allow our readers to hunt for the salaries of all the sheriff's employees. We would launch the database the same day the issue hit the newsstands.

I had taken Yoste off cover stories for two weeks because I wanted him to focus on a feature on Wittman's maritime park petition drive. However, he still needed to do a couple of news stories.

Yoste walked the staff through the story ideas that he and I had discussed: gang violence in the middle schools, a county commissioner getting contracts for an aide's husband, city staff sharing photos of nude women using government email accounts, and Sheriff Ron Frost's last hunting trip.

Unimpressed, Mal said, "That's nice, but which one can you deliver by Friday?"

"Gang violence," said Yoste, more than a little offended that she had called him out again.

I kept the meeting moving. "Doug, send me a progress report on the petition story. You may have a difficult time interviewing Wittman. I'm not one of his favorite people."

"I've already gotten him to answer a few questions," he said, "and, yes, he hates you."

Smiling, he added, "He likes me, though."

Two years out of the journalism school at the University of Florida, Yoste missed his hometown and the fishing it offered. Though he had worked for the *Tampa Tribune* for eighteen months, the *Herald* showed no interest in hiring him, but Doug filled an important hole in our paper. An investigative publication without investigative reporters doesn't last long.

"Will you make deadline on that story, too?" asked Mal. She was more of a managing editor than a production manager. She made sure we published an issue every week.

Her tattooed and pierced husband Teddy laid out all the articles, designed the covers, and did most of the photography. Mal handled the design of the ads, determined the space for the editorial and ads, and sent it all to the printer by 6 p.m. on Tuesday—that is if Doug turned in his copy on time.

Though weird and dramatic, Jeremy never gave Mal problems on Tuesdays. Any holdup would be Doug's fault. He was a good reporter and could weave facts together well, but he was slow. I had no idea why he never improved. Mal and Roxie beat him up every time he missed a deadline. Still, at five thirty on a print night, he would be found staring at his computer screen looking as if somebody had asked him to move large rocks with his mind. Hollow-eyed and scared, he struggled to ignore the sighs and nasty comments from all around him and type out his article.

"Ted," I said, "get with Doug on the cover. Mal, I will want more room for my editorial and plan on the letters to the editor being longer than usual. We will print all the hate mail as long as it's somewhat coherent."

"What about my stories?" chimed in Jeremy. "What am I supposed to do about the art galleries?"

"Get off your ass and walk down the street to the galleries. Take Teddy with you to take photos," I said.

"Yeah, Jeremy," said Mal, "whoever heard of an A&E writer that's afraid to do face-to-face interviews or listen to bands in person?" She understood that Jeremy might use the ruckus as an excuse for not meeting a deadline. Since Mal was the master of all deadlines, it appeared I had her for an ally, at least for this meeting.

"I'm not the problem around here," Jeremy said. "I make my deadlines."

He directed his full bravado at our production manager, like a child standing in front of a mechanical pony outside of Winn-Dixie telling his mother that he wasn't afraid. "And I listen to plenty of bands in person."

"Yeah, right," said Mal.

We wouldn't hear from Jeremy again for the rest of the morning. He couldn't wait to take a call from his boyfriend and discuss his woes over another cigarette in the alleyway behind the building. Roxie was another matter.

Ad sales were the lifeblood of our free newspaper. We didn't have paid subscribers. Ads covered our costs. We had no reserves, and my savings had dwindled steadily since the Hines article was published.

I told her and the rest of the staff, "We've been here before, guys. The story was the right thing to do. Hines is a fake and stole taxpayers' dollars that were intended to support nonprofits that struggle even more than we do to make ends meet. We can never hide from the truth."

"But it's my commissions," Roxie said, not wanting to give up just yet. Big Boy walked into the conference room and put his head in her lap. The sales director scratched him behind his ears.

"Roxie, we have our Best of the Coast issue in six weeks. We will make up the lost ad sales, and besides the trial will be over soon."

The paper normally sold about $45,000 to $50,000 worth of ads in the Best of the Coast issue that listed the best restaurants, shops, and businesses in Northwest Florida. Roxie knew it, and her commissions would start rolling in before her honeymoon trip.

"Email me the list of cancellations," I said to her. "I will call or visit those advertisers by Friday."

Meeting adjourned. Big Boy headed back to the couch while the rest of us went to check our email.

The office was one large space with exposed, ancient bricks and lined with windows that faced Palafox and Intendencia streets. The sun rushed through the uncovered windows and skylights making the room seem stark. The space had two small bathrooms and a break room that doubled as a conference room. My loft apartment occupied the top floor. Below sat Frank's Pizzeria.

The building had been around since the mid-1800s. Before we moved in, it was a punk club where Green Day, The Wallflowers, and numerous less memorable bands played on their way to Atlanta, New Orleans, Orlando, or Austin. Before that, it had been a jazz club that hosted Al Hirt and Fats Domino. And before that, my barber Eddie told me that it was a "high-class" strip club, which meant the strippers had all their teeth. Before that, nobody remembered. The office was haunted, if only by residual punk angst.

Most visitors loved the feel of the office. Governors, state lawmakers, and anyone seeking national, state, or local office dropped in at one time or another. The staff worked on six-foot long plastic folding tables. Papers were spread everywhere. Framed covers of old issues covered the walls. The space looked how the office of an underdog alt-weekly should. It was cool.

My head was killing me, and the caffeine wasn't helping. Summer Kay, our receptionist, walked over to my desk. She had handled the phones while we held our staff meeting.

"Hi, Boss." Tall and skinny with long brown hair with a touch of red on the tips, Summer had a fondness for tight jeans and eighties rock band T-shirts. Today, it was Culture Club.

She handed me my phone messages and told me that the day's deposit was $3,485. The first two messages were to call the state attorney's office—not likely. Another message was from Bree asking that I have a beer with her at Intermission at 6:00 p.m.

When I asked Summer about Bree's call, she elaborated, "She said she had a possible news story. She also wanted to know how you were you feeling."

Dropping her voice to a whisper, Summer said with a concerned look on her face, "She told me about Jace Wittman. Are you okay?"

"I could use some ibuprofen, but other than that I'm fine."

Outside my window, I watched the Palafox Street secretaries and administrative assistants stroll out to early lunches. Their dresses weren't quite as crisp as they had been earlier, but the view was inspiring.

Big Boy strolled over, ignoring Summer, and begged to go outside. Usually Summer took care of the dog's needs, which weren't many, during office hours. I guess he wasn't a Boy George fan.

5

Big Boy and I sat on a bench in Plaza de Luna at the foot of Palafox Street. I tossed the dog a crust of Frank's Pizzeria pizza as I finished the last of my Diet Coke. A refreshing breeze drifted off Pensacola Bay. Laughter and shrieks of delight came from children playing in the fountain in the center of the park. Their mothers gossiped on a nearby bench as they watched their kids play and the charter boats head out to the Gulf of Mexico. I fought the temptation to take the rest of the afternoon off.

"Holmes, the sheriff wants to see you."

I looked away from the water and saw Captain Peck Krager leaning against the hood of his car that he had parked in a loading zone. Peter "Peck" Krager, the stereotypical Sheriff Frost henchman, stood five foot six and weighed about two hundred and ten pounds. The buttons on his shirt screamed for relief, and his white T-shirt peeked through the gaps.

Krager was that former third-string offensive lineman in high school that never got to play, never lettered, but bragged about his championship football team. His grades weren't good enough for college, and the Navy rejected him because they knew he was a sociopath. "Peck" was short for speck.

The deputy kept his hand on his Taser while he talked to me. His belt looked like Batman's utility belt, but not the Christian Bale Batman, more like the Adam West version, filled with gadgets: handcuffs, pistol, two cell phones, nightstick, flashlight, and Taser stun gun.

Krager had been a mall security guard before Ron Frost won his first term. After he had worked hard on the campaign putting up signs and handing out flyers, Frost rewarded him with a shiny badge, uniform, a pistol with real bullets, and his very own patrol car.

The diminutive deputy had a toothpick in his mouth that he rolled back and forth.

"Hi, Peck. Couldn't you wait until the dog finished his meal?"

Undeterred, Peck growled, "Sheriff Frost wants to talk with you. Get in the car."

I stood, as did Big Boy. Peck took a half step toward us. His right hand never left his Taser. He stood as straight and tall as possible and tried to block our path on the sidewalk. He must have been wearing lifts because his head almost reached my chin.

I gave Krager the "Walker Holmes" stare and Big Boy stiffened and uttered a low growl. The deputy backed off a little.

"Not a chance," I said. "Have other commitments. Tell Frost I will meet him at the Garden Street Deli at three thirty for coffee. You can tag along."

Then I added, "And tell the sheriff to bring the records we requested three weeks ago."

I walked past Krager and headed up Palafox Street towards my office knowing the deputy wanted badly to use his stun gun on me. I heard the car door slam, and Krager sped past me with his siren blaring. I made a mental note not to drink outside of the city limits for the next few weeks. The Pensacola Police Department and Escambia County Sheriff's Office never crossed jurisdictions. The police rarely harassed me. On the other hand, there were times I felt Sheriff Frost had promised bonuses to his deputies if they could find a reason to arrest me.

My cell phone rang. I didn't recognize the number, but what the hell? Things had already gotten all screwed up. Maybe I had won the lottery . . . that's if I could win without buying a ticket.

A bank teller said, "Mr. Holmes, this is C & P Bank."

I felt a knot form in my stomach. She continued, "You are a month behind on your loan payments. We need $3,500 before next Monday."

"Thank you for the reminder," I replied. "I can drop off a check for $1,500 this afternoon and should have the balance of the payment due paid by next week."

"What reason should I give my superiors for the late payment?" she asked.

Because my staff needs to eat, I thought to myself, but said, "We had a lull in collections, but everything is picking up with Best of the Coast coming up soon."

The call ended without major hostilities, but there went my deposit. Money passed through the paper's checking account like beer flowing from a tap directly into a urinal without me even serving as temporary storage.

Roxie had been right about the Hines article's impact on our cash flow. Within days of the article's publication, two condo projects tied to Hines, his bank, and his law firm canceled their long-term advertising contracts with the paper, costing us about six grand a month. What hurt even more was that they all paid on time, a rarity in Pensacola.

The truth was, the newspaper had never been on solid financial footing. I convinced a couple of businessman to invest in it in 2002. At the time the daily newspaper dominated the local media, and I saw an opportunity to cut into their market share. Rueben Crutcher and Jackson Chipley agreed to put up $200,000 each, and we published our first edition.

We had no contingencies to deal with Hurricane Ivan. In the days after the storm nearly wiped Pensacola off the map, Crutcher and Chipley told me that they weren't interested in any more cash calls, which forced me to use my credit cards to keep the newspaper afloat.

The challenge of making the monthly payments on the credit cards and our startup loan ate up a substantial part of our cash flow. I struggled to keep the paper alive from week to week, but that was my secret. If my advertisers and the politicians knew of my possible collapse, they would do everything they could to push me off the precipice.

The day was hot. Lawyers, secretaries, and government workers crowded the sidewalk, heading back to their offices after having lunch. A few runners passed me. *Show-offs*, I thought.

My cell vibrated again as I walked up Palafox. Summer said, "The printer called. They won't print this week's issue unless we hand deliver a check before two o'clock this afternoon."

Summer was calling on her cell phone from the conference room so the rest of the staff wouldn't overhear the conversation. For someone so young, she had strong motherly instincts and looked out for the paper and me.

Shit.

"Cut the check and go ahead, write another for fifteen hundred dollars for C & P Bank," I told her.

"But that's leaves us with little cash in the account for payroll on Friday. We will need to have two more good deposits. I'm not sure that will happen."

"Summer, you bring the printer his check, but do it right at 1:55 p.m. They probably won't deposit it until tomorrow. I will handle the loan payment after three. We should gain at least two days before the checks hit our bank account. Print out a collections report, and I will try to make a few calls to our customers."

"Your call list keeps getting longer and longer," said Summer. "You know, you are making me an old woman fast."

I said, "What's old to you? Thirty-one?"

Summer laughed nervously. Before she hung up, I asked her to call Bree and tell her that I would meet her that evening.

As I approached the corner of Intendencia and Palafox streets where our offices stood, I saw the lunch crowd still packed Frank's Pizzeria, which leased the ground floor. The entrance to our office was in an alley that opened on Intendencia Street, an unremarkable gray metal door with a small red "IN" sticker on it. We prided ourselves on being hard to find. Fewer nuts walked in that way.

Upstairs the staff had begun work on next week's issue. Teddy and Mal, who had been with the paper the longest, five years, had an old rug under their work areas that clearly marked their territory. It had a real homey feel, and it always felt good entering their workspace.

As a practical joke, the couple had placed duct tape on the floor around Jeremy's workspace to mock his constant haranguing for privacy. Empty Starbucks cups and Diet Coke cans were tossed all over his area.

Jeremy was on the phone finishing his music interview for the next week's issue. He was telling the musician about his days working for VH1, MTV, MSNBC, and Entertainment Tonight. We had no proof that he actually had, but Jeremy enjoyed the storytelling so much that no one questioned him about it. No one cared anyway.

Big Boy strolled to Mal's desk, stretched out on the rug under it, and shut his eyes. He was taking his afternoon nap.

"Mal, the cover story is a go," I said, amazed at how quickly Big Boy could doze off. "I'm getting the records from Frost his afternoon."

She looked at Teddy and asked, "Do you think that will give us enough time to load the information into the database and test it before next Thursday?"

Teddy removed his headphones. You might have thought he listened to heavy metal while he worked, but he didn't. He liked jazz and played it soft enough that he could still follow the conversations around him when he wanted to hear them. He always perked up when Mal spoke.

"As long as we get the information in a digital format, preferably a spreadsheet, Kyle said it wouldn't take him long to upload the data," he replied.

"Well, that is how I requested the payroll data be given to us, but Frost might screw with us," I acknowledged.

"What's the backup plan if he hands you a bunch of printed reports?" Mal queried.

"We split up typing the data into a spreadsheet for Kyle."

No one was happy about that option.

Roxie signaled for me to join her in the conference room. I shut the door behind me and sat next to her at the table.

"Walker, I'm really worried," she said. "This possible suicide is freaking out some of our most reliable advertisers. AmSouth Bank and Hankin's Toyota have asked us to hold off on their upcoming ads. They haven't cancelled, but they didn't give me dates when they wanted to restart their advertising."

Their contracts had penalties for early termination but none for suspending ads. They could stay out of the paper indefinitely.

"Do you think it would help if I made an appointment to see them?" I asked.

Roxie shook her head. "We've been telling them to trust us; the trial will reveal the truth. Now the advertisers don't want to be collateral damage in the escalations of this fight between Bo Hines and you."

"This isn't some personal vendetta. The guy's a crook."

"You can tell yourself that, and I want to believe you. I really do, but the general public and our advertisers are losing faith. Walker, we're hemorrhaging cancellations and I can't stop the bleeding."

I reached out and touched her forearm. "Roxie, we handled this before when we reported on deputies misusing Tasers on nearly every traffic stop when they first got the stun guns. Their union called our advertisers and bullied our distributors. When the grand jury issued its report and Frost was forced to rewrite his policy manual, the advertisers came back."

"This is different," she protested. "Sue Hines was popular. Her death is working against us. I'm having trouble making appointments for sales calls to replace the advertisers we're losing."

I got up and walked to the window. Two blue jays were attacking a squirrel trying to cross Jefferson Street. He dodged them as they repeatedly swooped down and cut off his path to either side of the street. The squirrel made a dash for a power pole and was hit by a car. The driver didn't stop.

I said, "Be patient. The sales will come back."

"No, Walker, this is not the same as before. A woman took her life because of your reporting."

"Her death is not my fault," I maintained.

"Keep telling yourself that while you destroy this paper," said Roxie. "The *Insider* is more than Walker Holmes. We all depend on this paper for our livelihoods."

She began to tear up. "Dammit, if my commissions dry up, I won't be able to pay for my wedding. Brad is already getting cold feet."

Brad, her fiancé, made pottery that had yet to attract much artistic praise or commercial success. Roxie had met him at Peg Leg Pete's on Pensacola Beach. She was a waitress, Brad a bartender. The two opposites were attracted to each other and began dating. She helped him sell his pottery at arts and crafts festivals along the coast. Brad was funny and entertaining. It also didn't hurt that he had movie-star good looks and her parents loved him.

I had seen Roxie's potential in sales and enticed her to join the paper after the beach's summer season ended and her tips fell off. Roxie was ambitious, liked fine things, and loved the challenge of making the sale.

She kept her five-seven frame slim by doing Pilates four times a week. As her sales commissions at the *Insider* rose, she swapped her TJ Maxx wardrobe for Of Mercer, ordering their dresses, suits and blazers online. She kept her hair blond and her nails and toenails manicured and painted.

The only thing that took away from her polished, professional look was a starfish tattoo on her right ankle, which she refused to discuss no matter how many times Mal and I asked her about it. Brad didn't know the story behind it either.

Roxie put her head in her hands. I placed my hand on her shoulder to comfort her.

"There will be a trial, justice will prevail, and this fickle town will thank us for exposing a criminal."

"How can you be so sure?"

"The facts are on our side."

"I hope you're right."

So do I, I thought.

When I got to my desk, I dealt with phone messages, and then I logged on to my computer and checked my email. Looking out the window, I saw it had gotten too hot for people to be moving. Only a few cars were driving on the streets. I had thirty minutes before I met with Sheriff Frost.

My mail was unremarkable—a few hate messages and a dozen or so press releases. Hate email usually started with "Holmes, you liberal puke," and then told me how this person or that organization had bought me. They often challenged my manhood, intelligence, religious faith, or patriotism. I counted on four or five such messages after every issue. On slow days, I responded to them. Today was not a slow day.

I went upstairs, put on a fresh shirt, and headed out the office door with my notepad and cell phone. I told Summer to call me in thirty minutes. "If I don't answer, send Ted to the Garden Street Deli."

Summer nodded. I wasn't afraid of Frost, but our relationship had never been good.

Over the past six years, Frost had invited me several times to tour his offices and the county jail. I had refused each time. The last thing I needed was to be "accidentally" locked in a room with a serial killer. About once a month I would get a call from a mutual acquaintance who offered to serve as an intermediary and help Frost and me "patch things up."

The standard line was, "Please stop mocking the sheriff. He's doing the best he can under the conditions." I never quite knew what they meant by "under the conditions," but somehow Frost always made himself out as the victim.

My standard response was: "I have no personal issues with the sheriff. I don't like pregnant women being tasered in Walmart parking lots, but that's just how I am."

Summer handed me the check for the loan payment. "Please don't forget to drop this off."

She would make someone a good wife, if he liked Culture Club.

I began my four-block walk to the Garden Street Deli. *This would be fun*, I thought.

6

When I entered the Garden Street Deli, Sheriff Ron Frost was sitting at a table for four in the middle of the room, sipping black coffee and staring straight ahead. It was thirty minutes before closing, and the restaurant had no other customers.

Turned over chairs were set on top of all the other tables. A black teenager mopped the checkerboard floors. He wore black slacks and a Bob Marley T-shirt. I immediately smiled and thought of the Marley anthem, "I Shot the Sheriff." The teen looked up and winked. He got the joke without me even saying a word.

Frost was oblivious to his surroundings. He was cadaverously thin and hunched over like a vulture as he sipped his coffee. He wore his signature brown suit with a cream-colored shirt and string tie. His Stetson matched the color of the shirt and had been place in one of the chairs at the table. He had a small badge on the lapel of his jacket.

Having served six years as the Escambia County sheriff, Frost had survived four grand jury investigations and several ethics complaints. His campaign war chest rivaled that of any US senator. No one messed with Sheriff Frost—except for me.

Frost nodded as I walked in and motioned for me to sit down. The waitress put down her newspaper and brought me a cup of coffee, then moved away from the table as quickly as possible. Firework shows were better seen from a safe distance.

The sheriff and I had initially gotten off to a bad start when I wrote an April Fools' article about him using the department's helicopter for pizza delivery. Little did I know that he had actually done so. Sheriff Frost didn't like people laughing at him.

When he came to the *Insider* to complain, his gun got caught in the arm of the old lawn chair that I had put by my desk. Back then, I used lawn chairs for office furniture. Frost couldn't get up without dragging the bright orange chair with him. No, Sheriff Frost didn't like to be made to look ridiculous either.

Frost had tried several times to put me out of business. Peck and the goon squad picked up papers from the racks and threw them in the nearest dumpster. They visited advertisers and pressured my investors. In the end, nothing worked. We still published every Thursday. I still wrote. He won reelection in 2008. We had reached a stalemate. I couldn't put Frost out of office, and he couldn't stop the presses.

Our latest game involved public record requests. The Florida Public Records Law gave the public access to local and state government records, including all documents, papers, letters, photographs, films, sound recordings, and other records that were made or received in connection with government agency business. The Florida Supreme Court further enforced the law by ruling that public records encompassed all material prepared to "perpetuate, communicate, or formalize knowledge," which expanded the law to cover emails, text messages and voicemail.

The law had made it possible for the public and news media to understand how and why elected officials and other government officials made decisions. There were certain exemptions of course, but the deputies' salaries were public record.

Though the state statutes were on our side, nothing was straightforward when you dealt with the Escambia County Sheriff's Office. We sent our requests via email, and Frost always did his best to figure out why we needed the information and dragged out delivering the records for as long as possible.

When I sat down at his table in the Garden Street Deli, Frost smiled and shoved a folder across the table. He said, "Here is the salary spreadsheet that you requested."

"Thank you, this only took four weeks," I said tapping the folder. "We asked for the information in a digital format."

"Our records department will be emailing it to you later this afternoon."

He shrugged his shoulders and took another sip of coffee. I waited and drank from my mug, too.

"Holmes, you are a hard-ass. I don't know why you and I can't get along. People tell me you are a reasonable fellow."

It was my turn to shrug and take another sip.

"Word is out that you oppose my request for raises for the deputies," Frost continued. "I'm losing deputies to higher paying jobs in other counties, to the Florida Highway Patrol, the Pensacola Police Department, and the Florida Department of Corrections."

True, the starting salary for deputies was about five thousand dollars less than other law enforcement agencies.

"The budgeted three-percent average merit increase the commissioners approved meant less than seven hundred dollars a year for my deputies," Frost said, getting more passionate and sincere with each word. "A rookie deputy in Escambia County with two children is eligible for food stamps."

Frost placed both elbows on the table, cradling his cup in his bony hands, and took a big sip.

"Sheriff, last fiscal year you had two and a half million dollars budgeted for personnel that you didn't spend on pay increases," I pointed out. "You spent nearly two million on office furniture and renovations, a helicopter, and computer systems. The rest you returned to the county. You should be able to find money for your pay raises somewhere inside your $80-million-plus budget."

Frost's eyes blazed. "We streamlined our operations and found we didn't need all the positions in the original budget," he said. "As a constitutional officer of the county, I had the authority to spend those funds on those items I felt would improve public safety and reduce expenditures in coming years. Didn't you read the press release?"

Frost had banned the *Pensacola Insider* from all ECSO press conferences. We received no press releases from his office.

He said, "We chose not to use the money on salaries because we couldn't guarantee that the funds would be there in future years. It would be unfair to the men and women who are risking their lives every day."

The injustice of Frost's situation almost warranted tears, but instead I took a sip of coffee.

"Frost, what you are not saying is that many deputies are far from being underpaid. A master deputy's salary averages sixty-two grand a year, while a senior deputy's annual salary in the mid-fifties. You have twenty-five sergeants making that. All are excellent salaries for this market."

I saw that Frost wondered how I knew this. He almost interrupted me but instead drank from his coffee mug. I waited him out.

"Holmes, I don't know where you're getting your numbers, but I've got deputies working two jobs to make ends meet."

"Yes, but most of those jobs are off-duty security work that Captain Peck assigns."

"Listen, I've lost forty-two deputies this year. Part of the problem is that people are retiring, but a major reason for the losses is the inadequate pay."

We both leaned back in our chairs, and Act II of the drama began.

"Okay, Sheriff. Your concerns are duly noted."

The sheriff had other things on his mind. "My people are wondering about your connections to Sue Hines," he said. "Can you account for your whereabouts yesterday?"

"Screw you, Frost." I barely held back my anger.

"No need to raise your voice, Holmes," said Frost. "The state attorney wants to know if you have an alibi just in case it comes up."

"I haven't seen or spoken with Mrs. Hines for weeks. We worked late last night getting the paper out and grabbed a beer at Intermission afterward. Besides if the state attorney wanted to ask me a question, he would have called me himself."

"We may need names of people who saw you at the bar."

"Screw you, Frost," I repeated with a little more volume and edge to my voice.

The sheriff raised his deep baritone voice. "Don't give me that crap, Holmes, or I will take you into Investigations in handcuffs."

Frost's temper was legendary. Things happened when he lost it. None of them good. When he divorced his first wife, they had a bitter fight over a lake house in north Santa Rosa County. The house burned to the ground days after he signed divorce papers and before his ex could insure the structure. The cause was never determined.

Frost caught himself. He took a deep breath and another sip of coffee.

"You really get my goat, Holmes. I promised my chief deputy that I would try to work this out with you. You aren't good for my blood pressure."

"Sheriff, if you want a statement from me, call my attorney. Otherwise, look elsewhere for your scapegoats."

Frost sat his cup down, pushed back from the table, and stood up. The grim look on his face indicated the conversation hadn't gone as he had wanted. Again, I made a mental note not to drive my car outside the city limits.

"Remember I tried to work with you," he said as he headed for the door. Mal wasn't going to be happy. Frost clearly had no intention of emailing us digital files of his payroll.

My cell phone vibrated as Frost walked out of the deli. Summer had perfect timing. I delivered the loan payment to the bank and prayed that tomorrow's bank deposit would be a good one.

Only half a block from my office, Intermission sat across from the Escambia County Courthouse, which made it an excellent place to eavesdrop. Narrow like most of the bars and restaurants along Palafox Street, the bar itself stretched the length of the front room. Small tables with two or three chairs were arranged on the tiled floor in no particular pattern in the space between the bar and the dartboard, Golden Tee, and other video games on the opposite wall. Pool tables sat in the back by the restrooms.

The menu was limited—pretzels and, if you were lucky, peanuts. Nothing on tap, but every bottled beer imaginable stocked the coolers behind the bar. It was Wednesday happy hour, so there was no live music, but Journey played on the jukebox as I walked in wearing my fourth white button-down of the day.

Maybe I should cut back on my walking and use my Jeep more so that I didn't go through so many shirts in a day. I did a quick calculation and decided my laundry bill was still cheaper than a tank of gas.

The bartender handed me a Bud Light and brought me a basket of pretzels and nuts. I smiled. Things might be looking up.

Bree Kress walked in, and the bartender sucked in his gut and rushed to take her drink order—Bud Light. She had left her cover-up in her car, and the tattoo sleeve on her right arm almost took my eyes off her athletic frame. She had muscles and curves, and everyone in the bar noted her arrival.

Ignoring the attention, Bree smiled and gave me a hug.

"That was quite a show you put on at the cafe this morning," she said with a half smile. "How's your head?"

"Throbbing but this should help," I said as I took a swig of my Bud Light. "Thank you for your help. I'll get the shirt back to you after I do laundry."

"Keep it. The owner has no idea how many shirts we have in inventory. She'll get a kick out of seeing you wear it when you walk Big Boy."

Everybody on Palafox knew Big Boy. Bree had even taken him a few times on her daily runs. The dog thought the crowd stopped to look at him when they ran. Bree acted like that was why, too.

Bree had interned with the newspaper when she was in college, filling in for Mal when she took off for her annual summer concert tour, Bonnaroo, Summerfest, and Essence. She had finished at the top of her graphic design class at Pensacola State College. Now 32, she was one of the most sought after freelance graphic artists in the area.

She had some financial success designing logos for bands that were inspired by their music. Her posters for their concert tours sold well, and she had also designed our last two Best of the Coast award posters. She wanted to get into the corporate world and help with branding, but the companies in Northwest Florida weren't willing to pay much. I knew that she was interviewing with agencies in New Orleans and Atlanta.

"How's the job search going?" I asked her.

"Walker, that's why I wanted to talk with you," she said. "I think I'm going to get a job offer from one of the top firms in New Orleans. It's my dream job."

"Great! You have a gift for design," I said. "If you need a reference or anything, I'm in your corner."

She said, "I've already given them your name and number, but that's not the problem."

Bree paused and gathered herself. "I was so stupid and probably blew it and any future good job outside of this shithole."

"What are you talking about?" I asked. "Nothing can be that bad. You're too talented to stay here."

She looked at me, fighting back the tears in her eyes. "I was so stupid."

"What? Did they throw something at you during the interviews that you weren't prepared for?"

"No, the interviews went well . . . but the background check worries me, and they are not done with that."

"If there's a post on Facebook or somewhere else on social media, I've got friends that can take care of it," I assured her.

"This is bigger than that," Bree said. "I got drunk a month or so ago and did something I regret."

"What?" I asked, signaling the bartender to bring us another round.

She pushed back her brown bangs, and said, "This town is so difficult for women like me. Single, in my thirties, intelligent. All the good guys are married. Those who aren't have so many issues—they are sadistic misogynists or mommy's boys or focused on their careers or Peter Pans that never grew up."

I hoped she didn't include me in that group of misfits.

Bree took a sip of her beer and seemed to be gathering her emotions before saying, "A woman has to have her defenses up at all times."

I nodded in agreement. "What happened?"

"I was celebrating how well my job interviews had gone with my girlfriends," she began. "We had dinner and drinks. Somebody suggested we end our night with shots at The Green Olive. Have you ever been there?"

"No," I said.

"It's a dive, but sort of cool, I guess. One of my friends wanted to meet her boyfriend there, and another said she knew the owner and could get us free shots of Fireball. I didn't have my car so I was at the mercy of the group."

I didn't interrupt her, knowing that she needed to tell this at her own pace.

She continued, "The owner, Monte Tatum, came over to our table. When he found out what we were celebrating, he bought us a round."

"He's a little old for your crowd, isn't he?" I asked.

Monte Tatum was a Pensacola rich boy—a fortysomething hipster wannabe who was a few years older than me. During his twenties and early thirties he bounced around from job to job until his dad died, leaving him a chain of dry cleaners in Escambia and Santa Rosa counties. To everyone's surprise, he didn't piss the money away.

Tatum bought out his sisters, cleaned up his act, and ran for District 4 seat on the Escambia County Commission and lost a tight race. The *Insider* had endorsed his opponent, which didn't make Tatum a fan of mine. After the election he sold off the dry cleaning company and purchased The Green Olive, where it was rumored that he may have returned to his earlier ways.

Bree's story wasn't one I wanted to hear. I tried to only show empathy in my expression.

"I was already pretty drunk by then," Bree said. "He's pretty good-looking and was dressed professionally and smelled nice. And he had good manners, never too pushy or forward."

Bree took another sip of her beer. She kept pulling back her bangs and playing with her bracelets. This wasn't easy for her. This woman read F. Scott Fitzgerald, E. M. Forster, and Flannery O'Conner. She volunteered at the Pensacola Humane Society and took care of rescue dogs.

Bree continued, "Gradually my girlfriends began to peel off. I was left with Tatum who kept buying me drinks. I remember kissing him, but little else. I woke up the next morning in his bedroom."

That son-of-bitch, Tatum, I thought. I had heard he had a way of breaking down women's defenses by appearing to be a little dopey and harmless. He spent a great deal of money on his looks and clothing to pass as being younger than he was. He splurged on his dates by dining at Jackson's and other expensive restaurants, but he was careful never to come on too strong at first.

When the women began to relax and settle into what they thought might be a nice relationship, he'd pounce. His conversation would get crude and sexual. His hands would be all over them.

If a woman was offended, Tatum backed off. He'd say she had either misunderstood his actions or he had misinterpreted her interest in him. The next day he would send her flowers, or maybe an expensive gift, but would cross the line again in a few days. The cycle of aggressive behavior would continue until the woman realized Tatum wasn't capable of any meaningful long-term relationship. There was a reason the 48-year-old man had never been married. She would stop taking his calls. If she was lucky, he'd get bored with her and moved on to other targets. I had heard some dark stories about his "breakups" that had not ended smoothly.

Bree said, "I know, I know. I see it in your eyes. You think I was stupid to hang around Tatum and not just leave when my girlfriends disappeared."

"Stupidity has nothing to do with this. I'm holding back my anger," I said. "Do you think you were drugged?"

"I don't think so," she said. "But there's a bigger problem than regretting a one-night stand or being taken advantage of by this nasty guy."

"What?"

"I found evidence that morning that he'd videotaped us having sex. When I confronted him later, he even bragged about how good I looked in it," she said. "I've begged and threatened him, and even offered to buy the damn video, but he refuses to destroy it, saying it's part of his private conquest collection."

I set down my beer and clenched my fists. I wanted to punch someone, something.

Bree continued, "If the video ends up on some sleazy website, I'm ruined. I can't stop thinking about him and his buddies getting high and watching it every night."

I stilled my temper and tried to reassure her. "The chances of your new employer finding out about this are slim. I wouldn't worry about it."

She shook her head. "I can't live having this over my head. Tatum's cruel enough to send it to them."

Bree was right. Tatum might not be the brightest candle on the cake—after all, it took him seven years to graduate from the University of Southern Mississippi where coloring was his major—but Tatum relished singling out people to harass and bedevil, and he was very good at it. He always had to have an enemy to defeat. He had spent thousands of dollars trying to discredit the man who beat him in the commission race. He had his bartenders create a blog that regularly attacked anyone Tatum believed had slighted him. I had been mentioned several times on the site.

Bree had reason to be concerned.

I said the only thing I could. "I will take care of it."

"How? You've been on his enemies list before," she asked. "What can you do?"

"I will find his pressure point."

7

The next few days we tried to focus on our regular routines at the *Insider*, but Pensacola wasn't going to let that happen.

The medical examiner, at the request of the state attorney, finished the autopsy and reported she had found that a combination of barbiturates and alcohol had killed Sue Hines. The deceased had been drinking heavily according to her husband and niece and had only recently started taking the Phenobarbital again, which had been prescribed for her epilepsy, to help her sleep.

Her husband said he had had trouble waking her before he went to the television station for his morning interview. After he left Sue had made it as far as the bathroom, where she collapsed and died of cardiogenic shock due to what the medical examiner determined was an accidental overdose.

Standing in his front yard, Bo spoke to the media that had camped out on his street. We watched the impromptu press conference that was streamed on the internet by the *Herald*. The *Insider* wasn't a part of the media entourage.

"I want to publicly thank the medical examiner for acting so quickly," Hines said. "This report will dispel any hurtful rumors that some have tried to promulgate on the blogs."

He announced that the funeral would be the following Monday at St. Joseph's Church, the downtown church founded in 1891 as a place of worship for Pensacola's Creoles and blacks. Sue had been one of the parish's biggest benefactors and sang in its choir.

When asked about the status of his trial, Hines said, "The state attorney's office has said they are reviewing the case and will have an announcement next week after meeting with my lawyers and the judge."

He looked directly into the camera. "I'm hopeful they will dismiss the charges and end this nightmare for my family."

I called State Attorney Hiram Newton to find out what they were debating. I needed that trial to happen and soon.

Newton and I had once been friends. We coached AAU basketball together when his stepson was attracting attention from college coaches. Over the years, I reached out to him and his assistants when I came across things that didn't quite look right, such as a county administrator giving "surplus" equipment to a fraternity brother, a city councilman voting to give a contract to his nephew's firm, or an escort service tied to a state lawmaker.

But when I reported on the high percentage of prosecutions of black teens in comparison with their white counterparts, Newton blew a fuse. Our research found young white males had a much greater chance of being offered pretrial diversion or work release than black teens. Newton didn't like being portrayed as a possible racist and said his office handled each prosecution fairly on a case-by-case basis.

The ACLU and NAACP tried to get the U.S. Department of Justice interested, but Newton had too much political clout. We no longer talked. He assigned Assistant State Attorney Clark Spencer to deal with me, which was fine. I liked Spencer more, and over beers the assistant state attorney once admitted, after I pledged to never repeat it, that he was happy I did the article on the prosecution disparity.

When my call was answered, the receptionist sent me to Spencer, even though I had asked to talk with Newton.

"What's this crap that you're reviewing the Hines case?" I asked. "What's there to review? He's a crook."

"Holmes, I'm ready to try the case, but the boss is worried his wife's death will make it hard to find a fair jury," said Spencer. "Hines' attorneys are going to place the blame on the missing executive director of the Arts Council."

"What about the mystery bank account and the ATM withdrawals?" I asked. "And the series of cash deposits in his personal bank account?"

"They will try to convince the jury that the deposits were his gambling winnings from his trips to Biloxi."

I said, "Funny, he never mentioned that before."

"Yeah, well his attorneys are good, but I think I can poke holes in their arguments," he said. "However, Newton knows the case isn't a slam dunk—gosh, I hate how he always uses basketball lingo—and he doesn't like to lose cases."

"Clark, we need the trial to happen sooner, not later."

He said, "I agree but Newton will make the call."

Spencer asked that I stop by his office after Sue's funeral on Monday. When I hung up the phone, I dialed Dare. The call went directly to her voicemail. I informed her about the medical examiner's report and asked her to call if she had any questions or wanted to talk. I hoped she would.

In the meantime, at the *Insider* we were focusing on the sales of the Best of the Coast issue. The advertising cancellations had slowed down, and Roxie shifted over to the ads for Best of the Coast. We needed to book the ads soon and give Mal and Teddy enough time to design them.

Best of the Coast picks were based on an online poll where our readers voted on the best restaurants, burgers, doctors, politicians, nail salons, and just about everything else the greater Pensacola area had to offer. The first year we received about three hundred ballots and sold a little over $7,000 in ads. This year we had over ten thousand votes cast. Summer needed three weeks to count all the ballots.

Summer, Roxie, and Mal reviewed the winners with me on Thursday.

"If I get started today, Mal and I think we can easily reach sixty grand in sales, which would be a 20 percent increase over last year," said Roxie. "Even better, we think we can get them to prepay before the issue runs."

Both Roxie and Mal wanted me to give Summer more hours to help track the sales and ad approvals, handle invoicing, and manage the collections for the special issue. They also wanted me to give her a bonus for doing the extra work.

Summer would never ask. She was the only one who knew the paper's bank account was on life support. She blushed as they talked about her, almost shrinking.

"Summer did the best job yet handling the tallying of the votes," said Mal. "I don't have the time to track all this crap. I'll be lucky to get all the ads finished and approved in time."

The other big task was gathering the email addresses for the winners. Roxie said, "The more prep work Summer does making sure we have the right emails and mailing addresses, the more ads I can sell."

"You don't have the time to do the administration and accounting stuff," Mal told me. "Besides, you're shitty at it."

I raised my hand. Typically, we had set aside 15 percent of the total Best of the Coast sales for a bonus pool, which usually went to Mal, Roxie, and Teddy because they put in the extra work. However, the most we had ever sold was fifty grand in ads.

"I've been meaning to give Summer a raise," I said. "Let's do this. Summer, we will pay you two and a half percent of the total sales for the Best of the Coast issue. After that, we will sit down and talk about increasing your hourly rate."

Summer nodded.

I said, "Does that make everybody happy?"

It did. They left the office for lunch and to celebrate Summer's new role.

Looking over the Best of the Coast report, I agreed they had enough potential customers to reach and maybe even exceed the goal. We only needed to hold out until those dollars began flowing.

Meanwhile, we got by. The Thursday and Friday deposits covered our checks and payroll after I made a second round picking up payments from advertisers. I coasted on the blog, posting occasionally about upcoming meetings and rewriting press releases. Wittman's petition drive still wasn't gaining much traction. It was time to sit back and hope the state attorney's office stayed the course and won the case against Hines.

Sue's funeral was set for Monday. The staff agreed with me that we wouldn't write anything on her death or her husband's pending trial until after the services. It was a Southern tradition that no one spoke ill of the dead until after the funeral. News tips would start to flow late Monday afternoon. I guaranteed it.

I talked with Summer Friday morning. Dressed in jeans and a Van Halen concert T-shirt, she had come to work early to finish entering the sheriff's office's payroll data into a spreadsheet for the database and begin her Best of the Coast assignments.

"What do you hear about The Green Olive?" I asked her.

"Not much. The place has gotten creepy. Some of my girlfriends still go because the drinks are so cheap."

I asked, "What do you mean by creepy?"

"The owner is too touchy-feely," she said. "Wants to hug or tries to kiss you on the cheek. He offers to buy shots, but nothing's really free in this world."

Smart girl, I thought. "Any pot or drugs being sold?"

"I didn't get that vibe, but who knows what happens late at night?" said Summer as she headed back to her desk. "The Green Olive isn't the kind of bar any girl wants to be at closing time."

At night I worked on the Frost cover story while Big Boy slept under the desk and jazz drifted over from Blazzues.

Ron Frost was a product of the Escambia County Sheriff's Office, where he started work in 1965. We had never been able to prove he had actually graduated from Pensacola High School or that he had even got a GED. He was hired because his father and three uncles worked there.

From the beginning, Frost displayed folksy charm. He didn't hesitate to do favors for the wealthy. Sons and daughters of the powerful didn't have to worry about DUI arrests.

In 1973 he almost lost his badge for changing an arrest report regarding a bar fight on Pensacola Beach. The naval aviators complained that their names were the only ones on the report, while a cab whisked away the instigators, sons of a beach hotel owner. The commander of the Naval Air Station complained that while his men sat in jail, their attackers went free. An unamused county grand jury indicted the arresting officer, Frost. The state attorney ended up freeing the aviators and dropped all charges. Frost never went to trial. The incident simply disappeared from memory. Only my mentor Roger Fairley seemed to remember this, and he had delighted in giving me every juicy detail.

With each new sheriff, Frost ingratiated himself with his boss. Each of the sheriffs needed someone like Frost under them. The first sheriff Frost worked for, Bud Long, was removed from office after a grand jury indictment for two counts of gambling. The grand jury had reviewed an extensive list of allegations of misconduct, neglect of duty, and incompetence and settled on the gambling.

Sitting on his back deck that overlooked Pensacola Bay, Fairley had told me the stories of Long's political career over drinks. Sheriff Long had also once been investigated for drunken, lewd behavior before minors. During a trip to Birmingham with the county school safety patrol, he invited the teenage girls, some younger than fifteen, to his hotel room and served them alcohol while only wearing a bathrobe. The incident report said he wanted to teach them how to "French kiss."

The advisor for the safety patrol program was Deputy Ron Frost, who testified on Sheriff Long's behalf and was promoted to sergeant after the state attorney refused to prosecute.

Later while awaiting trial on the gambling charges, Long was fatally wounded by his chief deputy, who mistook him for a burglar when the deputy pulled up into his driveway and saw the former sheriff climbing out his bedroom window. The rumor was Sheriff Long had been having an affair with the chief deputy's young wife.

Dan Sota succeeded Sheriff Long. He was investigated for letting family and friends fuel their vehicles at the county pumps. The man in charge of the fuel pumps was Sergeant Ron Frost.

Sheriff Sota had tough opposition when he ran for a second term. Escambia County Solicitor "Big Jim" Reilly, who had garnered attention for fighting illegal gambling, challenged Sota in the Democratic primary. One month before the election, a plot to kill Reilly was uncovered. Five men, three from Pensacola and two from the Mississippi Gulf Coast, were involved.

Fairley told me that the murder plot was never tied directly to Sota, but many felt the sheriff and the Dixie Mafia were behind it. Sota narrowly won the election, but was removed from office after Reilly's cousin in the Pensacola Police Department arrested him for DUI.

Sergeant Frost, who had run Sota's reelection campaign, was promoted to lieutenant before the DUI arrest. During the nineties, Frost rose to the rank of captain, serving as the public information officer for the next two sheriffs, which helped to build his name recognition. He handled the VIP parking at concerts and events at the Pensacola Bay Center, garnering more favor with Pensacola's power brokers.

Along the way, he changed his party affiliation from Democrat to Republican. When he ran for sheriff, Frost was swept into office as the county overwhelmingly supported all the Republicans on the ballot. At his swearing-in ceremony at Riverside Baptist Church, Sheriff Ron Frost told the audience "the era of the John Wayne-style deputy has come and gone."

He immediately dissolved the Street Crimes Unit, which was reportedly involved in many of the fourteen fatal deputy-involved shootings under his predecessor's administration. Frost brought instructors from the Martin Luther King, Jr. Institute for Nonviolence in Miami to Pensacola to train his deputies. A local civil rights group honored his efforts with its "MLK Man of the Year" award, making him the first white man ever to receive it.

We started the paper six months before Sheriff Frost was sworn into office. There never was much of a honeymoon for the two of us. Maybe it was the stories that Fairley shared, or perhaps it was just Frost's cockiness, but the truth was we never got along.

His words and actions never quite matched. While he constantly whined about not having enough money to pay his deputies, Frost loved to buy the latest "gadgets." He bought two helicopters and a mobile command bus that he showed off at the Pensacola Interstate Fair.

He also spent millions to renovate, reequip, and refurbish his administrative offices. Every office had a flat-screen television. While his deputies' pay remained flat, his administrative salaries nearly doubled, jumping from $1.68 million to $3.23 million.

When he bought his deputies Tasers, reports of abuse began to surface. Frost was forced to settle lawsuit after lawsuit. He reached a $150,000 settlement with a Pensacola teacher, who was struck with a Taser stun gun four times as he tried to comfort his pregnant wife after a minor traffic accident. The family of a high school honor student received a settlement of a quarter of a million dollars after he was tasered while riding his bicycle. The boy suffered severe brain damage.

Then deaths in the jail began to mount—six in two years. Frost tried at first to dismiss them as sick people who would have died anywhere, but after the sixth death, public pressure forced him to reorganize the facility. We had heard the changes were only cosmetic and anticipated another wave of deaths was on the horizon.

Despite the problems, Frost had easily won a second term. After the election, his Democratic opponent filed suit in circuit court against Frost and Peck Krager, alleging dirty tricks by the Frost campaign to hurt his efforts, including dispatching investigators to his former places of employment to dig up dirt on him and sending flowers to his home signed, "Love, Delilah." Frost settled that case, too.

We reported it all but got little traction from the other media. Apparently, I was the only one who didn't like Frost. Realizing that no news story or investigation would ever be big enough to knock him out of office, I had adopted the strategy of a thousand cuts, pointing out his miscues and abuses of power without too much hyperbole. The strategy appeared to be working. People were talking about finding someone to run against Frost next time.

The story on pay raises wasn't a home run, but it was a solid double. Frost had asked the Escambia County Commission to approve a special appropriation so that he could give his deputies a $4,000 a year raise, in addition to the 3 percent merit raise budgeted for all county employees.

The spreadsheet Frost gave me agreed with our research that many deputies weren't underpaid and nearly two dozen sergeants earned more than sixty grand a year. When I compared his payroll with sheriff's offices in other Panhandle counties, his troops were paid $3,600 more on average. His chief deputy made $135,000 a year. Five of his administrators made over $95,000. Damn, Peck made $85,000. You would think he could buy a better fitting uniform.

I smiled. This wasn't the kind of story Frost wanted published while potential candidates were trying to gauge if they could unseat him in the next election.

While I held off publishing anymore on Hines on the blog until after Sue's funeral, the *Pensacola Herald* had no such compunction.

Sunday morning, Big Boy and I took our daily walk. At the Circle K, where they ignored that I brought a dog into the store, I poured a big cup of coffee and bought the dog a ham and cheese biscuit. The sales clerk loved Big Boy.

The Sunday edition of the *Pensacola Herald* was on the counter with big photos of Bo and Sue Hines above the fold. Dammit. I paid for a copy, handing the inserts to the clerk. We found the nearest park bench, and Big Boy feasted while I read what a worthless piece of crap I was.

The daily newspaper had published a double truck on Bo and Sue. The spread had photos from their wedding with Rory Evans standing with the couple. They published a team shot from a charity softball game. I was in the back row, having played second base for Sue's team. The article was a beautiful obituary for a woman universally appreciated by the community.

A separate article focused on the circumstances surrounding her death. The reporter mentioned Bo's arrest, the *Pensacola Insider*, and me. Friends speculated about her death and how her husband's pending trial might have contributed to her state of mind. Wittman took a direct shot at me. He called for a boycott of my newspaper, blaming his sister's death on the *Insider* and me.

Reporters, both print and broadcast, had begun digging into my life. I suspected they would profile me soon, warts and all, before the Hines' trial began. They would recount some of my more infamous battles with politicians. The reporters wouldn't have trouble getting interviews with those I had exposed, who would offer quotes that questioned my sources and ethics without mentioning the facts backing up our articles. The pent-up frustration and anger toward me would be released.

Payback was a bitch, but I had earned it. In the early days of the newspaper, I had picked on both the daily newspaper and the local television station. I hadn't yet learned to deal with what Roger Fairly called my fatal flaw—the failure to hit the "pause" button and tone down my rhetoric before I published my criticisms.

Our first ad campaign drew blood: "A good newspaper for a town that deserves one." It didn't win us any fans at the daily newspaper.

At the time the *Herald* had come up with a promotion that let Pensacola's elite purchase decorative pelican statues. The Pelicans in Paradise was a public art project based on the CowParade project, which the *Herald*'s publisher witnessed during a trip to Portland, Oregon. He was inspired by the bovine statues scattered throughout Portland and saw an opportunity to make money.

Each fiberglass pelican was nearly five feet tall and weighed about seventy pounds. They were decorated by various artists, selected by the statues' sponsors, and placed at various outdoor locations around downtown Pensacola.

A total of forty-one pelicans were commissioned for the project. The first wave of twenty statues included a pelican decorated with bright flames and a spiked collar and anklets called "Flambo," "The Godfeather" (a mafioso pelican in a pinstriped suit), and "Pelvis the Elvis Bird" and "Peli-Queen Elizabeak," which were based on Elvis Presley and Queen Elizabeth I respectively. The paper got the city to pay to put them on display around downtown.

The *Insider* countered with cheap, plastic pink flamingoes that we planted next to the *Herald*'s pelicans. Our flock included "Flam-stripper," a flamingo in a thong that was ready to entertain SEC head football coaches, law enforcement officers, and whoever had a wad of twenties or a visa card; "Ramboingo," an attack Flamingo that could whip birds a hundred times its size, even ones made of fiberglass bolted to the ground and painted all pretty; and "Mini Bucks," the flamingo that represented all the call center jobs the Pensacola Chamber of Commerce brought to the area by offering wages lower than most third world countries.

At a music festival, we stole one of their banners, cut it up into little pieces, and sent the *Herald* editor a ransom note. Unamused, she threatened to arrest me for petty theft.

We also regularly posted clips of the television station's miscues—and there were dozens. When a prostitution sweep in the seedy part of Escambia County snagged the station manager, we published his mug shot.

No, our competition relished going after the *Pensacola Insider* and particularly me.

I spent my Sunday trying to find out more about Sue's last days. Dare hadn't returned my call. Maybe the medical examiner's report had satisfied her concerns about her friend's death, but I wanted to find out more about Sue's state of mind as the trial was set to begin.

If she wasn't having seizures, why take the pills? The Sue Hines I knew hated taking them. She wouldn't self-medicate to sleep. Sue would have run three miles or read Faulkner instead.

Unfortunately, I hit roadblocks everywhere I turned. Sue's friends and neighbors either wouldn't talk to me or hinted that I was only trying to cover my ass and deflect any blame for her death. Harden had disappeared and didn't return calls or answer text messages.

So I decided to get my mind off Sue and follow up on helping Bree with her situation. I had a source who always seemed to know what was happening in Pensacola's underbelly. I drove to Benny's Backseat, the last remaining strip club on the west side of Pensacola. At four o'clock on a Sunday, the club didn't have many customers, but Benny Walsh would be there. He auditioned new talent on Sunday afternoons after he attended Mass at the Cathedral of the Sacred Heart and took his mother and aunt to brunch.

"Holmes, what the fuck are you doing here?" Benny yelled as my eyes adjusted to the dark room. Benny sat on a stool in the far corner where he could watch the bar and the stage. He wore a powder blue polo shirt. Every finger had a ring, and his gold tooth shone when he smiled. The stage lights reflected off his bald head.

As I walked towards him, he whispered something to a stocky waitress with a Daffy Duck tattoo on her left buttock. By the time I sat down, a Bud Light appeared on the table. Benny didn't shake hands. He bumped fists.

"What's got you slumming, my friend?" he asked.

On the stage, a very skinny girl with a blonde curly wig twirled on a gold pole to Warrant's "Cherry Pie." She held onto the pole for dear life. The sailors at the foot of the stage placed bets on whether or not she would fall again.

"What do you hear about The Green Olive and Monte Tatum?" I asked. It was always best to go straight to the point with Benny.

"That piece of crap," growled Benny. "He ran up a seven-grand tab here and tried to walk out without paying. The girls had the boys hold him down until he signed the credit card receipt."

He added, "Then the bastard tried to get the credit card company to void the transaction. Thankfully, we had him on video pretending to be a big shot and buying rounds of drinks for the girls at his table."

"Anything on him creating sex tapes of women he sleeps with?"

"One dancer did go home with him once," said Benny. "She said the SOB had a mirror above his bed, a stack of porno magazines in his bathroom, and drawers full of sex toys but didn't mention a video camera."

We drank and talked about his business and the challenge of finding dependable dancers. Millennials weren't the best recruits. They didn't work well with the older dancers, always demanded the prime hours, and never wanted to wait their turn.

"And they're covered with weird tattoos," he said as he waved at Daffy Duck to bring us another round. "Not butterflies and roses. They've got the names of their boyfriends and pets on their backs. It's too much." But Benny understood stripping was a young woman's game. He would adapt.

Benny said, "There is a guy going around town paying waitresses, sales clerks, and strippers to perform in short hardcore videos. He said he planned to show them on the web."

Benny was old school and didn't touch hardcore porn. He tried to keep his girls out of making trips to South Florida to the adult film studios, but the money was too good—a thousand dollars for a weekend. The girls never told him how many videos were cut over those three days, and he never asked.

"This guy doesn't really care about their looks. Most of the girls work at Waffle House or Walmart," Benny said as he pretended to shudder.

"He sets up a camera, the girl takes off her clothes, and they make amateur porno flicks. For about twenty minutes' worth of work, the girl makes three hundred to four hundred dollars. The kinkier the sex, the more money she gets paid."

"You know his name?"

"Can't remember. He tried to recruit my girls, and I had him thrown out. Too many drugs tied up with porn. The ones he got to do it couldn't dance anymore. Too screwed-up. One got so strung out she wound up in rehab."

"Would you text me if you find out his name?" I asked. "Also, let me know if you can find out what Tatum has been up to lately."

"Sure. Why the interest in that pervert?" asked Benny.

"A favor for a friend," I said, knowing Benny would understand. I reached for my wallet to pay my tab.

"Your money's no good here."

I nodded thanks and walked out into the sunlight.

Three years ago, Benny's third ex-wife was in a terrible car wreck. We investigated the county road where the accident took place and found out the road contractor had not followed the construction documents. The newly opened road had a much tighter curve than designed, and the speed limit had been set too high.

His ex-wife had no chance of maintaining control of her Camaro at 45 mph when she hit the bend. She flew off the road, hit a tree, and spent three months in the hospital and rehab.

After we published our article, the road contractor settled for five million dollars. Benny no longer had to pay alimony. I got a lifetime beer tab at a seedy strip club and another news source.

That night, Big Boy and I watched the Dodgers beat the Braves. I poured some beer in his bowl and gave him a pile of pretzels, figuring we would walk it off in the morning.

On a legal pad, I listed a few questions for Frost that would round out my story on his payroll. I needed to try to get him on record. Otherwise he would claim the article was unfair.

On the next page, I wrote my notes on the conversation with Benny, which probably had nothing to do with Bree's dilemma with Tatum.

I nodded off as I tried to work up a to-do list on Hines for after his wife's funeral.

Most people avoid conflict and turn away from confrontations. Few people ever walk into a room where everyone wants to stone them. I tend to walk into those rooms often.

After Big Boy and I took our Monday morning constitutional, during which he belched continually, much to the delight of the running brigade, I showered, dressed, and headed to Sheriff Frost's breakfast spot.

Mama's Kitchen was located two blocks away from the county jail at the edge of a decaying shopping center. Faded stickers on the window promoted pancakes, fresh biscuits, and home-cooked meals. Squad cars filled many of the parking spaces. The sheriff's silver Tahoe sat right next to the front door in a handicapped parking space.

Frost sat with Peck and two uniformed refrigerators who only spoke in grunts and ate as if they had just learned how to use a fork. Thank goodness the waitress carried away their empty plates as I pulled up a chair to their booth.

"Holmes, we didn't invite you to breakfast," sneered Peck, who looked even smaller next to Refrigerator No. 1. The two humongous deputies started to straighten up, but it was taking a while for the brain signals to reach the muscles. Two more regular-sized officers pivoted their seats at the lunch counter in our direction.

"Captain Krager, there's no need to be rude," said Sheriff Frost. "I'm sure Mr. Holmes has a few questions for his article."

Turning to his bodyguards, he said, "I've got this. Go wait in the car."

Again, it took a few minutes for the two giants to disengage from the booth and make it outside. It was like watching two dinosaurs saunter off into the jungle. The lunch counter deputies paid their tabs and exited, too. Peck stayed.

After the waitress brought me coffee, I said, "Sheriff, the records show you've given pay raises every year for the last six to your administrators, but nothing to your deputies."

Peck's cheeks started to redden. Frost remained calm, not taking his eyes off me.

"And each year you return millions to the county's general fund," I continued. "Why haven't you put some of the money toward increasing the starting salaries for deputies and cut some of your administrative overhead?"

Frost said, "You don't understand politics, Holmes. The taxpayers like to see budget dollars being put back and not wasted."

"But your budget keeps increasing."

Peck interjected, "The people want safe streets, and they're willing to pay for it."

Frost silenced Peck with a glare. This fight was between him and me. The hired help was to remain on the sidelines.

"I've reviewed some of the personnel files," I said. "Why aren't you doing job performance evaluations and tying raises to them?"

"The unions wouldn't stand for it," he replied.

"What about your administrators and department heads? They aren't in the union."

Frost said, "Well, I can't start treating my employees differently."

"But you have. Take Peck. His salary has doubled since you took office."

"A good leader rewards loyalty," said the sheriff with a little more tension in his voice. The veins in his neck began to swell. I think he knew what I was going to say next.

"Your brother, Amos, must be exceptionally loyal," I said. "In four years, he has gone from corporal to sergeant, lieutenant, captain, and then to major. Some might call that nepotism."

"You smug little pissant," yelled Frost as he slammed the table, spilling everyone's coffee. "I'm done. You print one word about my brother, and you will feel my wrath."

He stood up. "Peck wants to destroy that worthless rag that you call a newspaper, but I've kept him off your butt. No more." Frost poked me in the chest. "If you make this personal, then it will become personal."

Peck got up, too. "This is going to fun," he said. "Only a dumbass screws with the sheriff."

The waitress brought me the check after they left. I paid for the coffee and all their breakfasts. I was a dumbass.

At the *Pensacola Insider* offices, Mal had reined in all the editorial parts of the issue and only had a few outstanding ads. She had filled the holes caused by the last-minute cancellations with ads for local non-profits that she kept on file. Maybe those free ads would buy us a little goodwill in the community.

"Did you give Big Boy beer last night? His burps smell awful," she said as I passed by her desk. The dog was asleep underneath it.

I just smiled. "Let's move the staff meeting to this afternoon," I said to no one in particular. Everyone was in his or her own world anyway. I followed up with a group email explaining that I would be attending Sue Hines' funeral.

At my desk, I posted a teaser on the upcoming Frost cover story to my blog, which I knew would impact his blood pressure. I did one more read through of the article, adding a few remarks about my morning coffee with the sheriff. I kept Amos Frost in the article. Then I emailed it to Roxie for copyediting. After handing off the issue to the team, I went upstairs to dress for the service.

In the rain outside St. Joseph's Church, I stood with hundreds of others as they filed in for the service. I chose to stand in back when I got inside, surrounded by the drenched street folk that saw the funeral as a chance to get out of the downpour.

When I left my cadre of sinners who pretended to sing the hymns so the ushers wouldn't remove them, I felt the eyes of the congregation on me as I stood in the communion line. Fittingly, the bishop ran out of hosts as I reached him. He didn't even offer me a blessing, just a faint nod.

As I walked to the back, unblessed and without grace, I imagined Sue popping up from her casket and asking, "Why, sweetie? All we did was care for you."

Bo and his grandparents stared straight ahead as I passed them. Nestled in between Hines and his brother-in-law sat Julie Wittman, Jace's teenage daughter. Her red hair was pulled back in a ponytail, and she was crying into a handkerchief. Her uncle had his arm around her shoulder, comforting her.

Jace Wittman didn't take his eyes off me. His eyes glinted when the bishop didn't give me communion. Monte Tatum sat two pews behind Wittman by himself.

The bums must have held a conference while I was gone because they gave me a wide berth when I returned to my place. They probably were worried that I would hurt their reputations and future handouts if anyone in the church saw me with them.

I didn't walk over to the parish hall after the service. Martyrdom didn't suit my personality. Neither did three bean casseroles. Instead, I strolled across Government Street to the state attorney's office to meet with Clark Spencer. I needed to be sure they stayed with the prosecution.

Spencer specialized in white-collar crimes and loved wearing sweater vests, even in the summer. Humor wasn't one of his strong suits. His breath smelled of chili and onions, which meant he had eaten lunch at the Dog House Deli. The mustard stain on his tie confirmed my deduction.

He said, "Bowman Hines' attorneys want to cut a deal. Their client says the Arts Council executive director stole the funds. For immunity, he will testify against her."

"You've got to be kidding, Clark. He's had ample opportunity to share that explanation before."

I listed the opportunities on the fingers of my right hand. "When I tried to interview him for my article, when the auditors reviewed the Arts Council's financial records, and when your investigators tried to question him. He's guilty."

"The death of Mrs. Hines has made the defense attorneys more creative," said Spencer. "I think they fear her death points to his guilt, and they're scrambling."

"Wait a second," I said holding up my hand. "The daily newspaper and others have been not too subtly blaming me for Sue's mental state.

Bo Hines and her brother have fed that rumor. Now, you're saying it works against Hines."

"Walker, not everything is about you," said Spencer, as he scraped off the dried mustard he had just noticed on his tie. "None of us know what jurors may think about Sue Hines' sudden death, but I agree with his attorneys. It's a bigger problem for them than our side."

"I thought your boss was having second thoughts about prosecuting," I remarked.

Spencer shook his head. "I spent an hour this morning with Mr. Newton walking through the case. He is considering the immunity deal, but I think he will give me the green light to proceed."

"This is bullshit. Bo is the big fish. He's not this saint that everyone in the community believes he is. He is the mastermind behind the embezzlement scheme. Besides, no one knows where the executive director is. I haven't talked to Pandora Childs in weeks."

Clark kept his cool. "Mr. Newton is up for reelection in two years. Sheriff Frost is in his ear, denouncing you every chance he gets."

He continued, "The judge will delay the trial for a week to allow Hines to deal with his wife's death, which actually helps me. Hines' request for a speedy trial had cut short our trial preparation, but the judge's postponement has also given his attorneys time to negotiate with my boss. I will push to go to trial, but Hines may have the clout to pull off an immunity deal."

"Dammit, Clark. The press is vilifying me. The trial is how to prove what we reported is the truth."

"Yelling at me, Walker, does no good. Grow up. Your bad press isn't my problem."

"Screw you," I said, then walked back into the rain to my office. I had to find Childs. She had last been seen when investigators confiscated her computer and all the checkbooks. The twenty-six-year-old Emory University graduate had only been the executive director for fifteen months. She had no roots in the community and few friends.

Childs had let me interview her for the Hines article, but I hadn't connected the dots at the time. Later when my questions began to turn aggressive and pointed, "no comment" was her only reply. Attractive in a bookworm sort of way, she dressed well, liked apple martinis and an occasional joint. She had no visible tattoos, although I suspected she had either a rose or butterfly somewhere on her body.

Back at my office, I wrote "Pandora Childs" on a yellow Post-it Note and stuck it on my computer screen.

At the staff meeting, we went around the conference table. Mal proudly reported all the editorial was in, even Doug's. Roxie had a few questions about my cover story before she could finish copyediting it.

"Sheriff Frost and his deputies aren't going to be happy," she said. "But the readers will love it."

Teddy showed us sketches of his cover ideas. We chose a caricature of Frost sitting on top of a pile of money. We might as well go all the way.

"When can we have an A&E story on the cover?" asked Jeremy.

Mal said, "When you write one worth a shit."

Jeremy stuck out his tongue but didn't take the bait. Doug begged for another week on his cover story on the park petition. Mal voted against it, and I agreed with her. We needed to move on it before the petition drive gained any momentum.

When we adjourned, Summer pulled me back into the conference room.

"Today's deposit was anemic," she whispered. "We don't have the money to pay the second installment on the loan that you promised to bring to the bank."

"Don't worry about it," I said. "We'll have the money in a week or so to get caught up."

"We have to pay the print bill tomorrow or they won't put us on the press."

"Did we have enough money to cover all the paychecks we cut on Friday?" I asked.

"Only because Mal, Teddy, and I agreed to hold ours until today," she said.

Dammit. I said, "Thank you, Summer. We need to hold out a little longer. This will pass."

I hoped.

Summer handed me a handful of phone messages and a press release that had been faxed to us. Who the hell still used fax machines?

The press release read:

Open Meeting – Save Our Pensacola Tonight
6:00 p.m. New World Landing
We can stop the $100M maritime park.
Refreshments served.

Jace Wittman wasn't wasting any time. He buried his sister in the morning and was holding a public meeting hours later. He obviously wanted to capitalize on the attention Sue's death had received.

"Open" meant open, so I set out to crash Wittman's little naysayer meeting. My mood was foul enough already. Why not walk straight into a den of snakes?

Besides, who could resist the allure of free refreshments?

10

On the way to the meeting I thought about what Roger once told me, "Pensacola—old Pensacola—loves nothing more than stopping progress, especially when a wealthy Yankee is proposing it."

The maritime park had begun as a public-private development to revitalize downtown Pensacola after Hurricane Ivan. Wealthy real estate developer A. J. Kettler, who had built several high-end condominium projects along the Gulf Coast and also owned the city's minor league baseball team, the Pensacola Pilots, was looking to build a new stadium. And the University of West Florida had benefactors willing to build a maritime museum.

The city would issue bonds to provide $40 million to remediate the former industrial site on Pensacola Bay and build the stadium. Kettler would build a $16 million office building. The university would construct a $20 million maritime museum. The rest of the forty acres would be open for commercial, retail, and residential development.

It was a brilliant plan, with an excellent mix of public and private use. The build-out of the project would put over $300 million on the tax rolls and create about 1,000 jobs. *Florida Trend* hailed the maritime park concept as one of the brightest developments on the horizon.

The city council members loved the plan—with the exception of Jace Wittman. Wittman had taken a strong position against it for the single reason that his high school nemesis, Stan Daniels, was A. J. Kettler's attorney. His grudge against Daniels trumped any argument about the benefits that might be derived from the proposed development.

Despite fifteen months of public hearings and city council debates on all aspects of the project, Wittman claimed the public had been left out of the decision. His first referendum to stop it for this reason had failed. But now that the building was about to begin, he had a new petition drive focused on rescinding the construction contract.

Wittman had a group of loyal followers that I had labeled "naysayers" during the 2006 referendum. They were suspicious of any changes proposed for their city, especially if it involved spending tax dollars, and they loved Jace Wittman. The naysayers saw him as their champion, the one who believed all their wild conspiracies and promised them the keys to power. He was their Moses, a voice in the wilderness telling the city leaders to repent and forget their wicked progressive ways.

As I pondered this unfortunate truth, I realized the rain had stopped. Steam rose off the hot pavement as the business day subsided. Workers piled out of the Escambia County Office Complex opposite the *Insider* offices. Secretaries and their supervisors wandered across the street to Blazzues and Intermission to commiserate over a few beers about how they only got four weeks of vacation and the stupidity of the county commissioners before they headed home.

A herd of runners thundered down Palafox Street. Downtown bars had running clubs that offered pasta and cheap beer. The afternoon runners, older than the morning crowd and about twenty pounds heavier, jogged or walked past me in their too-short shorts. Me? I'd rather pay the extra dollar for my PBR and skip the lasagna on a plastic plate.

When I walked into the meeting room at New World Landing, a boutique hotel on south Palafox, I expected to see a bunch of old farts wearing tinfoil hats, drinking warm punch, and eating soft sugar cookies. I wasn't too far off. However, they had left their hats at home, probably because the tinfoil interfered with the sound system.

I had taken it on the chin earlier at Sue's funeral, but not tonight. I got a sick pleasure from walking into rooms like this one. The crowd reacted to me the second I entered and signed the guestbook. A perceptible shudder could be felt, as if someone had found a fingernail in their punch, but was too polite to say anything.

I sat in the front row with my black notebook and recorder. Wittman and his brain trust huddled in the corner next to the punch bowl and cookies. I looked around and didn't see a pile of stones in any of the corners, which only meant they hadn't planned ahead.

Wittman's Save Our Pensacola attracted two groups of people—military retirees who hated anything they believed might increase their taxes, and old Pensacola families that resented anyone changing their town. The military retirees always talked about their tours of duty and how Pensacola didn't measure up to other cities. From their vantage point, community leaders were idiots and never did anything right.

The old Pensacola crowd began every conversation with a statement about how many generations their family had lived in the area. They tolerated the military retirees because they were worker bees that did the tasks they would never do like knock on doors, gather petition signatures, and put campaign signs in yards.

The Save Our Pensacola leaders wouldn't ask me to leave. After all, they had complained about the city's lack of open meetings. The daily newspaper and the television reporters stood in the back of the room. Two very slight men in cheap suits with their photographers and cameramen shook their heads and grinned at me. Apparently they expected fireworks.

A couple of retired military types sat on both sides of me, not saying a word, but they looked hard to see what I was writing in my notebook. Pensacola attracted such retirees from Michigan, Ohio, and Illinois. They complained about everything while getting their health care for free at the Navy hospital and buying cheap goods and groceries at the Corry Station PX Mall.

They filled their days attending city council meetings, writing letters to the editor that quoted Fox News and Rush Limbaugh, and trolling internet forums and blogs looking for chances to prove their brilliance.

I wrote in my notebook for my chaperones to see, "The crowd is warm and happy to see me. Their medications must be kicking in. There is a smell of Bengay, talcum powder, and Old Spice in the air. I hope the Depends hold out."

The two men sitting next to me snorted. Having failed to intimidate me, they stood and moved to sit next to the refreshments to guard against reporters eating the cookies. They muttered "asshole" under their breaths as they left me.

A lady in red polyester pants with a head of orange-tinted hair opened the meeting with a prayer to "Our Lord and Savior." I didn't think she meant Wittman, but I bet he did. The room didn't have a flag, so they said the Pledge of Allegiance to Wittman's lapel pin.

The woman sat down at the head table with a gangly fellow who turned out to be her husband, and Wittman. Her chair creaked as she plopped down. My escorts stood and stared at me from their vantage point near the sugar cookies. I barely suppressed a laugh and kept my head down while I wrote.

"Ichabod" thanked his Technicolor wife before launching into a diatribe about all the sins of Kettler and the flaws of the maritime park. The retired UWF professor, who said he was a sixth-generation Pensacola native, droned on and on. A few of the faithful in the crowd appeared to be nodding off. The reporters were getting restless, and I noticed them checking their cell phones. Wittman nodded with a fixed phony smile and stroked his gray goatee. He kept looking at the door and checking his Rolex. After nearly thirty minutes, he stood and took over the meeting.

Wittman was a big man, a former athlete whose waistline had expanded as he had gotten older. His black hair with a few strands of gray was still full, and he wore a white polo under a Ralph Lauren blue blazer and loafers without socks. He didn't have his brother-in-law's natural charm and perfect manners, but he commanded attention when he spoke.

"Thank you, Professor Ellis," he said. Looking at the other reporters, he continued, "I see the legitimate, nonbiased press is here for this very important meeting."

Professor Ellis and his wife stared daggers at me.

"We, the people of Pensacola, don't want this park." Wittman's words set off a round of applause and a chorus of "amen" from the crowd. "The downtown crowd is trying to force this on us. We shouldn't be paying for a baseball park for a millionaire's hobby team."

Wittman towered over the podium. He reminded me of William Jennings Bryan when he gave his famous "Cross of Gold" speech at the 1896 Democratic National Convention. Wittman had the same religious fervor that I imagined the upstart Bryan had when he delivered his closing line to his speech on using silver to value the US dollar: "You shall not press down upon the brow of labor this crown of thorns, you shall not crucify mankind upon a cross of gold." Then the crowd went wild, rushed the stage, and swept him in as their presidential nominee. Bryan would later lose to William McKinley.

The Save Our Pensacola crowd edged towards the same level of hysteria. Wittman was charismatic and a master of twisting his opponents' words and programs. He knew how to manipulate this audience and the media.

He shouted, "We CAN do better!"

"Yes, WE CAN," I heard a familiar voice yell from the back. Bowman Hines walked into the room, welcomed by applause and a hug from his brother-in-law.

"Jace is so right," said Hines, dressed in the same dark suit that he wore to his wife's funeral, "which is why I'm handing Save Our Pensacola a check for $10,000." Facing the audience with his arms spread, he continued, "This is our town, our land, and we are the only ones who should decide what we do with it."

More applause. I noticed the reporters were lapping it all up. The park project was in trouble.

"This check is just a down payment on my commitment. My late wife would have never wanted to see such valuable property handed over to some outsider. Sue would want me to stand with her brother against this boondoggle."

I couldn't remember Sue ever taking a stance on the maritime park.

"Sue loved nature," Bo continued. "I donate this money in her memory so that we can have an open waterfront park that the entire city can enjoy."

Hines spied me in the audience. He pulled back his shoulders and stuck out his chest as if daring me to say or do anything. He said, "We will stand together as one community and take back our park for our families and future generations to enjoy. Let Kettler build his ballpark elsewhere."

As the crowd cheered, Wittman's daughter, Julie, slipped into the room. Thin, with the broad shoulders of a swimmer, she had the same athletic figure as her late aunt. She must have arrived with Hines.

Wittman said a few more words, thanked the crowd, and walked over to the "legitimate" reporters with Hines, who motioned for his niece to stand at his side. He wanted the entire family in the photo that would grace tomorrow's front page.

Hines beamed confidence. He smiled and answered every question, all the while keeping his arm around his niece's shoulder. He wanted to project that he was the hero who had suffered an unbearable loss, and with his family by his side, he would rescue the city in the name of his beloved wife.

I walked out and headed to the hotel's bar, 600 South. Pensacola had only a few high-class bars. This was one of them. The waitresses had no visible tattoos, wore short black dresses, and noticed when your glass was three-quarters empty. Plus, 600 South didn't have a running club.

I ordered a Jack and coke to celebrate my surviving three near stonings in one day, a new Walker Holmes's record. As I sipped my drink, an African-American man sat down beside me. He was slim but well-built, possibly a triathlon athlete. He had too much muscle to be just a runner, and he carried himself like he was either a cop or Marine Corp officer. Being in no mood to do anything but drink alone, I ignored him.

"You Walker Holmes?" he asked after the bartender handed him his Crown Royal, no ice.

"Guilty," I said, looking ahead as I watched through the mirror behind the bar the Save Our Pensacola supporters milling in the parking lot.

He extended his hand. "I'm Alphonse Tyndall, Mr. Holmes. Joyce Blake is my aunt."

I shook his hand and turned toward him. "How's your aunt?" I asked.

"She is living with my mom in Memphis," he said. "Still hurting, but doing much better. I wanted to buy you a drink and thank you for helping her when no one else would."

Three years ago, an Escambia County deputy ran over Joyce Blake's son, Andre. The patrol car's dashboard camera captured the teenager's homicide. The video shows the vehicle chasing Andre, who is riding a bike, and the officer shouting at him to stop. We hear the enraged deputy muttering about him being a black kid as he catches up with Andre and tries to shoot him with a Taser from his window, and then we see the officer suddenly veering into him and pinning him under his car.

It was a senseless tragedy that never should have happened, but Sheriff Frost blamed bad parenting for the death. He claimed the boy was snooping around a construction site at three o'clock in the morning and his deputy was just doing his job.

A coroner's inquest agreed with Frost. I did not. I lost sleep over the boy's death. I saw it as my failure. His death was only the tip of a much larger iceberg. Poverty, racial disparities, and a failing public education system were at the root of the problem.

In break rooms, at lunch and dinner tables, and on internet forums, people blamed Andre or his mother for his death. "Why wasn't he at home at 3:00 a.m.?" "Why didn't he stop?" "He's a thug; he was packing a gun." They wanted to blame his mom because they didn't want to admit the same thing could happen to their children—that is if they lived in Brownsville where their teenagers rode bikes because they didn't have cars, and if their children felt they needed a gun to protect themselves but knew if they were found carrying one, they could end up in prison forever, and if they lived in constant fear of being racially profiled and chased down by the police—or if their children lived in a world that had crushed their dreams long ago.

Joyce Blake's pastor agreed to set up a meeting for me to interview her, and our paper told her son's story. We also posted the patrol car's video on the blog. After the backlash, Frost eventually had to fire the deputy, which didn't make him happy. Our reporting won a victory for the Blake family and cleared Andre's name. It added to the list of grievances Frost had concerning me.

I asked, "What brings you to 600 South? Don't tell me it's a coincidence that you're having a drink here."

Tyndall smiled. "My aunt told me how you never backed down in your reporting on Andre. You always would walk right into the middle of the fight. I've been following the Sue Hines story, saw the announcement of the Save Our Pensacola meeting, and took a chance you might be there. I lingered in the back of the meeting room and followed you into this bar."

So much for my powers of observation.

"Alphonse is a pretty big name to carry around," I said. "Do you have a nickname?"

Most white people in Pensacola didn't know that many of the black men they knew had two names—the ones they gave their white co-workers, and the ones their friends called them.

Alphonse smiled. "Razor because I never could grow a beard. I'm pleased to finally meet you, Mr. Holmes. My aunt speaks highly of you."

"Call me Walker or Holmes," I said. "Please skip the mister."

"Using 'mister' is part of my military background," he explained. "I spent six years in the Air Force as a judge advocate officer."

I asked, "Are you with a local law firm, Razor?"

He shook his head. "I'm on the Florida attorney general's Child Predator CyberCrime Unit."

According to the Federal Internet Crimes Against Children Task Force, Florida ranked fourth in the nation in volume of child pornography. The CyberCrime Unit protected children from computer-facilitated sexual exploitation.

The Florida attorney general set up five regional offices to work cooperatively with local law enforcement agencies and prosecutors to provide resources and expertise. Pensacola had one of the regional offices. The identity of the staff at those offices was confidential information, but we knew they were active. Last month, the task force, in conjunction with local, state, and federal law enforcement officials, arrested twenty-six individuals across the Panhandle for targeting children.

"You've been busy," I said. "The work must wear on you."

Razor said, "Getting the sick bastards off the streets makes it worth the effort. Unfortunately, new ones pop up every day."

So we drank. Our second drink was to "Operation Yellowtail," the name of the bust operation last month. The third was in memory of Sue Eaton Hines. The fourth was for the maritime park because Razor loved baseball. And the last was for short black dresses.

Razor and I exchanged business cards and agreed to drink again soon.

As I got ready to head back to the loft and Big Boy, the bartender handed me an envelope. "A woman told me to hand this to you before you left," he said.

"What did she look like?"

He shrugged, "I don't know . . . fat."

I opened the white envelope when I got back to the loft. A single, off-white piece of stationery fell out.

It was Sue Eaton Hines' suicide note.

11

Jace Wittman had always thought of himself as special. Like his brother-in-law, Bo Hines, Wittman was a miracle. He was the fifth child in a brood of six, which in and of itself didn't make him special, except for the fact that his mother had had three miscarriages before his birth.

His mother always called Jace her gift from Saint Theresa. Every miscarriage took its toll on Mary Alice Wittman, but the Roman Catholic Wittmans didn't believe in birth control. Jace Francis Xavier Wittman's birth proved God still loved his mother, and even though she would eventually have another child after him, a girl, Jace would always be the special one.

His older brothers teased him and often ganged up on him, but nothing ever dimmed his belief in his predestination to greatness.

"No matter how many times we hit him," his older brother Frank would tell friends, "Jace would never back down from an argument."

Jace was never wrong, and his mother made sure the Wittman siblings understood it. No one could ever tell her that Jace wasn't perfect. When he was caught with matches and gasoline setting a neighbor's shed on fire, Mary Alice blamed his friends for egging Jace on.

On the baseball diamond, Jace was the best baseball player. He had gloves for batting, fielding, and running the bases, a trio of bats to use, and real cleats. Jace pitched and played shortstop when not on the mound. The biggest kid on the field, he led the league in home runs—that was until Stan Daniels' family moved from Gulf Breeze to Cordova Park when the governor appointed his father to a county judgeship.

Stan played with a hand-me-down glove from his older brother. He wore Keds, not baseball cleats, and used whatever bat the coaches handed him. But he could hit homers from the right and left sides of the plate, and his fastball was unhittable.

Roger, whose nephew played on Stan's team, remarked, "It was something watching the Daniels kid come up to bat. He was thin and wiry, with lanky, rust-colored hair that fell straight over blue eyes. Everything seemed effortless for the boy."

Jace hated him, and so did his mother. When Stan was the altar boy at St. Paul's, she wouldn't take communion.

Both Stan and Jace made the Little League's all-star team. At the team party at the Wittman house, Jace beat all his teammates on his brand-new ping-pong table playing, of course, with his own special paddle.

Then Stan took off one of his flip-flops. Using it as a paddle, he beat Jace in three straight games. Mary Alice had her husband put the table on the street after the party. Jace never played ping-pong again. Neither did Stan.

Both boys went to Pensacola Catholic High. Stan didn't try out for the football team his freshman or sophomore years. He worked at his grandparents' grocery store after school. His parents were fine with that. They wanted him to learn the value of a dollar and how to handle customers.

Jace quarterbacked a rather mediocre team, which won its district but never progressed far in the state tournament.

The coaches watched Stan in PE and convinced him to try out his junior year. He not only won the starting position but also quarterbacked the team to two consecutive state titles. Jace was moved to tight end.

Stan got a scholarship to Florida. Jace went to Louisiana Tech and never forgave Daniels for stealing his thunder and proving that he wasn't as special as his mother and he thought. Within a year, the Louisiana Tech coaches kicked him off the team. There were rumors that he had gotten a professor's daughter pregnant—something never mentioned in polite social circles.

Stan, meanwhile, was injured his sophomore year and never started a game at Florida as quarterback. He still earned a UF letter after the coaches switched him to be the long snapper on punts and field goals.

Stan went on to law school, worked two years with the state attorney after graduation, and then joined one of the big firms in town.

Both Jace and Stan returned to Pensacola and married girls that were best friends at Pensacola Catholic High. The wives never expected Jace and Stan to get along, which was a good thing since they didn't.

Jace went back to school at Pensacola State College until he flunked out. He got a job as a bartender at a Warrington dive, The Barrels. His career changed when his father died in a boating accident, and his mother married Bruce Eaton, Sue Hines' father. Jace became an agent for Eaton's real estate firm.

Though their wives stayed close, Jace and Stan rarely crossed paths. Stan became a managing partner of his law firm and president of The Florida Bar. His firm, one of the oldest in the state, mainly handled the legal affairs of corporations, specializing in the utilities, health-care systems, banks, insurance, real estate, and construction industries. They partnered with large out-of-town firms to defend the tobacco and pharmaceutical companies when they were sued in Florida courts. Whether the lawyers won or lost their cases, Daniels' firm always got paid.

The animosity between Jace and Stan came primarily from Wittman. Stan never commented on Jace and their high school days. For his wife's sake, he tried to keep his relationship with Jace civil. But Wittman saw every success of Daniels as something that was stolen from him.

Jace floundered as a realtor, largely because he spent more time playing softball and hunting on the Eaton's land in South Alabama than selling real estate. When Stan's firm hired him to handle a land deal on Pensacola Beach, Jace botched it so badly that his stepfather was forced to rescue him. This gave Wittman even more reason to hate his rival.

Then Jace somehow got himself elected to the Pensacola City Council. In politics he found the adoration and attention that was sorely lacking in the rest of his life. He positioned himself as a rebel who was an environmentalist and advocate for the people. He didn't win many council votes, but he never lost an election until the maritime park controversy.

The proposed project was a no-brainer for most people. The city would take polluted waterfront property across from city hall that it owned, use bond money to remediate it, and create a public-private joint venture to revitalize downtown Pensacola that was still struggling to recover from Hurricane Ivan and the 2008 recession. It was progressive thinking outside of the box, something that Jace would naturally support.

But there was one big problem for Jace. It turned out Stan Daniels represented A. J. Kettler, the owner of Pensacola's minor league baseball team who wanted to use the ballpark proposed for the site for the Pensacola Pilots' games. Jace could not let Stan take credit for the renaissance of downtown Pensacola, which would happen if Daniels' client got a piece of the maritime park

Wittman found every reason to oppose the plan to build the park. So no matter what Stan or anyone else said to persuade him that it would be the best idea for the city, Jace refused to agree that the maritime park would revitalize Pensacola. Stan even had the bishop try to intervene and mediate the dispute between Jace and Kettler, the baseball team's owner. But Jace wouldn't budge.

When the Pensacola City Council finally passed the plan for the park by a 9-to-1 vote, Jace immediately began a petition drive to rescind the decision. It became a vicious battle. There were no bounds to the lies and half-truths that Jace spread to stop the park. He focused primarily on the baseball park, overlooking the maritime museum, office building, and other components of the project. As far as Jace was concerned, the battle over the construction of the maritime park boiled down to whether to have a ball field for the Pilots. Jace called the public-private venture a "land grab by a millionaire carpetbagger," completely ignoring Kettler's sixteen-million-dollar investment in the project.

The *Pensacola Insider* supported the construction of the new maritime park and expressed enthusiasm for the addition of a ball field. I created a weekly feature in which we tackled Wittman's lie of the week. My blog became particularly effective in bedeviling the councilman and his cohorts. I rapidly rose on Wittman's enemies list, though never high enough to supplant Stan Daniels.

The referendum to build the park passed with 57 percent of the vote. A year later, Wittman lost his council seat. His wife died of cervical cancer while he was running for reelection, and he and his daughter moved in with Bo and Sue. The couple had plenty of room, and Sue provided a motherly influence for her niece. Besides, Jace had been forced to sell his house to pay for the cancer treatments.

Wittman's new petition drive sponsored by his political action committee "Save Our Pensacola" was his final attempt to stop the park and deny another victory for Daniels and his client.

Wittman's goal was to cancel the building contract and force a new contract that didn't include construction of the ballpark. He needed to present a petition signed by 10 percent of the city's registered voters—about 3,700 signatures.

One more time it was Jace Wittman versus Stan Daniels. Jace could not—would not—let Stan beat him again. Any collateral damage didn't concern him.

He had to win.

12

The note was written on cream-colored linen stationery that was monogrammed "SEH"—Sue Eaton Hines. The message was one sentence:

"Sweetie, no more lies."

There were water stains on the paper. Tears, maybe. Was this Sue's suicide note? How could I be sure? And if it was, what the hell should I do with it? I had to publish it, didn't I?

I couldn't take this to Bo Hines. He wouldn't let me in the house. Even if he did, why would he help me? This could be damning to his trial. Obviously, his wife killed herself because of his lies. Right?

I shouldn't have had that last bourbon and coke. The walk four blocks to the loft helped sober me up some. I found Big Boy bouncing all over the place, so I attached the leash to his collar, and we headed out to find Dare. Maybe she would recognize the handwriting. She wouldn't answer my phone call, but she would meet me the door at her house if she saw me with Big Boy.

It was after nine, but Dare stayed up late. If her porch light was on, we would ring the doorbell. To hedge my bet, I texted her: "Coming over with BB. Have new info on Sue." Half a block later, I sent a second text message: "Please."

While we walked toward Aragon, Dare texted back: "K."

Dare lived in the trendy downtown neighborhood, Aragon, which was built on the site of a former housing project one block north of Pensacola Bay. Twenty years ago the city fathers realized, with the help of local developers who made large contributions to their campaigns, people would pay top dollar to live downtown near the bay. Why waste the view on poor black people?

The city relocated the housing project residents with the understanding that Aragon would have a quarter of its lots set aside for first-time homebuyers. The catch phrase for the project was a "new, urbanist, traditional neighborhood." Really, that's how they described it when the developers presented the drawings to Rotary Clubs in the area.

The developers moved the poor people. Expensive townhouses, cottages, park houses, side-yard houses, small cottages, and row houses replaced the tenements. The developers made millions, and the city added thirty-five million dollars to the tax rolls.

What about the first-time homebuyers? They turned out to be the sons and daughters of the developers and their buddies. Nobody else could afford it. No blacks and none of the offspring of the families that had been moved off the property lived in the new Aragon homes.

Dare resided in a two-story row house in the middle of Aragon. Big Boy and I reached her house in about twenty minutes. A lot of beautiful trees lined the streets between my loft and her house. Both the dog and I took advantage of more than a few of them.

The front porch light was on. Big Boy made a dash for Dare's front door as soon as he saw it, jerking his leash out of my hand. Hearing the jingle from his dog tags, Dare opened the door and greeted the mutt with a hug and kiss. She unhooked his leash, and Big Boy ran in and immediately jumped up on her couch. I followed the pair and shut the door behind me.

"I'm still pissed at you for suggesting that Sue committed suicide," Dare said over her shoulder as she sat next to Big Boy, who put his head in her lap. She was dressed in a red Ole Miss polo and navy blue shorts, and wearing pearls, of course. Spread out next to her laptop on the coffee table were financial reports and contracts.

"I know, I know. Isn't everyone mad at me?" I replied. "That's my superpower, pissing people off."

"Stop right there, Walker Holmes," Dare interrupted. "You brought Big Boy here to soften me up, but it won't work. The dog is always welcome. You? I'm not so sure about. Just tell me what you found."

I handed her the note. She turned on the light next to the couch and grabbed her reading glasses off the coffee table. She folded herself back into the couch. Dare read the note maybe three times, handed it back to me, and got up and left the room. When she came back five minutes later, she had a tissue and her eyes were watery.

"Did Sue write that note?" I asked, quietly.

"Where did you get it?"

"From a fat lady, but that's not important," I said.

Dare glared at me as if to say *really?* "Your wisecracks aren't as funny as you think," she added out loud.

I said, "That's what the bartender told me, really."

This wasn't where I wanted the conversation to go. I pointed to the stationery in Dare's hand. "Dare, did Sue write the note?"

"I think so. Sue had a unique writing style, a mix of cursive and print letters. There was no rhyme or reason to it, except it worked for her." She paused. "I think I have a thank-you note she wrote me a few weeks ago."

Dare went to her study. I heard her rummaging through her desk. Big Boy had fallen asleep and was snoring. She brought back the thank-you note. It, too, began with "Sweetie," written nearly identically to the suicide note. We appeared to have a match.

Dare started to sob. I held her for a few minutes until the wave of tears passed. Then I walked into the kitchen and poured us both cups of coffee. Good old Dare, she always had a pot of coffee brewed. She followed me, and we sat around the large island in the middle of the kitchen.

"I still can't believe it," she said. "What lies is she talking about? What has Bo done? Sue worshiped him. Is it about the Arts Council money?"

"I don't know," I said between sips. "It could be the missing funds. It could be something far worse. The state attorney's office is debating whether to prosecute Bo. His lawyers are trying to get an immunity deal in exchange for him testifying against the council's executive director. Bo could walk away from this with a slap on the wrist. Nothing to die for."

Dare started to tear up. "You are an asshole. You're talking about my best friend's death."

"I'm sorry. Really I am, but help me figure this out. Did you hear that Bo is now supporting Jace Wittman's petition drive? He gave it ten grand tonight."

"What?" She looked up and set down her cup. "That makes no sense. Sue told me that Bo's company could get some subcontractor work at the park."

Dare stood and looked at a framed photograph on the counter. It was her, Rory, Bo, and Sue on Hines' yacht, all wearing huge smiles.

She turned to me. "Those men should be thinking about Julie. That poor girl has lost her mother and her aunt. Sue told me her niece had become sullen and withdrawn lately."

Dare refilled her cup. "She quit the swim team. Her grades fell. Sue was struggling with how to connect with the girl."

I said, "Would Jace or Bo listen to you?"

She shook her head. "No, Bo is too heartbroken, and Jace is too full of himself as always. Maybe I will reach out to Julie."

We sat and drank coffee, each caught up in our own thoughts. Big Boy continued to snore in the next room. Before I did anything with the suicide note, I needed to have an expert verify the handwriting.

My rush to publish a controversial story had gotten me in trouble before. Frost had tried to shut down my paper over an article regarding him and one of his hunting buddies. In sworn testimony to a Florida Ethics Commission investigator, Frost had downplayed any personal connection with a vendor to whom he had given a five-million-dollar communications contract. The sheriff said he had no close relationship with the company's owner and spent little time with him outside of the office. The investigator specifically asked about the rumor of hunting trips, which Frost denied.

When the daily newspaper printed a photo of the two standing over a moose they had killed in Wyoming in 2008, another communications vendor filed a complaint with the state attorney's office, calling for an investigation of Frost for official misconduct, perjury, and false official statements. Clearly, the two were friends and hunting buddies.

We published an article on the investigation. Frost claimed the audiotape of the interview had been doctored and demanded a retraction. I refused. Two weeks later, the court reporter sent out a corrected transcript. After repeatedly listening to an audiotape of Frost's statement, she determined that the sheriff hadn't said he had never hunted with the new vendor. She corrected the transcript to say: "I hadn't hunted with him this year."

The complaint was withdrawn, the case closed, and no further action was taken against Frost. State Attorney Newton said that errors by court reporters were rare but not unusual. We had to admit that we had never listened to the tape. The newspaper was forced to print a retraction, even though we had only reported on what the complaint had said. Frost publicly threatened to sue us but never did.

Clark Spencer told me, "I've used court reporters for years, and this doesn't happen often. There was no indication that this was anything other than an honest mistake by the court reporter."

Peck delivered copies of the retraction to our major advertisers, and I spent weeks doing damage control to rebuild our image. Much later, I learned the court reporter's son had been hired by the sheriff's office.

"I need to be sure the note was written by Sue," I said, refilling my coffee cup. "Would you mind if I take your note and have an expert compare it with the one I was given tonight?"

Dare slid both notes across the table to me. She picked up her mug again and drank, her face thoughtful. "Does today's donation to Save Our Pensacola have anything to do with the note?" she asked. "Is Jace involved in this, too?"

"I don't know."

Slamming down her empty mug, Dare said, "Then what the hell do you know, Walker?"

"If the note is Sue's, I know I have to publish it," I said.

Then I put down my coffee cup and walked out the back door, heading for home. Big Boy would spend the night with Dare. No reason for both of us to lose sleep.

13

Walking back to the loft, I texted Gravy, my attorney: "Meet me for breakfast at CJ's Kitchen 7 a.m."

William "Gravy" Graves Jr. handled most of the newspaper's legal issues. When local officials didn't want to comply with a public records request or had any legal issue, I called Gravy.

Gravy was in his early forties, a committed bachelor, devoted ladies' man, and one helluva trial attorney. Witnesses changed their underwear after he deposed them.

He got his nickname for his daily breakfast regimen of biscuits and gravy at CJ's. No matter how late he was out the previous night, Gravy could be found every morning in the corner booth of the little diner on the western edge of downtown eating two big, open-faced biscuits smothered in creamy sausage gravy.

Gravy held the record for the shortest term on the county commission, twenty-three days. Fifteen years ago, Commissioner Joe Willis died suddenly of a heart attack on the weekend before the election while watching his beloved Florida Gators lose yet another football game when a last-second field goal veered wide right.

The governor despised the candidate who won the seat and refused to appoint the man to finish the last three weeks of Commissioner Willis's term. Gravy was dining in the next booth at the Silver Slipper in Tallahassee when he overheard a conversation among the governor's staff and offered to be a three-week commissioner.

Since then, Gravy and I toast whenever a county commissioner's tenure hits the twenty-four-day mark. His record would never be broken.

At 7:05 a.m. Gravy sat in his spot, already making headway on his biscuits. He had the daily newspaper spread out in front of him. Dressed in Levi's and a starched blue buttoned-down shirt, he looked fresh and ready to take on the day. He smiled at me broadly. I, on the other hand, felt and looked like crap.

Gravy ignored the circles under my eyes and waved to the waitress to bring me a cup of coffee.

"Before you tell me your latest crisis, did Sheriff Frost hand over the payroll records you needed?" he asked.

When I nodded in the affirmative, Gravy said, "Do you have any idea what I went through to get them?"

He said he had a client in his office last week when his cell phone kept vibrating.

"I didn't have time to look at it, and it would have been rude."

The phone would rest every few minutes and then start vibrating again until he finally turned it off. A few minutes later his secretary knocked on the door and handed him a fax with a four-word message: "Call me! Sheriff Frost."

Gravy said, "I excused myself and called Frost's office. They patched me straight to his cell phone."

Frost told him that he would hand over the records I requested not because he gave a rat's ass about Walker Holmes or his rag newspaper, but because he respected Gravy. And officers of the law should respect each other.

"He wanted me to know I owed him a favor," said Gravy. "And he would hold me liable for how you used those records."

I asked, "What did you say?"

"Thank you, Sheriff," said Gravy, laughing.

He finished his last bite, threw his napkin on top of the plate, and pushed it away. He asked, "What's your latest crisis?"

I handed him the note.

"Who is S E H?" Gravy asked.

When I told him, he whistled.

"It was delivered anonymously to me last night," I said between sips of coffee. "Dare confirmed it's Sue's handwriting."

Gravy's smile disappeared. "Well, you need to hand it over to the state attorney."

"I'm going to let you give it to them but not until I verify the handwriting," I said. "Do you know someone who can do the analysis if I give them another sample of her writing?"

He said, "There's a retired forensic tech in Mobile I've used before. My paralegal can drive it over to him, and we'll probably get a reply in a few days, depending on how busy he is." Gravy looked me in the eyes, "Once it's analyzed, what will you do?"

"I'll publish it," I said. "Then, you can deliver it to the state attorney's office."

Gravy said, "The state attorney won't be happy that you publish it before handing it over to his office, but as long as it's Sue's handwriting they can't do much more than complain."

"It's Sue's handwriting."

"If it's not, you might have to deal with an obstruction of justice charge, but it will be more bluff than reality," said the attorney. "No one believes this is a homicide. There is no active investigation."

Gravy pointed to the front page of the daily newspaper spread out on the table. The headline read "Hines Honors Wife, Opposes Park."

He said, "However, anything you write will look like you're attacking Bo Hines to clear your name. You'll be playing into his argument that that you're a tabloid publisher out for big headlines to attract readers and that you're trying to sell ads at his expense. Is that wise?"

"Don't worry. I'll use words like 'appears to be,' 'possibly,' and 'awaiting confirmation by experts' to cover my ass."

Gravy just nodded and stared ahead while the harried waitress brought me the omelet I had ordered. After she had walked away, he asked, "What else do you want from me, other than being your errand boy?"

I told him about Bree and Monte Tatum. Gravy and Tatum graduated from Pensacola Catholic High, though Tatum was about six years older. I knew there was some bad blood between them, but not quite sure why.

"He's an asshole," Gravy said. "That sounds exactly like something he would do. He could never get a date like a normal person."

As I tried to stomach the omelet, Gravy continued, "Tatum liked to hang around good-looking younger guys with pretty girlfriends. He came over to FSU when I was in school and hung around the fraternity house, even though he was in his mid-twenties. He partied with the young couples, bought them drinks, and got them drunk. Then he'd start feeding the girl cocaine on the side. The girl got hooked and would do anything with Tatum for more."

He took a sip of his Tab. Who still drank Tab, especially for breakfast? I wondered.

"I had this girl I was seeing when I first moved back to Pensacola. Joy was a bank teller, a sweet girl, beautiful. We were in bed one night. I got up to go the bathroom, and she was gone when I returned. Joy left in such a hurry she forgot her phone on the nightstand. The phone log showed she had just received a call from Tatum. When I confronted her about it, Joy told me he had coke for her."

I said, "I thought Tatum had cleaned up his act and was all respectable now."

"Maybe but a guy like that doesn't ever change," Gravy said. "Tatum dumped Joy two weeks after I ended our relationship. She couldn't give up the coke and went to jail for writing bad checks. I worked out a plea agreement and she eventually moved to Orlando."

"Could you put out a few feelers and see if any other women have stories like Bree's?" I asked.

"Sure, but others may be too embarrassed to talk."

"Give it a shot. I will ask Harden to do the same," I said.

Gravy nodded and started to gather up his newspaper.

"Anything else you need from me?" he asked.

"What do you think will be the fallout from the suicide note?"

"Like I said, the state attorney will be pissed if you go public with the note before giving it to him. If his wife wrote it, Bo Hines looks guilty as hell. The prosecutors will have to take him to trial. Hell, the public will demand it."

Gravy took another sip of his Tab. "Part of the town will applaud your investigative skills. The others will hate you for it. It definitely will help you sell papers."

"My papers are free."

"Then you're a dumb ass."

"I know."

"You never cease to amaze me," Gravy said, folding up the wrinkled papers. "I've never seen someone so focused on self-destruction, but I'm glad you're here. I will try to smooth things over with the state attorney."

"Gravy, all this is somehow linked. Posting the note on the blog will be how we fish for more leads. Maybe someone will want to talk once they read it."

"And the nuts will crucify you," Gravy said as he got up to pay the bill. "But you're used to that."

I gave him the suicide note and the sample of Sue's writing Dare had given me. I didn't mention that the cover story on Sheriff Frost's payroll would be on the newsstands Thursday morning. Gravy might have wanted to have me committed to a psychiatric ward.

When I got back to the office, Big Boy was lying at the backdoor. Dare had tied his leash to a nearby lamppost and a note was attached to his collar.

"I fed him two spicy burritos for breakfast. Have fun! —Dare."

Big Boy passed gas all the way up the stairs. He didn't even acknowledge that I was walking behind him. After a shower, I felt better. The dog demanded I take him for a walk. Considering his breakfast, I agreed. Fortunately, a cool breeze blew off the bay.

I picked up a copy of the *Pensacola Herald* as we walked and read about Hines and his brother-in-law's performance at the Save Our Pensacola meeting during Big Boy's many pit stops. The two lavishly praised Sue and were quoted saying their efforts to stop the park were to create an environment-friendly park to honor her memory. One section would be kept completely natural and off-limits to even the public. They weren't going to let a carpetbagger ruin the people's waterfront. A. J. Kettler could build his ballpark elsewhere.

Hines hinted his "legal troubles" were behind him, and his attorneys had indicated all charges against him might be dropped.

"It was a witch hunt perpetrated by someone trying to make a name for himself, someone I thought was a friend," Hines told the reporter,

who was more than happy to include it in the article. "We have cooper-
ated fully with the authorities, and they agree I'm innocent."

My old friend aimed one solid shot at me. "And once all the charges
are dropped I plan to sue Walker Holmes and the *Pensacola Insider* for
libel and defamation, and I will win. It's time we end the negative influence that they have had on Pensacola. I can't bring back Sue, but I
can avenge her death."

14

The paper ran smoothly for a change. Mal had received the last outstanding ad, and she had printed me the pages for one last read through. No matter how many times you looked at the pages, there was always something you missed. Roxie took a break from working on the Best of the Coast sales and looked over the pages, too. The only one missing was Doug. Mal and Roxie made sure I noticed his absence.

"You've got to quit babying him," said Mal, in a voice loud enough for everyone to hear.

"He's fine and still growing into the job," I said.

"But he isn't getting better at making deadlines."

For the next two hours, we worked on the cutlines and pull quotes, and Mal loaded the pages up on the printer's FTP site. Mal and Teddy's friend Kyle completed the database with all the salary information so that readers could search online for the pay of their "favorite" deputies. We tested the web page, and it worked splendidly.

"Frost's head will explode when the issue hits the stands tomorrow and he realizes how easily voters can check out his payroll," I said to Mal and Teddy.

"It could make for some uncomfortable nights for you," said Teddy.

"I'll do more walking than driving," I replied. "This is a nice change of direction from all the Hines reporting."

"But how many chainsaws can you juggle?" chimed Mal. "One slip and you lose a limb."

We all laughed, but Mal did have a point.

Summer pulled me aside and asked to talk with me in the conference room.

"My paycheck bounced," she whispered.

"How? Everything looked fine yesterday."

She said, "The bank put a hold on the McGliney check for some reason and didn't give us credit for it. They returned my check and the Gulf Power payment NSF."

"Give me some time," I told her. "I'll take care of it."

After thirty minutes working my way up the food chain at the bank, a vice president agreed to release the deposit. Unfortunately, the amount wouldn't show up until after midnight. Meanwhile, Summer had to worry about her rent check and car note payment.

"I'm sorry," Summer said after we had gotten the bank to release the deposit. "I should have held my paycheck until I knew the funds were available."

"No, this is my problem," I said. I had some cash in my savings account and withdrew enough to cover her check.

Handing her the cash, I said, "Go ahead and take off the rest of the afternoon. Give your landlord and the finance company cash for your payments, explaining that there was a screw up with your bank account."

"You don't have to do this," she said.

"Yes, I do. I'll also cover any bank charges."

Summer looked relieved. I said, "Let me buy you dinner today."

"Okay," she said as she went back to her desk to get her purse and keys. "Remember I'm vegan," she added.

Of course, I thought. "What do vegans eat?" I texted Gravy. He replied, "Try oysters. They don't have a central nervous system."

"Huh?"

Gravy answered, "They don't feel pain like other animals so you may get away with it. I'm not sure that the strict vegans buy that explanation, but living on the Gulf with all our seafood has some of the local ones willing to make an exception."

After spending a good part of her afternoon covering her bad checks, Summer had a friend drop her off at the office at six o'clock. She wore a bright orange sundress, make-up, and looked spectacular. I asked if she would like to eat at the Atlas Oyster House.

"Sure, I love oysters," she said.

We sat on the Atlas deck that overlooked Pitts Slip, a marina outside the Port of Pensacola that opened to Pensacola Bay. In the distance, the traffic had backed up on the Three-Mile Bridge. Flashing lights signaled an accident at about the midpoint.

A light breeze came off the water, and the temperature had dropped to the high seventies. The place wasn't crowded but had a respectable number of patrons.

Summer pulled at her brunette hair as she talked, twirling it around her finger. I couldn't tell if it was a nervous habit or just a habit. She had originally moved to Pensacola from Michigan with her Navy aviator boyfriend. When I asked where in Michigan, she held up her palm, which resembled the state, and pointed to a spot a half-inch below her index finger. Summer said, "I grew up here."

Her boyfriend had earned his wings and was transferred to Corpus Christi. Summer decided to stay. "I wasn't cut out to be a Navy wife. Playing second to his naval career wasn't for me."

She had a soft voice and a wicked smile. The waiter immediately became infatuated with her, which meant we had no trouble with service. Our beer mugs were never empty.

Summer had worked for the newspaper since mid-April. The first time I met her, she walked into the office and said she loved the paper and wanted to join the staff. Mal and Roxie liked her, so I hired her for twelve dollars an hour. If those two didn't like her, Summer wouldn't have had a chance. Yoste, on the other hand, was my hire, which somewhat explained his difficulties.

After two dozen oysters and half as many beers, Summer began to tell me why she loved the paper and put up with my bullshit.

"I've never worked at such a cool place, where what we do matters," she said in a voice that was maybe a little tipsy.

"You're a good fit," I replied. "You brought some order to the business side of the paper."

Summer straightened up and said, "Well, I should. I majored in accounting and had half a semester to go on my MBA when I moved here with the asshole."

"I'm sorry about the check issue today," I said, "but I appreciate how you handled it."

She leaned towards me. "Well, I used to be a dope dealer."

Yes, she had a slight buzz going. She threw the line at me as if it were a nerf ball, wondering if I would catch or drop it. I tried not to show my surprise.

"I don't do it anymore, but selling pot paid for college," Summer said flashing a sly smile. "No one ever suspected a wholesome coed of being a big dealer at Eastern Michigan."

She explained how she had run her business, never letting anyone buy on credit, and avoiding trouble with her suppliers. She made it sound like she had sold Girl Scout cookies.

"When I was in high school I smoked pot and sold really small amounts," she said. "When my supplier learned I had been accepted to Eastern Michigan, she told me how much money I could really make and offered to give me six ounces at a time."

I looked around to see if anyone was listening to our conversation. Summer lowered her voice a fraction. "I would sell that in about ten days, keep about seven or eight hundred dollars, and return the rest of the cut to my supplier, who would give me another six ounces. I did that through undergrad and grad school."

I asked, "Did it impact your studies?"

"No, although developing the self-control to not smoke all my stuff was the hardest part. The dealing itself wasn't that difficult. It took maybe fifteen minutes to put everything into dime bags for the week, and you need organizational skills to work around people's schedules and make deliveries."

"How did you find customers?"

She laughed. "It was a college in icy Michigan. Everybody smoked weed. The most money I made was when I was an RA in the residence hall. People would literally come knocking on my door for drugs, and there were parties in the building every night. I was always in demand."

"And you made enough to cover your college expenses?" I asked.

Summer nodded. "My tuition was covered by my scholarship. I paid for, like, almost all of my expenses through dealing. I used it to feed me, go out, cover my car payments, and buy all my clothing, books, and supplies."

"Do you miss the money?"

"No, I miss the excitement, which is probably why I was attracted to the *Pensacola Insider*. You give me my excitement fix every day."

"You seem to really like the *Insider* team," I said.

"I do. Mal is so cool. She's well-read and very organized," Summer said.

"She really is the brains of the paper," I said.

"She and Teddy are a great couple," she remarked. "I don't think there's a more talented, creative couple in Pensacola. I've seen other alt-weeklies in other cities. The *Insider* is special."

I nodded my agreement with her assessment.

She continued, "Roxie is the perfect salesperson for this paper. She fights for clients and challenges you on their behalf. And I love her clothes."

"How about Jeremy and Doug?" I asked.

"You and Mal give Jeremy too hard of a time. He can be a box of kittens, but he knows art and music."

"You're probably right," I said. "It's just too easy to pick on him, especially with all of his melodrama."

"Walker, he's your A&E writer. Doesn't melodrama come with the job?"

I laughed. "You have a point."

"I also hate to see Doug and Mal always at odds," she added. "But Mal is probably right. He isn't really cut out for this paper. He has the coolest job in town—investigative reporter for the *Pensacola Insider*. Girls would love to date him and hear his tales, but all he wants to do is fish."

I nodded. "I'm hoping he will come around and see the value of our reporting."

"I don't think it will ever happen," Summer said, "but I love your optimism."

I ordered some edamame and a small house salad to get a little more food into her. She got her second wind and wanted to talk more about the paper.

Sipping a water with a slice of lemon, she asked, "Has it always been this way? So, hectic and with such constant pressure?"

I took a gulp of my beer and looked out at the traffic on the bridge. "It's like walking a tightrope without a net, but our reporting is important. The *Insider* is the equalizer for the powerless and voiceless in this community. Often it seems like we are the only ones standing up for justice and against corruption. But somebody has to be Horatius on the bridge, standing in the gap fighting off the horde."

Summer said, "I can't imagine Pensacola without the *Insider*. I've seen how people look forward to their issues. I'm proud to say I work here."

"I make it sound more heroic than it is," I said. "But we have done a pretty good job of keeping our finger on the pulse of the community and picking the right side of most issues. Financially, I think it will start paying off at some point. Advertisers follow readers."

She asked, "What's your exit strategy?" Summer's accounting and MBA sides were showing.

"Originally our goal was to corner enough of the advertising dollars in this market to force Barnett to buy us out and merge the *Insider* with the *Herald*," I said. "Then we were hit by hurricanes Ivan, Dennis, and Katrina. The economy fell apart. Barnett figured that putting us out of business was easier than buying us."

She asked, "What about your investors?"

I laughed. "They are looking for an escape clause without losing the half million they invested."

"Surely they are pleased with the investigative reporting."

I shook my head. "No, they are more often upset that we uncovered their favorite politicians and the backroom deals of their friends. Our early board meetings were epic battles over editorial control and the finances. My investors haven't written a check to help us in years."

"How have you survived?"

"Hubris and credit cards," I said.

After I paid the tab I walked Summer to a cab and headed back to the loft, where Big Boy anxiously awaited his nighttime walk. Forty-five minutes later, we were in bed asleep.

That night I dreamed of Mari.

By the second semester of my second year at Ole Miss, Dare and Rory were an item. Dare had less and less time for me, though she got me dates with her sorority sisters for the big parties. Rory would finish law school soon and ask Dare to marry him. I wasn't sure how I felt about it, but my feelings didn't matter.

I began working for the college newspaper, *The Daily Mississippian*. The juniors and seniors got all the cool beats and big stories. Sophomores did the fluff pieces unless we could scoop the upperclassmen with a story or topic that they hadn't thought of. Scooping them became my obsession, of course.

The *New York Times* published a story on the rise of suicides on college campuses that had gotten some attention. I went to interview the telephone operators that handled Ole Miss's twenty-four-hour crisis line.

That was how I met Mari Gaudet, a psychology major from Eunice, Louisiana. Petite, dark-haired, and olive-skinned, she had no interest in being interviewed, especially by a skinny frat boy in khakis and a white button-down shirt.

Mari took the volunteer job seriously. Twice that semester she had talked students out of overdosing on pills. She had a calming voice and a big, genuine laugh. Her coworkers said she had regular callers, lonely students who needed someone to help them navigate adulthood.

They also told me that she had recently broken up with a football player and had little interest in dating. They clearly didn't think I was in her league. She was also a GDI, a God Damn Independent, who hated anyone tied to the Greek system. I later learned that Mari had dealt with too many suicidal coeds who had failed to make it through sorority rush.

After three phone calls and two visits to the crisis center, she agreed to do the interview at the library. She refused to meet for coffee or a drink, not wanting to give me the wrong impression.

I did my homework on suicide and its prevention. My knowledge on the subject and my questions impressed her. She even smiled a few times and laughed once.

The article had a huge impact, making it to the front page, but below the fold. The Associated Press wire picked it up, and other student newspapers and a few dailies published the article with my byline. The chancellor even appropriated a few more dollars for the crisis center's budget. The senior and junior reporters hated me, but I didn't give a shit. I became addicted to journalism.

I sent Mari a thank-you note but received no reply. I thought of dropping by the crisis center or even calling the hotline but chickened out. Dare might have helped me figure Mari out, but she was focused on picking out her dress for the engagement party in anticipation of the "big ask."

A month later, I skipped my afternoon political science class and headed to Rowan Oak, my favorite getaway on the edge of the campus. Rowan Oak, the ancestral antebellum home of William Faulkner, was built in 1844. The white, two-story house stood on over twenty-nine acres not too far from the square in Oxford. Rowan Oak was open from dawn to dusk. Five dollars covered the cost to tour the home, but walking the grounds was free.

I liked to explore the grounds and had only been in the house once. A couple of times, I met the old groundskeeper who remembered Faulkner and shared a few stories about the odd little man who won the Nobel Prize in Literature in 1949.

The University of Mississippi owned the property and preserved his papers in the Faulkner Room on the third floor of the J. D. Williams Library. Every day when I walked from the Pike House on Fraternity Row to my classes, I read the Faulkner quote memorialized on the back exterior wall of the library: "I decline to accept the end of man . . . I believe that man will not merely endure, he will prevail."

When I sat on a bench at Rowan Oak, I channeled the man who wrote about a decaying South coping in the aftermath of its Civil War defeat, integration, and the Civil Rights Movement, a man whose works were rarely taught in Mississippi classrooms because he made the state come to grips with its past.

In the dream, I did what I did once or twice every month during the four years I was enrolled at Ole Miss. I parked my 1969 blue Camaro at the gate and walked up the narrow driveway between two rows of trees. As I approached the brick walk to the house, I veered to the right and down a slope to a bench overlooking a creek. It was my private spot not visible from the house.

Mari was sitting on the bench, just as she had twenty-two years ago, staring away, sobbing. She was upset because she had failed to prevent a suicide. I had helped her cope with the loss at the time. It had been the pivotal moment of our love, the one time I did something right in a relationship.

I rushed to her, wanting to hold her in my arms, longing to touch her skin again, smell her hair, and kiss her lips one more time. The harder I ran the further she was from me. I shouted her name repeatedly, but she wouldn't look my way. Then, as if an invisible tether had snapped, I fell forward flat on my face, got up, and rushed toward Mari. But I kept stumbling. I yelled, but she still didn't hear me as I approached. As I reached out to her, Mari faded away. I stumbled over the bench and over a cliff.

I awoke, covered in sweat, crying her name.

15

It was 5:00 a.m. I dressed, put Big Boy on his leash, and started running north on Palafox. I didn't wear my headphones or bring my cell phone. The dog knew this outing would be different, but he willingly came along.

I had to run Mari out of my system.

We ran past the San Carlos Hotel, "The Gray Lady of Palafox." Built in 1910, lumber magnate and shipbuilder Frasier Bingham envisioned it would rival the upscale hotels in New Orleans, Mobile, and Atlanta when it opened on the first day of Mardi Gras celebrations. Over the years, a series of owners would expand on the north and west sides of the hotel, adding a ballroom and office and retail spaces.

For decades, Pinckney Hall ran his business and political empire from the penthouse suite of the San Carlos. He controlled railroads, banks, and lumber mills across the state. He hated unions, liberals, and Yankee carpetbaggers, and he kept his businesses racially segregated until Attorney General Bobby Kennedy threatened to shut them down.

An infamous miser, Hall fired a manager for using two paper towels to dry his hands in the restroom. His First Gulf Beach Bank had marble floors and oriental rugs but not a single hot water tap in the entire eight-story building.

Hall had a five o'clock weekday ritual. He and his business associates and buddies would gather for cocktails. They toasted "Confusion to the Enemy!" with Jack Daniel's whiskey. When the CBS News began at 5:30 p.m., all conversation and movement ceased. Hall took his news and Walter Cronkite very seriously. After the news concluded, the group moved to the Executive Club for dinner.

Hall died in 1991 at the age of ninety-four. The San Carlos Hotel ceased operations the following year and had been vacant for almost two decades. A proposal to convert it into retirement apartments failed to materialize. The current rumor said the federal government might buy it, demolish the hotel, and erect a new federal courthouse.

As we ran past the hotel, I almost stumbled on a shattered piece of mortar that had fallen off the building.

At the Wright Street intersection, we moved past the Perry House. Charles A. Boysen, Swedish consul to Pensacola, began construction of the two-story house with porches that wrapped both floors in 1867. Governor Edward A. Perry completed the house in 1882 shortly before he became Florida's fourteenth governor, serving from 1885–89.

A Massachusetts native and a graduate of Yale, Perry moved to Pensacola in 1856 to practice law. During the Civil War, he joined the Pensacola Rifle Rangers, which elected him captain. He later commanded the Florida Brigade in General Robert E. Lee's Army of Northern Virginia. Twice wounded, he was discharged as a brigadier general.

While he was governor, Florida adopted a new constitution and cleared out the last visages of Reconstruction. An outspoken opponent of the carpetbaggers, Perry made sure the Northerners never owned his home that overlooked downtown Pensacola. He bequeathed it to the Scottish Rite of Freemasonry. His antebellum home had been the Scottish Rite Temple in downtown Pensacola for more than a hundred years.

Big Boy and I began to run up the hill. My anger about our cash flow issues, Bo Hines' irritating confidence that he would be cleared, and the possibility I could lose everything prevented me from slowing down. Big Boy seemed to understand and didn't lessen his pace. The grudges of Hall and Perry drove us harder.

Breathing hard, I pushed us past the "Our Confederate Dead" monument in Lee Square that was erected in 1891 and ran across Cervantes Street into North Hill.

Once there, I fell to the ground in Alabama Square. My chest was nearly exploding. Big Boy laid panting beside me. Getting up, I cupped my hands and gave the dog water from the fountain. His tail began to wag again. I sat on a bench and watched the sun rise.

In my head, I heard Mari say, "Why is everything a fight with you? Why can't you let go of some things?"

I said aloud to no one, "Because I have to," as I petted Big Boy who had his head in my lap.

When Big Boy and I walked down from the loft, we found Summer at her desk working on the Best of the Coast database. She wore a Guns N' Roses T-shirt and white jeans. She looked up and smiled but stayed focused on her work. Big Boy crawled under her desk, exhausted.

On the blog, I posted a teaser for tomorrow's cover story:

INSIDER HAS ECSO PAYROLL

This Monday, the *Insider* received the Escambia County Sheriff Office's payroll. A sortable database will be uploaded for viewing on Thursday.

When I finished reading the daily newspapers online, I clicked back on the blog. I had a dozen comments in less than an hour, none of them complimentary of Sheriff Frost. This issue would do very well.

Summer walked over to my desk. She looked worried.

"I wanted to check our bank balance because I didn't want us to be blindsided again," she said. "The check to the printer hit our account last night. We don't have the funds to cover the overdraft. Plus, the bank will tack on a mountain of service fees if other checks bounce, too."

Dammit, I thought. When would this tape stop playing?

"Okay, we've got until ten o'clock before the bank manager decides to honor the checks or return them," I said. "That gives us two hours to round up $2,500."

Summer interjected, "$3,250."

"Ok, $3,250. Print out the receivables list. I'll visit those within walking distance who have invoices for advertising older than thirty days. Everything we bill is due upon receipt, but we always have to chase down advertisers for checks."

"They're good people but everyone is hurting," said Summer.

I replied, "That's why we need the maritime park to help draw more customers downtown for these restaurants, bars and shops."

For the next ninety-five minutes, I walked the streets of downtown Pensacola. Several of the businesses weren't opened yet, but I knocked anyway. After ten stops, I headed to the bank with six checks totaling $2,700 and handled the rest with the last of my savings. If we had a fair deposit today, I could drink tonight.

Back at the office, I discovered that I had left my *Insider* staff unattended far too long. My "ace" reporter Doug Yoste hadn't shown up for work. Roxie was battling a new wave of angry advertisers wanting to cancel their ads. Sheriff Frost must have stirred the business owners up. Jeremy was talking about moving to Austin, Texas, and checking job listings on Craigslist. Teddy had his headphones on, oblivious to the world while editing photos for the next issue. Mal remained pissed at everyone, particularly the absent Doug.

"He's too juvenile for this job. He doesn't get this paper," Mal said as Big Boy nuzzled her leg. Her mood was black today. "You can go on your crusades, but somebody has to write the news. This paper can't only be a long rant by you."

"Yeah, it can't all be me either," Jeremy piped in.

Starbucks cups filled his trash can to the brim. I didn't know how many were from this morning. Why had I hired the sloppiest gay A&E writer in the world?

Mal's glare stopped the writer before he went off any further. Jeremy scowled at her and stormed out for a smoke.

"Mal, I will deal with it," I said.

Summer waved for me to join her in the conference room. She said, "You have a visitor."

Sitting in a chair was a large, dark-skinned man. It was Tiny, wearing a suit and looking very serious. He said, "Mr. Holmes, I'm here for my cover story."

"Tiny, that's quite a suit," I said admiring his three-piece gray pinstripe suit, red shirt, and black tie. It was tight, but not shabby or threadbare. The only thing that took away from his sartorial splendor was his running shoes.

"I have important things to say," he said pulling on his jacket's lapels and straightening his tie. "Important people wear suits."

I looked at Summer. She knew I didn't have time for this, but Summer also understood that it was my policy to listen to the stories of whoever walked into the office. It wasn't always worthwhile, but we would listen. I usually assigned the interviews to Yoste, but his absence took away that option.

With her eyes, Summer begged me to do the right thing. Big Boy walked in and jumped up to lick Tiny's face. He had also decided that I should listen to the "mayor of Palafox."

"Okay, let's have a good visit, Mayor," I said pulling up a chair. "Summer, grab my notepad and have Teddy take photos of Tiny while I interview him."

"Is that okay with you, Tiny?"

"Most certainly."

Summer handed me my notepad and sat down next to Tiny.

Not knowing how I would use this story, I interviewed Tiny the same way I would a governor, state representative, or a real mayor. Big Boy and Summer would have it no other way.

Since I recalled that Tiny had served two tours in Iraq, I began by thanking him for his service. He replied, "When I came back, some at the VA clinic called me a 'hero.' I ain't no hero. I'm a survivor who somehow has to make my life worthwhile for those guys who died. They died, I didn't."

For the first time, I noticed small Arabic script tattooed on his right forearm. I asked, "What does that mean?"

He said, "The end of life is death."

I wasn't ready to follow up on this startling piece of information. Instead I asked Tiny when he had left his home in southern Mississippi. He explained he had joined the Army Reserve in 2004 to better himself when he was twenty-two.

"I couldn't find work in Hattiesburg, Wiggins or McComb," said Tiny. "Not many paying jobs for black men with no college education in Mississippi. My mom thought the military would give me skills that I could use to build a life—at least one better than hers."

He spoke with little emotion in his voice, not looking me in the eyes. Tiny petted Big Boy while he spoke. He clearly had something important to share and was struggling not to break down.

"They taught me how to be a man. I got discipline and self-esteem. People saw more than the color of my skin when I was in my uniform."

Tiny stared down at the dog, gathered his thoughts and continued. He said, "It was like, like I was a superhero or something. I was no longer a former high school jock and a screw-up. I was a soldier."

After basic and advanced individual training, Tiny came home to his unit in the Mississippi National Guard at Camp Shelby, south of Hattiesburg, Mississippi.

"They said don't even unpack your bags," Tiny recounted, "because in three weeks I'd be in Iraq." Though the air conditioning was blasting, Tiny was sweating. He loosened his tie and undid the top button of his shirt.

"Take your time," I said.

Summer got up to bring him a glass of water.

He nodded thanks to Summer and continued to pet the dog. I motioned to Teddy to take a break from taking photos.

"Mostly rode escort in the hottest damn place on this earth. I thought Mississippi was hot. Iraq was much worse," said Tiny. "When I wasn't part of some convoy, I manned security checkpoints and gates at the bases, checking visitors and vehicles for weapons, bombs and other crap."

He said, "Could never let down my guard. All I heard was stories of some soldier relaxing and being blown into pieces by a fucking IED or suicide bomber."

Tiny caught himself. He looked at Summer and said, "Sorry, Ms. Summer, I promised myself I wouldn't curse."

She nodded for him to continue. "I've heard the word before."

He continued, "My buddy Jake got killed when a suicide bomber attacked his checkpoint in Fallujah. From then on, I could never relax. Fear crept in . . . it wouldn't let go of me."

He got up and walked over to the window. He turned to face us and said, "Fear gnawed at my soul. The more I saw, the more I began to pull back from life–mine and my friends. If I cared about life, the more pain I suffered when somebody was killed."

Summer glanced at me. Big Boy put his head in her lap. The dog was comforting everyone in the room.

Tiny said, "My mind found new ways to mark the passage of time. Every time my truck drove past a mile marker, I thought that's another mile that I was still alive."

He injured his foot on the battlefield when his vehicle hit an IED. Tiny didn't say much about the incident other than mumble a few words about watching his fellow soldiers die and bleed, hearing moans and groans, and smelling death and infection all around him.

"I was lucky. The docs at Walter Reed saved my foot, and PTs taught me how to walk again. They put me with two soldiers from my unit. One lost both his legs, and the other had his back broken when his gun turret was hit by a rocket-propelled grenade. Guys missing body parts filled the beds around us. No one gave a damn what I had seen or felt. They just wanted my ass out of the hospital as quickly as possible."

Tiny received no counseling for post-traumatic stress disorder, but he did get prescriptions for painkillers anytime he asked for them. He said, "Pills made the fear and all other emotions go away. I felt nothing."

When I asked him how it went when he returned home, he said he had no one to tell about his war experience. He told us, "Probably wasn't another Iraq War veteran for thirty miles. Everybody else wanted to talk about *American Idol, Survivor* or some crap like that, while what mattered most to me was having A/C, running water, and fresh groceries."

Without his soldier identity, he felt disconnected from his family, friends and the civilian world. Once again, Tiny couldn't find work. He wandered up and down the Gulf Coast for a couple of years, living on the streets and making do.

"Never stole anything. Never got arrested. Drank, popped pills, and waited to die. Hell, I was supposed to have died in Iraq like Jake and my buddies. Why should I live?"

Tiny took a sip of water and shut his eyes. "What right did I have to live while Jake and others didn't? I thought about killing myself several times, I really did, but God always put someone in my life whenever I came close to doing it."

While in Pensacola, Tiny ran into someone from his unit who hooked him up with drug abuse counseling and PTSD therapy.

"A doctor helped me reconnect with my feelings. Pushed me to write down those things, those emotions that I couldn't talk with others about," Tiny said. "Told him I ain't no writer, but he wouldn't let up. The first few entries in my journal were just words, no sentences. I had forgotten how to feel. How does anyone write about feelings when they don't have none? But I got better at it. Words became sentences and I began to face my fears, my guilt about living and all the emotions that had gnawed at me for so long."

He said the counselors got him a job in the kitchen of a local restaurant, but it didn't work out because he had trouble following directions from his supervisors. However, they continued to work with him and found him volunteer work at a homeless shelter.

"I liked helping in the shelter. Got to work around parents and their kids, see how they acted with each other," said Tiny. "Seeing them in normal situations helped me reconnect with life. See what normal was."

He then said that it had been a little over two years since he last contemplated suicide. He no longer drank or used drugs and had been clean for over a year. He had moved into a group home for veterans and now helped out at the downtown coffee shop before volunteering at the homeless shelter in the afternoons.

"See homeless vets every day in the park downtown," he said. "The owner lets me take them the day-old pastries. I try to talk to them, but mostly I listen. I understand their pain and feelings of loss. Others walk by them as if they're invisible. I thought maybe you, Mr. Holmes, could tell my story and get people to understand these are real people who just can't figure out how to live in this town."

I said, "Tiny, we would be honored to tell your story. Maybe we can even interview a few of the homeless vets in Ferdinand Plaza."

He nodded, looking exhausted and appearing relieved that he gotten all this out without collapsing. He said, "This is the first time I told this to anyone outside of the home or treatment center. The place is a military town, but it ignores the vets sleeping on park benches. We need your help."

"We will help," said Summer as she looked at me. "Won't we, boss?"

"We will, but it will take us a few weeks to pull this together," I said.

Tiny said, "I know you're a busy man."

"Not too busy for this," I said. "It's an important story. I'll come by Bodacious Brew next week or so, and we can talk more."

Tiny stood up, smoothed his jacket, fastened his top button, and straightened his tie. He reached over and kissed Summer's hand.

"Thank you for your hospitality, Ms. Summer," he said. "Good day, Mr. Holmes."

As I walked back to my desk I thought, *Pensacola never ceases to amaze me. There are people with stories all around us. Our newspaper needed to survive to tell them.*

Roxie yelled with her hand over the receiver on her phone, "When are you going to deal with this Hines-Wittman crap? Once the Frost story hits, I won't have any customers. You're killing me!"

"Offer them free upgrades," I told her. "This will pass."

Everyone turned away from me. I walked over to my desk, where someone had posted a note to call Stan Daniels. I reached his secretary, who asked me to drop by at eleven o'clock, which gave me about forty-five minutes before I had to head out.

Dare called to say she was heading to New York City.

"Had this trip planned months ago," she said. "Promise me you won't do anything with the suicide note until I get back. And join me for brunch on Sunday."

I agreed, knowing Gravy's expert wouldn't have finished his analysis until then anyway.

I posted another article to the blog:

ECSO IS TOP-HEAVY

Escambia County Sheriff's Office appears to be top-heavy when you compare it to the operations at the Pensacola Police Department (PPD).

To manage its 112 police officers, PPD has 20 sergeants, 5 lieutenants, an assistant chief, and the chief. The department has as a supervisor for every 4.2 police officers.

To manage its 243 deputies, Sheriff Frost has 72 sergeants, 35 lieutenants, 8 captains, a major, chief deputy, and himself.

The county sheriff's ratio of supervisors to deputies is 2.1. In other words, Frost has twice as many supervisors for every officer on patrol than PPD.

Plus, the Escambia County Sheriff Office is spending 335 percent more to supervise its deputies than PPD does to supervise its police officers.

Within ten minutes, my cell phone vibrated. The caller ID read "Frost." I ignored it. The phone vibrated again. The text message said: "Hi, this is Alphonse. Could you meet today for lunch at H&O?"

I replied, "Yes, 12:30? But u r buying."

Then I headed over to Daniels' office.

16

Stan Daniels and I had become acquainted during the 2006 park referendum fight. We didn't have a lot in common. The rich and powerful of Northwest Florida flocked to his firm. I took up for the 'little guy' and tried to tell the stories of those with little money or influence. I had more in common with the trial attorneys that took Daniels' clients to court.

For that reason, I didn't think I could ever like him. His idea of making a better Pensacola meant making his friends richer. Me? I thought of helping that single mom holding down two jobs trying to feed her five kids. I didn't begrudge him, though, and realized he went to bed every night thinking what a great job he was doing for the community.

He slept. I rarely did.

Daniels came from behind his desk and greeted me when his secretary escorted me into his office. You could imagine him beating out Wittman to be the Catholic High quarterback. Unlike Wittman, Daniels was still slim and athletic. On the wall were pictures of him crossing the finish line at the Boston and New York City marathons—just another reason for Wittman and me to dislike him.

"A. J. wanted me to meet with you about Wittman's new petition," Daniels started. He was charming and sincere when he spoke, with a bright, winning smile. Okay, maybe I liked him a little.

"He wants your take on it," he continued. "Will they get the 3,700 signatures to force another referendum? How will Bo Hines' endorsement impact the success of this new petition that will halt the building of the baseball stadium?"

"Tell Kettler that it's too early to tell," I said. "Wittman has been clever this time. His petition challenges the award of the construction contract. The city charter allows any citizen to conduct a petition drive for a referendum on any vote made by the council. He has ninety days to present the signatures to the city council, which is a tight timeframe to gather them. Wittman needs to aim for about 4,500 because not all of the signatures will be valid city of Pensacola registered voters. However, if Hines bankrolls the effort, Wittman might get them in time."

"Should I try to meet with Bo?" Daniels asked. "We've served on a few boards together. A. J. has made some pretty big donations to his fundraisers."

"That's your call," I said. "If you do, don't mention my name."

Daniels nodded.

I continued, "Stan, we will be battling the same misinformation as before, the same lies. The petition and subsequent referendum give Wittman and his followers another opportunity to attack Kettler and the baseball team. Hines' push to create this nature reserve in Sue's memory adds a new dynamic to the debate. I can't be sure how that might impact people."

"Sue had a lot of friends," Daniels observed. "People will want to honor her."

"Agreed," I replied. "Does Kettler have the stomach for the fight? He could take his team elsewhere. I've heard Biloxi is building a baseball stadium and would be interested in the Pilots."

Daniels said, "They have reached out to A.J., but he considers Jace a bully. He refuses to let a bully stop a project that he sincerely believes will turn this place around. My client will continue to fight for this park."

"Okay," I said. "There's one thing that has bugged me about Hines' theatrics at the Save Our Pensacola meeting. His road construction company was one of the subcontractors for the site work at the maritime park. He stood to make money on the construction."

"Your article on missing Arts Council funds and his arrest got him dropped from the project," said Daniels. "His company was not part of the construction contract approved by the city council at the end of May, thanks to you. On June 7, Jace announced he would try to force a referendum to reverse the vote."

I noticed on his wall a flip-flop mounted on a plaque. I asked Daniels about it.

"My old all-star baseball team gave it to me at a 45th reunion party," he said. "It's about a silly ping pong match I had with Jace when we were all ten years old. It's a trophy of sorts."

I nodded, letting him know that I'd heard the story about the way he defeated Jace. I said, "I guess Wittman didn't want to show up for the reunion."

Daniels replied, "He did come and wasn't too amused. It didn't help matters any when a couple of buddies and I played a prank on Jace later."

"Jace has always left his truck unlocked. So we were able to attach under his truck's steering column a great item from an Annoy-a-tron Pack we had found online. It was a battery-powered small circuit board with a magnet that set off loud beeps at random intervals."

He laughed. "I forgot about it until my wife told me a month later how Jace and his wife had driven to Atlanta with a mysterious beeping noise driving them crazy. They had stopped at two dealers to try and locate the source of the sound. Jace was ready to sell the truck."

I laughed, too. "What happened next?"

"I confessed to my wife that I did it," he said. "She made me call Jace, apologize and remove the circuit board, but our classmates didn't help smooth things over. For weeks they greeted him with "beep" whenever they saw him."

I said, "Jace doesn't believe in forgiving and forgetting, I guess."

"Few in Pensacola do," said Daniels. "I'm tired of Jace's pettiness and bullying. Maybe we can put an end to it by killing this petition effort."

"You don't really believe that, do you?"

"Think positively, Mr. Holmes."

We talked twenty or so more minutes about the petition drive. Daniels didn't make any other comments about the acrimony between him and Wittman. He wanted to talk primarily about the petition, Hines, and how to get the baseball stadium built.

"My reporter, Doug Yoste, is working on a story about the petition. Can he interview you and Kettler?"

"Yes, we can set it up," he said. "But I think he is traveling in Canada with his family this week."

As I drove over to H&O Cafe, Summer called. I almost didn't pick up the phone, but I owed it to her to answer.

There was no hello or other pleasantries. "The printer wants another check before they print the issue," she said. "What do I do?"

This issue was too big to delay printing. "Cut the check. I'll be back in an hour. Tell them we will deliver it by 2:30."

Again, we would take advantage of the bank float. Missing the 2:00 p.m. bank cutoff would buy us another day or two. Goddammit, this was getting old.

Blocking the negativity from my mind, I parked in the oyster shell-covered parking lot behind H&O, navigated around a few deep puddles, and walked in to meet Razor.

Located at the corner of Hayne and Gonzalez streets almost under the I-110 overpass, the H&O Café was one of the first black-owned restaurants in Pensacola. Hamp Lee and his brother Booker opened the place in 1922 and named it for their wives, Hattie and Ola.

The H&O was first a grocery with a lunch counter and poolroom in the back. A popular hangout in the all-black Eastside neighborhood known for good soul food, it was listed in USA Today's "Top 10 Iconic Soul Food Joints" a few years back.

In the 1950s, "Little Book," Booker Lee's son, nearly lost the restaurant when he almost beat a customer to death. The legend was a pregnant woman had tried to sit on one of the counter stools in a very tight, short skirt. Noticing how exposed the woman was, a man sitting nearby shouted, "My, my, I'm looking at paradise."

Little Book, who stood over six and a half feet tall and weighed about three hundred pounds, took offense to the remark. One version of the story had the woman as his girlfriend. Lee came from behind the counter, dragged the man outside, and began beating him with a belt. He was arrested and charged with aggravated battery. Judge Beckham let Lee off with a fine. Ever since a sign hung over the H&O Café lunch counter: "No Pregnant Women Allowed on Stools."

Little Book passed away in 1999. His nephew Curtis ran the place now. The grocery store and poolroom had long been abandoned, but the restaurant with its counter, five booths, and a handful of tables still operated twenty-four hours a day, seven days a week, just as it had done in the 1920s.

When visiting Pensacola, politicians, and celebrities made sure to eat a meal at the H&O Café. On the wall were photos of Rosa Parks,

Muhammad Ali, President Bill Clinton, Michelle Obama, and local champion boxer Roy Jones, Jr.

Curtis looked up from a copy of last week's *Pensacola Insider* when I entered. He said, "Finally found time to read you, I just knew you would show today. It's meatloaf day."

"Hi, Curtis. Meatloaf, mac & cheese, fried okra, and collard greens. What's better than that?"

"Five hundred dollars in my pocket and a fine, big-butt lady on my lap," he said laughing as he got up to make my plate.

I said, "Only if Ms. Delores doesn't catch you."

Percy Sledge was playing on the jukebox. You had to love a joint that played its jukebox during lunch. In the corner booth sat Alphonse Tyndall. The special agent had less than half of the meatloaf special remaining on his plate. A group of dusty day laborers sat at the long table by the window. The rest of the place was empty. Curtis's daughter Natalia sat by the phone to handle any takeout orders, playing on her cell phone. The girl was eighteen and curvy, which explained why her daddy wanted to keep her in his sight.

Razor smiled and greeted me as I sat down. Natalia brought me my sweet tea in a Styrofoam cup and a plate of hot cornbread.

"Thanks for meeting on such short notice," he said, as he reached for a piece of cornbread. "I moved back more than two years ago after living in Atlanta for nearly a decade and eating at all kinds of restaurants there and other big cities, including New York and DC. This may not be the prettiest looking establishment, but none of their food can touch this place."

The jukebox switched to Nat King Cole's "Mona Lisa." I said to Alphonse, "This is one of my breakfast haunts on the weekends. Always can find a story here."

Natalia delivered the lunch special with a bottle of hot pepper sauce.

Razor said, "You know this town better than I do. I've been away too long."

"I'm glad you called," I said. "I think a lot of your aunt, and having another source in the attorney general's office is always good."

"What we discuss has to stay off the record until I say you can publish it, okay?" he warned.

"As long as we are honest with each other, then there will be no problem," I said. "Everything can be on background. We can decide later what needs to go in print or on the blog."

"Fair enough."

We ate our meals quietly for a few minutes. He wanted to ask me something, but I wasn't going to rush him.

"Razor, what's your background?" I asked after Natalia poured us more tea.

He said that he had gone to Howard University on a football scholarship. When he graduated with top grades, several alumni encouraged him to go to law school. He worked as a graduate assistant for the football program and enrolled in Howard University School of Law.

"It was tough, but the alumni stayed on my case. They weren't going to let me be a football coach or pharmaceutical salesman," he said.

He graduated with honors, passed the bar, and went to work for the Federal Bureau of Investigation, first in Los Angeles, then Chicago and Atlanta. He became an expert in catching hacking rings that operated in the cyber underground.

"I sort of made a name for myself a few years back," Razor said. "An international hacking ring devised sophisticated hacking techniques to compromise the encryption used to protect data on forty-four payroll debit cards, and then provided a network of "cashers" to withdraw millions from over 2,100 ATMs in hundreds of cities in the United States, Russia, Ukraine, Estonia, Italy, France, Japan, and Canada. They stole nine million dollars in a span of fewer than twelve hours before we realized what happened. We caught them operating out of an internet café in Boca Raton."

When the Florida attorney general wanted to set up his Child Predator Cybercrime Task Force, he called Alphonse Tyndall first. Razor agreed, but only on the condition that he could work out of Pensacola.

"I've operated under the radar here. Passed the Florida Bar. Started coaching youth football and basketball with the Southern Youth Sports Association. And I'm an usher at Mt. Zion Missionary Baptist Church."

"What do you tell people when they ask what you do?" I asked, finishing my last bite of meatloaf.

"I say I work for the state."

As I moved on to a bowl of banana pudding, Razor got to the point about why he wanted to meet me.

"Benny says you've been asking about a porn crew shooting videos around here," he said, fixing on my eyes. He waited for my reaction. We weren't friends yet.

I set down my spoon. My normal routine was to bluff my way through conversations like this, especially when I didn't know much. The other party would usually share everything, thinking I already had the information. With Razor, I told the truth.

"Benny is a talker," I said, taking a sip of tea. "He brought up the porn thing. I was checking on something for a friend who made a mistake."

Razor relaxed a little.

I asked, "What does a porn ring have to do with child predators?"

"A couple of girls taped are still in high school," he said. "We're close to shutting it down and don't need any blog posts or news stories tipping them off."

He explained to me how this operation was much bigger than just a few guys selling homemade porn videos on the web.

"They have set up a subscription-based website called 'Deb's Playpen,' using Tor in the dark web," Razor said.

He explained that Tor was software that enabled anonymous communication on the web. Created by Naval Research Laboratory employees to protect Department of Defense communication, The Onion Router, or Tor, later became available for free.

Computer geeks began to direct web traffic through the free worldwide, volunteer network consisting of more than seven thousand relays that concealed a user's location and usage from anyone conducting network surveillance or traffic analysis. Hackers loved it.

"The website has over than twenty-seven thousand members and two thousand videos," he told me. "Several feature children. The members not only download videos created by the website but also share photos and videos of the minors freely, thanks to Tor's ability to conceal online users' identities and locations."

"Is the Pensacola crew a supplier for the site?" I asked.

"Most of the child porn has been supplied by users, but I think this area may be the headquarters, which is why we're so sensitive to being exposed before we arrest anyone."

"Can I get an exclusive?"

Razor laughed. "I will make sure you get a copy of the documents we file with the courts. That's the best I can do."

During a break in the conversation, Curtis poured us more tea and brought us the tab. Tyndall grabbed the ticket but he had something else he wanted to discuss before we left.

"Walker, I'm thinking about running for sheriff in 2012. What are my chances?"

"Let's see," I said. "A black Democrat—I assume you're a Democrat"—he nodded yes—"with a very low public profile running against a two-term Republican sheriff that crushed his opponents the last two elections. Not good."

"That bad, huh?"

"Bad but not impossible. The luster of Frost is wearing off. People are tired of his thugs and backroom deals. I just don't know if they're ready for a black sheriff."

He said, "Raising money won't be a problem. My friends around the country will write checks."

"You need to start building some name recognition. The election is a little more than two years away."

"I need to finish this operation first," Razor replied. "Then I plan to join the Rockwell Theisen law firm."

One of the top trial law firms in the state, Rockwell Theisen had three floors of Jackson Towers. T. A. Rockwell wasn't a fan of Sheriff Frost.

"Nice career move," I said. "Do they know you want to run for Escambia County sheriff?"

"Yes, the firm represented Aunt Joyce. Mr. Rockwell said he would do anything to help me. He's onboard."

"Well, that could alter the dynamics of the race," I said. "When you make the switch to the firm, we'll do a profile of you. You need to find a charity fundraiser to chair, and you've got to make the rounds to the black pastors."

I finished my tea and Tyndall paid the bill. As we walked to our cars I told him, "This will be a long shot, and you might not win on the first try. But I will help."

We shook hands and agreed to have beers again soon. *Another crusade*, I thought.

Mari would have been pissed.

17

When I got back to the office, Doug Yoste was huddled at his desk. Fittingly the rest of the staff had ostracized him. His excuse for missing the morning meeting was that his power had gone out, shutting off his alarm clock. No one bought it. His sunburned face and neck gave away that he had been fishing again.

After fifteen minutes of my third, and maybe final, "Come to Jesus" meeting with him about responsibility, deadlines, and teamwork, Doug filled me in on his research for the petition story. He had been busy calling all the principal players.

According to Doug, most of the Save Our Pensacola wackos were completely caught off guard when Wittman announced another petition drive. They saw the park project as a done deal, but right around when the police arrested Hines, Wittman fired up the PAC again.

"I got a hold of a Mrs. Ellis and her husband last night," Doug said, reading from his notepad. "They say they are members of the executive committee of Save Our Pensacola. Mrs. Ellis hates you and tried to get me to understand how evil you really are."

Yoste didn't defend me, only asked questions. Mrs. Ellis was the lady with the orange hair who had run the meeting at New World Landing.

"Professor Ellis called you the 'Spawn of Satan' before he gave me a twenty-minute lecture on how the economic analysis for the park project was flawed," Doug said. "Neither of them ever met Bo Hines before Monday night, but they were happy to have him and his money."

The prior petition attempts had been underfunded. Wittman depended on free publicity from the daily newspaper, local talk radio shows, and anybody who believed in conspiracy theories, UFOs, and the Illuminati. He had never matched the money Kettler threw out for advertising and mailers to counter the naysayers. Hines' money would be the great equalizer this time.

Wittman told Doug, "We must remember that the residents and taxpayers of the City of Pensacola own the proposed development site. I can't sit idly and watch the city council hand over our valuable waterfront property to some millionaire for his hobby baseball team."

Wittman insisted he based the petition drive on the hundreds of phone calls and emails that he had received to stop what he liked to refer to as a "giveaway" to Kettler. He never mentioned Stan Daniels.

After Monday night's announcement by Hines that he was joining forces with his brother-in-law, Doug tried to get a quote from him and got nowhere, but he promised to continue trying.

I gave him Stan Daniels' phone numbers. Daniels would help him reach Kettler.

The outline for his cover story was due by Thursday afternoon, and he needed to talk with Teddy and Mal about the artwork. The firm deadline for this copy was the following Monday morning. Doug agreed to not go fishing until after the final draft was turned in.

Mal and I tested the payroll database a few more times. The searches worked perfectly.

She said, "Do you think people will really want to look up the salaries?"

"Hell yeah," I said. "Frost's employees will check out each other's pay. Girlfriends will want to learn how much their lovers make. And the public will see how Sheriff Frost rewards his henchmen."

I had gotten the idea from the Boston Globe. They had set up an online database of the salaries of all government employees in the state of Massachusetts. So many people had logged on to the site that it had crashed. This project had taken us four weeks to pull together. I expected similar results tomorrow.

Thursday morning, I heard the rain when my alarm went off. As I was about to roll over and go back to sleep, Big Boy jumped on the bed with his leash. He liked running in the rain. There must have been something primordial about it, or maybe he just enjoyed hearing me curse as he pulled me through puddles.

As we headed back to the office, bundles of the *Insider* wrapped in plastic bags were stacked on the doorsteps of downtown businesses. I loved the anticipation of a new issue hitting the stands, especially when it had a blockbuster as the cover story.

Whenever I had a story published in *The Daily Mississippian*, Mari had teased me about being like a child on Christmas morning rushing to find what Santa left for me under the tree. She had to put up with hours of me obsessing over a story, listening to me bitch about my editor and faculty advisor, and fretting that I wasn't good enough to do the story.

Damn, I missed her.

I dried Big Boy in the stairwell and stripped down to my boxers. My phone vibrated, and the display said, "Sheriff Frost." I passed on answering it. When I got out of the shower, there was a text message from him: "BIG MISTAKE."

With a cup of coffee and Big Boy next to me on the couch, I wrote my first blog post of the day pushing readers to the cover story.

CHA-CHING!

Who are the big winners in Sheriff Ron Frost's administration? The *Insider* has the annual salary for every employee in the Escambia County Sheriff's Office available online. You can search by name, job title, or salary range. Enjoy.

My phone vibrated. It was Rueben Crutcher, one of my investors. Crutcher owned the Pensacola State Bank. Well, actually his mother owned it and let him sit in an office off the lobby. I recruited Crutcher to invest in the *Insider* when I launched the newspaper because I had heard he wanted to get back at the society columnist at the *Pensacola Herald* for mocking his Mardi Gras court. Recruiting the banker was a decision I often regretted.

Crutcher liked to tell people he owned the paper, but he didn't enjoy any political pushback from the editorial content. He would email me story ideas that I deleted without reading. When he suggested an editorial position, we took the opposite side. We battled continually over the paper's coverage during our monthly board meetings. Then Hurricane Ivan hit. The bank and his family investments took major losses. He quit answering my cash calls to help keep the paper operating, and I quit calling board meetings.

We had reached a tenuous truce that would last as long as I didn't need any money. If I faltered, he would demand a board meeting and call for my ass.

"Walker, Crutcher here," he said, not understanding that cell phones identify the caller. "Just got off the phone with Sheriff Frost—what the hell are you doing over there?"

"Reporting."

"He's threatening to sue if you don't pull the story and write some type of retraction about his brother," Crutcher shouted.

"He won't. I had our attorney review the article," I lied. "Frost has nothing to sue us over."

"You think this is all a joke," he said. "It's important to some of us to have the sheriff on our side."

I remembered that Crutcher's son had been arrested for driving while intoxicated during spring break. It was his second such arrest, and for the second time the charge was dropped for insufficient evidence. Frost reassigned the arresting deputy to court security.

"Rueben, my contract gives me complete control over the editorial content of the paper," I said, trying not to sound smug. "Tell Sheriff Frost to call me."

"He said he did, but you wouldn't answer your phone."

I said, "I must have been in the shower. I'll take the next one."

Crutcher said, "The Hines story already has created enough problems. If Frost piles on, we're going to have to convene a board meeting."

"Nothing to worry about, I've got it under control."

"Sure you do," he snarled. "I got a call from your bank yesterday. You bounced some checks this week."

"Sales are picking up," I replied. "Best of the Coast is next month. Only a momentary cash-flow snafu."

"We'll see," said Crutcher as he hung up.

The rain got heavier. Thunder could be heard in the distance. Big Boy slept while the staff wandered in for our meeting.

Roxie said the Best of the Coast sales were ahead of last year. She praised Summer's help and said they would start billing for the ads next week. Doug gave a report on his Save Our Pensacola article. I didn't tell them about the suicide note since I hadn't verified its authenticity.

This was one of those rare meetings when everything clicked. Summer came into the conference room to announce that we had so many hits on our website that the server had crashed. I bought pizza for the staff to celebrate.

During the afternoon, the Frost payroll story went viral. The *Pensacola Herald* and the local radio and television stations ran stories on the salaries. One or two of the radio reports even mentioned the *Insider*.

At six, I got a text from Gravy to join him at Hopjacks, a pizza joint a block north of the office. Hopjacks Pizza Kitchen and Taproom attracted a young crowd. Each member of the waitstaff was apparently required to have at least two tattoos or piercings to be hired.

The place was packed. A concert at the music hall next door would open its door in about an hour. At first, I didn't see Gravy, but I noticed Bree at the bar with a few of her girlfriends. They were laughing and talking with the bartender. She didn't look in my direction, which was fine. I didn't have anything to report yet.

Finally I spied Gravy waving from a booth in a dark corner of the bar where he sat with two tanned, blonde thirtysomethings.

"Ladies, this is Pensacola's Thomas More," Gravy shouted over the din of the crowd. Empty beer glasses covered the table. It must have been three-for-one happy hour or else Gravy had started early. "He does none harm, says none harm, thinks none harm, but wishes everybody good."

The paraphrasing of the famous quote from the movie *A Man for All Season* flew—no, it zoomed—over the girls' heads. They both said in unison, "Hi, Thomas," and smiled. I didn't care enough to correct them. Neither did Gravy.

"These are the Ashleys," he said as the waitress handed me my beer. "They're both teachers on vacation."

"She's Ashley with a y, and I'm with double e's," said the girl sitting on Gravy's right. She obviously expected a reaction as she leaned across the table to show her freckled cleavage flowing out of her tank top. I never took my eyes off her forehead.

"Ladies, nice to meet you," I told Ashley and Ashlee. "Would you mind if I take Father Graves away from you for a few minutes? We need to talk about an incident that happened on his last campout with the altar boys."

Gravy's lips formed a thin smile. He wanted to kill me. I took a long sip of my beer as the girls found excuses to leave the table and Hopjacks as quickly as possible.

"Holmes, you are an ass," Gravy said. He was mad but understood we needed to talk. He was wearing black jeans and a pink polo shirt—not a good choice for someone trying to convince two Montgomery, Alabama, elementary school teachers that he wasn't the Roman Catholic Church's next lawsuit.

"I thought you asked me here to toast today's cover story," I said.

Gravy touched his mug to my Bud Light bottle. "Cheers. Did you ever talk with Sheriff Frost today? He kept calling me and bitching about you. He thinks you're treating him unfairly and that you could find similar salary structures within the city and county governments. He threatened to put you out of business."

"Frost will have to get in line," I said. "What was your reply to him?"

"I finally told him that nobody could do anything with you."

I laughed. "The web server crashed. Papers flew off the rack. The other media started asking big, bad Sheriff Frost questions. Hell, we even picked up a couple of new advertisers. Life is good."

Gravy's expression showed he had doubts about how I would survive another round with the sheriff. He said, "Please keep me out of this one. I've got several clients in the county jail and don't need them to have any problems."

"Problems?"

He said, "I'm trying to get them placed in pretrial diversion and avoid trials. Sheriff Frost could block it with one word to the judges."

"You worry, too much," I said. "Frost wouldn't take out his frustrations with me on you. He likes you."

Gravy drained his beer. "You messed with his family when you wrote about his brother . . ."

"But his brother works at the sheriff's office and holds a high-ranking position. It's fair—"

"You don't get it," Gravy interrupted. "You made it personal, and—"

"I didn't. This is—"

"Stop, Walker," said Gravy holding up his hand. "It's not your intentions that matter. It's how Sheriff Frost has taken the article. I need to lay low with the sheriff's office for my other clients' sakes and for you to switch to some other coverage to get Frost off my ass. Do a pet issue or something."

He waved to the waitress to bring us another round. I passed on the pizza since one was enough for the day.

Gravy said, "The rest of the town may love reading about Frost's payroll, but you understand how this works. Just as soon as you think you're winning, Pensacola kicks your legs right out from under you."

"I'm enjoying this while I can. We needed a break from the Hines and Wittman bullshit, and I've been trying to do the Frost story for over a month. We'll move away from the sheriff's office for a few weeks until his troops screw up something again."

Gravy ordered some hummus and pita chips, figuring I would need something in my stomach. I made a mental note to eat healthier—not any time soon, but one day . . . maybe.

"Speaking of Hines, my guy in Mobile said he would send me the handwriting analysis by Sunday," he said as he noticed another blonde walk into the bar. I wasn't going to have his attention much longer. Gravy asked, "If it checks out, what's your next move?"

"I will open the blog with it on Monday."

"Shouldn't you give it to the state attorney first? Spencer won't be happy, and his boss will forget you two coached ball once upon a time. You could score some points with them by showing you're cooperating."

"I don't want the state attorney's office to drag out its analysis of the writing," I said. "We need to shoot a hole in Hines' story lines that the charges are bogus and there might not even be a trial. Plus, I want public pressure on Spencer and Newton to prosecute."

Gravy said, "I really wish you would reconsider this strategy."

"No," I said, "we will break it and see how the cockroaches scramble."

Gravy finished his beer and ordered two Irish car bombs, a concoction of a Guinness stout, Baileys Irish Cream, and Jameson Irish whiskey. "You might be able to survive combat with the sheriff or state attorney, but not both at the same time."

"Harmony and peace are overrated," I declared.

He laughed, "Well, hell. Let's toast your victory while it lasts."

We downed the drinks and ordered two more Irish Car Bombs. I finished off the rest of my Bud Light. Gravy gave me time to let it all soak in. He finally asked, "Did you see Bree at the bar?"

"Yes, I didn't speak to her," I said. "Have you had any luck with Tatum?"

"His former bookkeeper has filed a sexual harassment complaint with the EEOC and a breach of contract lawsuit against him," Gravy said. "The harassment complaint probably won't go anywhere, but the lawsuit has legs. Tatum will probably settle before it goes to court."

"Will she meet with me?" I asked. "It can be off the record, at least initially. If she has any useful information, I can ask her later for quotes."

Gravy said, "Her attorney thinks she might talk with you, but it most definitely needs to be for background purposes. Nothing gets published without his permission."

"Okay, when and where?"

"I should have an answer in the morning," he replied.

The bar began to clear out as the concert hall opened its doors. Bar tabs were paid, tables cleared. Bree and her friends gathered their purses and headed to the concert hall. She saw us and waved. A few guys hung around the bar and the foosball table near the bathrooms.

Gravy said, "I can go with you to the state attorney when you're ready to deliver the note."

"I don't know. Let me think about it," I told him as I got up and went to unload the Irish car bombs and beers.

The bathrooms at Hopjacks were far from luxurious—a urinal, a sink, and a stall with a broken door.

The door to the restroom opened as I finished and headed to the sink. In men's restrooms the cardinal rule is to never look up, especially in small ones. I stepped toward the sink, and a large man, one of the foosball players, blocked my path.

"Excuse me," I said as I looked up. I moved my head just in time to dodge a punch, but he bull-rushed me back into the stall.

The quarters were too tight, and I couldn't fight worth a damn. I protected my face with my arms but left my midsection open, of which he took full advantage. Fortunately, my assailant was also hampered by the small space and couldn't step into his punches.

My attacker was built like an NFL defensive lineman. I couldn't push him back. If I fell, he would kick the crap out of me. One punch knocked the breath out of me. I doubled over for the second time since Sue's death. When I went to protect my stomach, two quick jabs hit the side of my head above my left ear. Another glanced my nose, not connecting fully but hard enough to start it bleeding. A left punch hit me in the mouth. He rammed me deeper into the stall.

Instead of falling to the floor, I rose quickly, pushing off the commode and somehow the back of my head connected with his jaw. The behemoth stumbled back dazed. I pushed him into the urinal. Water splashed on the floor and soaked his clothes. He slipped as he tried to get up. I broke for the door where I surprised his buddy, who I guess was the lookout.

The guy was short, more fat than muscle, and shocked to see me. He grabbed for me and grasped the collar of my button-down. I shoved him hard against the hallway wall. The shirt ripped as I pulled away and headed for Gravy and help.

The waitstaff surrounded me as soon as they saw me. My shirt was torn open, and I was bleeding from my mouth, nose, and ears. As I fell to the floor, I saw my attackers running out the back door—then I passed out.

I spent most of the evening at the emergency room at Sacred Heart Hospital. The doctor gave me five stitches above my ear and wrapped my chest to secure my bruised ribs. My lower lip and nose were swollen, but the nurse said ice packs would lower the swelling by morning. I had no black eyes, cuts, or bruises to my face. No one would need to know about the attack. I talked the ER into not reporting the incident.

I remembered one thing about my attacker. He wore a Hines Paving Company work shirt.

18

My head pounded. My ribs ached and made it difficult to breathe. Big Boy sighed and laid on the foot of my bed. I couldn't tell if he was worried or just disgusted with my constantly getting beaten up.

Sleep eluded me, even though I'd compartmentalized the fears of losing the paper, being penniless and forced to live in a jail cell with someone who thought I had "purdy hair."

Even on my best nights, the first few minutes after I climbed into bed were the worst, but somehow I could always place my anxieties in a nice little box in the corner of my mind, near the much larger crate of regrets and broken dreams, and nod off.

This was the worst night in a long time. There was no way to stop my whirling thoughts about Mari. Again and again I went through my ritual punishment of reliving how she died because of me. I watched myself covering the voters' rights rally in Holly Springs, losing track of the time, and failing to pick her up from the crisis center—and making the horrifying discovery that she never made it back to her dorm.

I thought about standing behind her family in the cemetery in Eunice as her casket was placed in her grave, her parents sobbing. I didn't have the courage to admit to them that Mari's death was my fault. No amount of rationalization would ever let me escape the guilt. If only I had not been so focused on writing the next big story and arrived at the crisis center when she finished her shift, Mari might still be alive. We would be married with three kids. But I was a self-absorbed coward who never owned up to her family about my role in Mari's death.

I finally drifted off into a troubled sleep and woke up forty minutes before my alarm clock was set to go off. My cell phone was vibrating and Harden was on the other end.

He said, "Officer down at Walnut Hill Holiness Church. This one will be bad. It's Sheriff Frost's brother, Amos."

When I arrived at the church, the rising sun reflected off the stained glass windows. Green and white Tahoes circled the site. Yellow tape shut off the parking lot. Sheriff Frost, Peck, and State Attorney Hiram Newton huddled next to the side door of the little white church.

I parked my car next to the railroad tracks and walked over to the crowd standing by the crime scene tape. Tyndall stood by a group of deputies away from Frost and Newton. He looked my way and gave a slight nod.

The deputies on guard didn't know anything. When the TV crew arrived, Newton walked over to the edge of the parking lot and addressed them. The state attorney wore a freshly pressed black suit and a maroon tie. He spoke with a deep voice that commanded respect. It wasn't difficult imagining that same voice putting the fear of God in the suspects he questioned.

"At approximately 4:20 a.m. a driver on Highway 99 noticed the blue lights flashing on what turned out to be an unmarked sheriff's office cruiser parked in a cemetery behind this church. The victim is Lieutenant Amos Frost, brother of Sheriff Ron Frost, which is why the sheriff isn't addressing you this morning."

He added, "No foul play is expected. We will have more after the medical examiner's report comes in. Our condolences go out to Sheriff Frost and his brother's family. That's all for now."

Thirty yards behind Newton, Sheriff Frost and Peck stood staring at me. They weren't thinking happy thoughts.

I talked to a few bystanders, but they hadn't seen or heard anything. They had rushed to the church when patrol cars with sirens blasting passed their homes. I walked back to my car, thinking about how I would write this up.

As I crossed the tracks to my car, someone shouted, "Halt, asshole. Put your hands on your head."

I turned around, and two deputies had their Tasers drawn and were standing in position ready to fire them.

"What?"

"Put your hands on your head. Down on your knees."

The deputy shouted his orders again. Others were getting in their cars a few yards away closer to the church, oblivious to my predicament. Frost and Peck did notice and stood by Peck's Tahoe nodding with approval.

I put my hands on my head and dropped to my knees in the mud. "What's the problem, Officer?"

A third deputy came up behind me and cuffed my right arm, and pulled it behind me. Pressed his knee into my back and pushed me flat on the ground. He pulled my left arm behind my back and cuffed it tightly, too. My ribs begged for relief. I grunted but held back a scream.

I started to protest. "What the—"

The deputy, who smelled of Axe body spray, leaned into me, putting his full weight on my back, which amped up my agony. "It's illegal to trespass on railroad property, Mr. Holmes. We're taking you in."

I tried to turn my head and face him. "This is ridicu—"

"Shut up, cocksucker," he said pushing me further into the mud. The pain shot from my ribs out to all parts of my body. I lifted my head and stretched my neck to avoid swallowing mud.

I heard a familiar voice. "That's enough."

The deputy eased the pressure, but remained standing over me. I wiped my face on my sleeve and tried to catch my breath without looking pathetic.

Alphonse Tyndall flashed his attorney general identification. "This man is here because I asked him to come."

"We're taking him to the station," said the deputy. "You can talk with our bosses about it there."

I had the feeling any ride to county jail wouldn't be swift or safe.

"Officer, the Florida Department of Law Enforcement and the FBI are standing behind the church," said Tyndall as he pulled out his cell phone. "Do I need to call them over here?"

Peck yelled, "Muncie, Gordon, Smitty! Uncuff the man. This isn't the time or place."

They removed the cuffs. I had trouble getting up. Razor helped me stand.

"What's wrong?" he asked. "You didn't land on the ground that hard."

I said, "I got in a fight last night. Busted some ribs. Let's act like we're talking for a few minutes while I catch my breath. I don't want Frost to see I'm in pain."

"What was the fight about?" Razor asked.

"A Pensacola ass-kicking, and my ass took the brunt of it," I said as I tried to stand erect without wincing.

"I can't stay here with you too long or my bosses will think I am sharing privileged information," Razor said.

"Will you?"

He laughed and shook his head no. "I'm walking back to the church. Frost is driving off. You should be safe."

"Why are you here?" I asked.

He said, "This could be linked to my operation."

And Tyndall walked away.

I drove the speed limit, came to a full stop at every stoplight, and did my best not to entice law enforcement to pull me over on the way back to the office. I got to Walnut Hill in forty-five minutes. The return trip took an extra thirty minutes.

The pain was tolerable but just barely. I had left the loft in such a rush that I hadn't thought about taking a pain pill. Covered in mud, I refused to look at myself in the car's rearview mirror.

When I opened the door to our building, I collapsed on the first landing. How did I climb the stairs last night?

Big Boy's tags jiggled from the office area, and Summer called after him as he ran down the stairs.

"My Lord, what happened to you? You look like you lost a fight with a mule," Summer said as she rushed behind the dog.

"I fell into a mud puddle," I said. I pushed the dog off me and struggled to stand.

"Let me help you."

"Before you do anything, help me take off this shirt," I said. "No need to get you muddy, too."

The shirt took a few tugs and moans to remove. Summer gasped when she saw the bandages wrapped around my chest. Fortunately, they weren't dirty. My shirt and T-shirt had absorbed all the mud and water.

"Who did this to you?" she asked. "What's happened in the last twelve hours?"

I said, "Get me up the stairs and let me change into some fresh clothes. I'll fill you in on the wild adventures of Walker Holmes."

Slowly we made it up to the third floor. Summer steadied me under one arm, while I kept a grip on the railing. Big Boy led the way, occasionally looking back to make sure we were following him.

Summer refused to let me fall on the bed without her first cleaning me up with a warm washcloth. While she removed the muck, I told her about Hopjacks and the Walnut Hill incidents.

"Please, nothing to the others yet," I said. "Give me time to tell them about it. I promise I will after I get some rest."

Summer made sure I landed gently on the bed, gave me two pain pills, and took Big Boy with her downstairs. Exhausted, I slept without any nightmares.

I got out of bed at 11:00 a.m. and texted Harden to meet me for a late lunch. The dog came up the stairs as I finished shaving and dressed. Summer followed. With her help, I put on a fresh T-shirt and white, button-down shirt. Big Boy started drinking out of the toilet.

"Today's deposit covers yesterday's check to the printer and most of this week's payroll," she said. "Sign these checks before you go."

"Summer, thanks," I said. "You told the staff about Hopjacks, didn't you?"

"Mal and Teddy already knew about it," Summer said. "Her sister works in the ER."

"Okay," I said as I put my hand on her shoulder to balance while I slipped on my deck shoes. No more tying shoelaces for a few days.

She said, "I didn't mention Walnut Hill, other than to say you drove up there early and needed to catch up on your sleep."

"Thanks. It's Friday. Everybody knows what to do. I'm headed to lunch with Harden."

"Is that smart?" she asked. "You look like a strong wind could knock you down. You need rest."

"I'll rest later and will sleep in tomorrow, promise," I said almost convincing myself.

Summer said, "I'll take Big Boy home with me so you don't have to walk him tonight and in the morning."

Big Boy looked up from the toilet and nodded approval.

19

Driving over to Bangkok Gardens, I got a text from Gravy: "Tatum ex-bookkeeper tends bar on Saturday afternoons. Call me later."

Bangkok Gardens was in an old Western Sizzlin' location that went out of business when Gayfers left the nearby Town and Country Plaza. The once thriving shopping center in midtown was mostly empty. Only nail salons, wig shops, and a bingo hall remained.

The restaurant was a popular lunch spot for sheriff deputies and bus drivers since it was within walking distance of the Escambia County Area Transit bus depot, Sheriff Frost's administration building, and "Castle Grayskull," the county jail.

An old Asian couple owned Bangkok Gardens, although we were never sure if they were Chinese, Thai, Vietnamese, or Cambodian. The restaurant had on its walls photos of royal families and Buddhist monks. Wooden cabinets lined one wall and were filled with Hummel figurines, Franklin Mint plates, and Furbies.

The menu only had a dozen items, each served with a spring roll and a cup of broth soup with a tofu cube and slice of mushroom floating in it. The AC hardly ever worked so customers jockeyed to sit close to the oscillating fans.

"You want pad thai?" one of the owners asked as I sat across from Harden. She wore a red blouse over a black skirt.

I ordered the pad thai and two Diet Cokes because she would never think to bring a second one later. Within minutes, her husband marched out of the kitchen and handed Harden and me the Tom yum kai soup, spring roll, and sweet and sour sauce before his wife had time to deliver our drinks. The couple had worked out this routine over the years.

Harden wore a short-sleeved, light blue work shirt, navy blue khaki pants frayed around the hem, and work boots. He looked like an auto mechanic on his lunch break.

"Do you do brakes?" I asked.

"Screw you, Holmes," he said softly so he wouldn't be overheard by the bus drivers sitting two tables away. "You called this meeting."

"What's the back story on Amos Frost?"

Harden said, "Good guy, a cop's cop. You went after him pretty hard in your article for his promotions under his brother, but the deputies liked him. You didn't win any fans in the force with this issue."

He continued in between spoonfuls of soup. "Amos was the kind of lieutenant that backed up his guys and gals and fought the battles that needed to be fought. He wasn't afraid to stand up to his older brother."

"Are we sure it was a suicide?"

He said, "Yes, he was on the phone with Sheriff Frost when he pulled the trigger."

"Damn, any details on the conversation?"

Harden said, "Frost hasn't shared it with any of my sources, but he might this afternoon. He has called a press conference."

Pausing to drink his green tea, he added, "I recommend you stay away and out of sight."

"Why? What do I have to do with his brother's suicide?"

He said, "Sheriff Ron Frost is a coldhearted, political animal. You wounded him with your cover story, and he wants revenge, even if he does it with his brother's death."

"He's covering something up," I said. "Something about Amos's suicide that he doesn't want the public to know."

He said, "Maybe, or you're the one trying to alter the narrative. This community has had two suicides tied to your reporting. You've got a problem."

"Thanks for cheering me up." I must have winced as I leaned over my bowl.

"I heard you got your tail kicked at Hopjacks," said Harden, who didn't look up from his soup. "Kicking your butt is becoming a sport around here."

"I'm still standing," I said.

"Just barely, Holmes. You can't keep taking these beatings."

There was genuine concern in his voice.

I said, "I'm okay. Just need to be smarter and more aware of my surroundings."

"Have you ever thought about carrying a gun?"

I shook my head. "No, I can't."

Too many thoughts of Mari popped into my head. Having a gun in the loft wasn't a good idea on long nights. Hell, I couldn't be sure that Big Boy wouldn't use it against me one night. I smiled at the thought of the dog with a gun. Not sure why I had a grin on my face, Harden moved the conversation into a different direction.

As the old man took our plates and his wife dropped off our main courses, Harden said, "You can't mess with these people and think everyone is going to be happy. The casualties keep mounting. Nobody can survive the kind of war you're waging. Nobody, not even Walker Holmes."

I didn't take the bait and spent a few minutes enjoying my pad thai. The bus drivers got up and went to pay their checks, never looking our way.

As I poured my second Diet Coke, I said, "Tell me what you know about Monte Tatum."

Harden hardly broke stride from enjoying his meal.

"Political wannabe. Wants badly to be elected to something, anything, but afraid of the possible fallout concerning his past personal life if he files to run again."

I asked, "What's he afraid of?"

"His club trolling before his dad died and left him the dry cleaning business," Harden explained. "One incident in particular. The bastard picked up some college kid one night. The coed was the mayor's daughter and ended up having to be taken to the ER for alcohol poisoning. Tatum's old man smoothed it over with the mayor and cops, but Tatum got banned from several night spots."

"Really? That made our boy Monte persona non grata on the club scene?"

Harden nodded. "The mayor had a lot of friends, and the bar owners didn't want the cops setting up DUI checkpoints near their operations."

"There had to be more to it than that," I said. The PI was making me work for answers.

"There was. Tatum pushed coke, not a lot, but he loved to prey on other guys' girlfriends. He messed up several of their lives. The bartenders got tired of his melodrama and used the mayor's daughter as an excuse to keep him out of their bars. Tatum eventually worked his way back in, but he had to tip them well for the privilege."

"How come I didn't hear about this during the election?" I asked.

"You're not from Pensacola, and this place tends to take care of its own," said Harden as he finished his red curry. "Most people see Tatum as a goofball with more money than common sense, but he still has a dark side. I once had some parents hire me to deal with him."

"What happened?" I asked.

"Tatum denied everything," said Harden, "but he left the girl alone after we had our little talk. Much of this was years ago. I haven't heard of any recent incidents. He has tried to become respectable."

I asked, "And owning a bar makes him respectable?"

"Well I did say he has no common sense."

"Ask around," I said. "See if there are any problems arising from the bar he owns."

"What does this have to do with the Hines case?" Harden asked.

"I don't know."

"Holmes, you're starting to run up a mighty big tab."

"I know, but I'm good for it."

Harden said, "Only if you're alive."

No shit.

20

Sheriff Ron Frost's press conferences were private, invitation-only affairs. He invited only select newspaper, television, and radio reporters. Held in a Castle Grayskull room that was only slightly bigger than a walk-in closet, Frost dominated the setting. A few reporters had complained that the chairs were lower than standard chairs so that the sheriff could seem even taller and more imposing than he was. Their complaints fell on deaf ears.

I had never received an invitation and never wanted to visit the Castle. Too many chances I might not find the way back out.

The press conference led the six o'clock news. The camera showed Frost flanked by his leadership team.

"My brother, Lieutenant Amos Frost, was a troubled man," he said. "The pressures of the job can wear on a man, and my brother took the responsibilities of his job very seriously."

A *Herald* reporter asked the sheriff about his last phone conversation with his brother.

"He had recently separated from his wife and was tired after working nearly thirty-six hours without sleep on a special investigation. Then this article by Walker Holmes came out, questioning his character and professionalism. He offered to resign if I thought it hurt the sheriff's office or me," he added. "I told Amos to stop talking such foolishness and come into the office. I thought I had him settled down, and then the phone went dead."

Frost appeared to be fighting back tears. He paused and gathered himself.

"We must do something about the sleazy tabloid journalism in this town," Frost said addressing the reporters in the room. "Over a span of two weeks, we have had two suicides because of Walker Holmes and his *Pensacola Insider*. The man is a menace."

The sheriff paused to let the words sink in. "Holmes hides behind freedom of the press and ruins lives and destroys this community. It's time the law-abiding, Christian people of this county put this man out of business."

I took two pain pills and went to sleep while I was thinking about the time I finally met Mari's family.

Bringing your boyfriend or girlfriend home to meet your family was an Ole Miss tradition. No relationship was considered serious until that happened. Mari passed the test with my family effortlessly. Her dry sense of humor won over my dad, and her manners impressed my mom. When my younger brothers pranked her, Mari not only laughed it off, she pranked them back.

My family was easy. Mari's would be a different story. She hadn't brought many boyfriends home to meet her family—only two during her first two years at Ole Miss. The Rebel football player she dated before meeting me never was introduced to her family. There was a good reason. Mari's father was a lifelong LSU season ticket holder for football, basketball, and baseball, and the boy wasn't worth the headache it would have caused Mari.

She had chosen a different path, forgoing the Bengal Tigers for the red and blue Ole Miss Rebels. Her parents supported their only child and defended her choice to her grandparents, aunts, and uncles. But their love for Mari didn't make it easier for the hated Ole Miss boys brought to Eunice, a little Louisiana town in the heart of the Cajun plains between Lafayette and Lake Charles.

Mari wouldn't tell me much about her family. She said it would have given me an unfair advantage. This was a test, and she wouldn't let me cheat.

The Gaudet family was old school. College boyfriends did not sleep under their roof with the daughter in a nearby bedroom. I would stay in the guest bedroom of Grandma Gaudet. Her family insisted I have breakfast with Mari's grandmother Saturday morning. If she liked me, she would invite her twin sister and Mari's uncles over to meet me. If not, I would pack my bags and head back to Oxford, like the last boy. Her dad would bring Mari back to the campus on Sunday.

We took my car to Eunice, arriving near midnight. I let her drop me off at her grandmother's house, and her Uncle Tom, who still lived with his mother, showed me to my room.

At 6:00 a.m. I woke, showered, and found Grandma Gaudet sitting at the kitchen table impatiently waiting for me. In her sixties, she was dressed in a purple jogging suit with gold tennis shoes. Her eyes were the same bright blue as Mari's, and her auburn hair had a little touch of gray at the temples.

"Good morning, Mrs. Gaudet. It's a pleasure to meet you."

In a voice raspy from years of smoking Kools, she said, "Call me, Grandma."

She poured me a cup of black chicory coffee. "Milk is in the refrigerator, sugar on the counter by the toaster."

I drank it black, no need to complicate the morning any more than it would be. "Thank you, Grandma."

She smiled. "Mari says you're a writer. What have you written?"

I told her that I had interned with *Commercial Appeal*, the daily newspaper in Memphis.

"Did you cover any murder cases?" she asked.

I nodded and told her about a trial I covered that had garnered some national attention.

The case had started when two marines heard a woman screaming in the woods near the Millington Naval Base north of Memphis. Minutes later, a beat-up, green Mercury station wagon nearly ran them over. The car was familiar around the base. It was owned by an air conditioning technician who lived in base housing with his wife, an enlisted sailor.

A few hours later, law enforcement found the mutilated body of nineteen-year-old Lance Corporal Suzanne Marie Collins. Covered with over a hundred wounds, she had been violated with a tree limb that had been shoved so far into her body that it punctured a lung. The autopsy showed her skull had been fractured with a screwdriver.

The cops arrested the repair man. His attorney tried to convince the prosecutors that he suffered from a multiple personality disorder. All the networks picked up the story of the gruesome, senseless crime.

"You see the body?" she asked as she poured me a second cup of coffee.

"No, ma'am, but I did see crime scene photos and read the autopsy report," I said, not mentioning how I almost vomited when I saw the photos.

She said, "Do you buy the story of his multiple personality that would mean he was too crazy to know right from wrong?"

"No, his story never made sense. He was wearing a bloody T-shirt when they arrested him. The screwdriver was found in his car. He claimed that he had been drinking at home. When he drove back to the liquor store, he accidently hit Collins who was jogging near the park, and he had offered to take her to the emergency room. He alleged that he couldn't remember many details after she got into the car."

I got up and added milk and sugar to my cup. "He said voices in his head told him to kill the girl. No one believed him, not even his wife and sister."

Grandma Gaudet smiled. "You know, I once served on a jury in a murder case."

It was then I knew I had won her over. Grandma Gaudet was an avid fan of true crime stories.

She told me about the trial. When she finished, Grandma Gaudet grabbed her gold handbag and said, "Come on, boy, we're headed to the slaughterhouse to get breakfast. Everybody will be coming over soon."

On Saturday mornings, locals crowded Eunice Superette & Slaughterhouse for fresh boudin. People lined up with coolers to fill with steaks and pork chops for grilling later in the day. We bought boudin for breakfast.

Grandma Gaudet spoke to everyone in line. They talked about the Friday night dance at the Knights of Columbus Hall and who drank too much and who left with who. She introduced me as Mari's friend from college. After they shook my hand and moved on, she whispered to me juicy pieces of gossip about them.

Back at Grandma Gaudet's house, I met her twin sister, Alice, and Mari's uncles and their wives. The men worked on offshore oil rigs, one of the most dangerous jobs possible. They poked fun at me for being a liberal journalist but were impressed that I had spent the two summers before my newspaper internship working on road crews laying asphalt.

Their hands weren't soft, and neither were mine.

Aunt Alice, the town librarian and family historian, gave me a quick tour of Eunice once we had finished our breakfast of boudin, saltine crackers, cracklin, and warm Pepsi.

The man who developed Eunice in 1884 had named the town for his wife, and in the center of town was a statue dedicated to its namesake. She looked like a Cajun Mary Poppins in a Victorian dress and hat.

Eunice's claim to fame was the Cajun Music Hall of Fame. On Saturday nights, the locals headed to the Liberty Theatre for the best Cajun and zydeco musicians in Louisiana. WCJN radio broadcasted the performances across the state.

Alice showed me the town's one-of-a-kind Nutcracker Museum, with a storefront that boasted the world's largest collection of nutcrackers. We walked into a Cajun music souvenir shop located in between the theater and museum. The owner's wife kept a sewing machine and spent her spare time making Mardi Gras costumes for everyone in town.

Around noon, Alice dropped me off at Mari's home. I met her parents and the rest of her extended family. Grandma Gaudet kissed me on the cheek and gave me a warm hug.

Mari beamed when she saw me surrounded by all her relatives. She kissed me warmly and whispered in my ear, "Thank you."

My alarm went off, and I awoke abruptly. I wanted desperately to go back to sleep and continue the dream, but no matter how hard I tried, I laid awake.

21

Over a pot of coffee, I read the Saturday edition of the *Herald*. Frost had successfully turned the media's focus, and possibly the community's, away from his top-heavy administrative payroll to my "sleazy tabloid journalism." The daily published an almost complete transcript of the press conference and promised more tomorrow.

Summer texted to say she would bring Big Boy over around four o'clock. They were going to the beach.

I researched Amos Frost online and sent out emails and text messages to various sources asking for any information on the man.

While he was a decorated lawman, Lieutenant Frost's personal life wasn't as stellar. Married and divorced twice, his marital problems seemed odd for a church deacon and "outstanding Christian." But this was Pensacola—Christianity and personal morality weren't necessarily the same thing.

A Waffle House waitress shared online that Amos Frost was leaving wife number three for a much younger woman. She had heard the girl, barely out of her teens, was pregnant.

Gravy called mid-morning. He said, "Let's talk about Eva Johnson."

"Who?"

Gravy said, "Monte Tatum's ex-bookkeeper who's suing him."

"Okay."

"I'm not sure she will go on the record," he said. "She's a little nervous, and her lawyer doesn't want to hurt her case. However, she will meet with you this afternoon when she starts her shift at three. You need to get there before the five o'clock crowd starts filling the bar. She's worried Tatum will find out about her talking with you."

"I'll win her over with my charm."

"You won't get another shot at her," Gravy warned. "Handle her gingerly. She does bookkeeping for a downtown real estate firm during the day and bartends at Intermission on weekends. She agreed to see you, but she's jumpy."

"Handling witnesses with care is my specialty," I said as I hung up.

A little before four o'clock, I walked into Intermission. A white button-down hid the wrap around my ribs. My Dodgers cap covered the stitches on my head. My ribs and head ached only dully.

The place was nearly empty. A NASCAR race, women's soccer, and a Miami Marlins game played on the televisions above the bar, and Aerosmith played on the speakers.

The bartender was a woman with black, curly hair and a dark complexion, maybe of Hispanic or Italian ancestry. As I walked in, she waved me to the corner of the bar away from a small group of drinkers.

I recognized her, not as Eva Johnson—her real name—but as Sparks Sinclair, the former Benny's Backseat stripper who had played a supporting role in the short-lived career of Alabama's head football coach a few years ago. The head coach had been in town for a celebrity golf tournament. When he left the dinner gala at Jackson's the night before the event, the coach ended up at Benny's with Sinclair and another dancer in the Champagne Room.

No big deal except he got drunk, mixed up his credit cards, and used his university one to pay the tab. An Auburn fan found out about it, and the coach got fired for misuse of university funds, and Sparks Sinclair got her fifteen minutes of fame. Benny loved the notoriety and even auctioned off what he claimed was the Champagne Room table where the coach had been entertained.

After she sold her story to *People Magazine*, Sinclair found Jesus, let her hair return to its natural color, and gave up dancing.

As an unnamed source who had danced at strip clubs from Miami to Atlanta, she helped us write a story on the mechanics of strip club operations. She used her *People Magazine* check to make a down payment on a cinder-block house on the beach. I heard she had gone back to school for a college degree before starting work as a bookkeeper. I didn't know it was for Tatum.

"Hi, Sparks," I said as she slid me a Bud Light.

She smiled, "I didn't know if you would remember me."

"You never told me your real name, but you aren't someone people forget easily."

Eva cocked her head back and smiled. "You're sweet."

She explained to me how six years ago she had married a cop named Johnson. She had finished her accounting degree at the University of West Florida, had a baby, and got divorced. After that she went to work for Tatum as his business manager and bookkeeper.

"Most of the time, he was all right—a little touchy-feely, but nothing I couldn't handle," said Eva. "I dressed professionally; it wasn't like I was showing off my cleavage. Had my son's picture on my desk."

She wiped down the bar as she talked. "He may have treated me different at first because of my ex, JoJo. Monte enjoyed a weird relationship with the cops. They laughed at him behind his back, but he always paid for their drinks, offered them nights at his condo, which he called the 'Love Shack.'"

I drank and listened.

"My split with JoJo was amicable." She gave a slight shrug. "He's a good father, but we drifted apart. It happens. JoJo moved to Tallahassee and went to work for ATF."

A couple of sailors stepped up to the bar. Eva took care of them and came back. She didn't miss a beat. She wanted to share her story.

Eva brought back a bowl of pretzels and another Bud Light. "After the divorce, Monte Tatum became more aggressive with me. Doing creepy things that somehow didn't sound quite so weird when I repeated them later to my girlfriends."

I asked, "Like what?"

"He invaded my personal space constantly, stood too close to me when we talked. He would pull up a chair, sit right next to me, and ask to go over the books. Regularly he leaned over my shoulder to view my computer screen and put his hand on my neck or shoulder. He bragged about his dates with people I knew and how good or bad they were in the sack."

"Did he ever mention taping his bedroom escapades?" I asked.

She shook her head.

"How about drugs? Did you get any indications he used drugs with the girls?"

Eva said, "I have heard the rumors about his past, but I had no hints that drugs were part of his lifestyle or the bar's operations. Our offices were in the SunTrust Bank building. I never went inside The Green Olive. JoJo warned me not to go there, ever."

"Why?"

She said, "I think it had more to do with the cops hanging around the place. He didn't want to have them gossiping about me or causing me any problems. You know how cops can be."

I nodded, not knowing exactly what she meant. "Did Tatum know you used to be a stripper?"

"Probably, I know that he and Benny had a history, but that was before I danced at the Backseat," said Eva. "I'm sure one of the cops mentioned it to him, but he was too afraid of JoJo to cross the line or say anything to me about my dancing."

"How did you handle Tatum's advances?"

"When I objected and asked him to stop, he acted innocent and told me I had misunderstood him," she said. "It was a lame-ass act, but I put up with it because I needed the job and the pay was good. Besides, I'd dealt with worse. He seemed to be all bark and no bite."

Eva said Tatum would stop for a few days after she objected, but it wouldn't be long before he'd start coming on to her again. He eventually began to ask her out to concerts and plays, even offering to pay for babysitters. She refused. Then he abruptly stopped hitting on her.

"It was like he had a shiny new toy that captured his attention," she said. "He ignored me, which I first thought was some silly mind game he learned reading *Esquire* or *Playboy*. But after a couple of weeks, I was relieved to have him off my back."

Intermission began to fill up, and I slowed down on my drinking. Eva juggled a dozen customers. She made each of them feel special, both men and women. Leaning into them and laughing, she expertly handled their drink orders.

The tips mounted. More than a few vied to take her home after work. At thirty-eight, she still was a crowd-pleaser. She must have driven Tatum crazy.

On the television above the bar, a teaser for the six o'clock news ran. Sheriff Frost was shown. Fortunately, there was no sound, but I was certain I was the topic.

Eva looked up at the screen. "Sad news about Amos."

"You knew him?" I asked.

She nodded. "From my days at the Backseat. He liked lap dances from the young ones. Passed out his business cards, just in case they got in trouble on the way home or needed a ride."

"I thought he was such a fine Christian."

She smiled and said as she walked away to serve another customer, "Everybody has to let off a little pressure."

While she tended to customers, I jotted down notes on cocktail napkins, sticking them in my shirt pocket.

"Walker, this is off the record, right?" Eva asked when she came back.

"Completely," I said. "This is all background, but I've had a few beers and don't want to forget anything."

Showing her a napkin, I added, "Your name isn't anywhere on this. I always protect my sources."

She handed me soda water with a lime. "I don't want to hurt my case. My attorney assures me Monte will settle to avoid depositions."

Eva then shared with me why she no longer worked for Tatum and the reason for her lawsuit. In March, Tatum began hanging around a guy named Cecil.

"A big dude," she said. "Typical gym rat. He and Monte talked about setting up a film production company. Monte started writing $10,000 checks to his production company. Two over ten days. Always after they had spent time viewing footage behind closed doors."

"Did you ever see any of the clips?" I asked.

"No, but the dude Cecil began coming on to me, very aggressively. Monte egged him on. They kept saying I had a great body for film and laughed about me doing a screen test."

Eva almost shuddered as she recalled the story. "I wasn't sure exactly what they were talking about it, but it was unnerving. I walked out."

When she returned to work the next day Tatum told her that she was fired. Eva asked for the ninety-day severance that was in her contract, and he told her to sue him, which she did.

"He tried to claim he caught me stealing, but I kept a backup of the books on a flash drive. I can account for every nickel."

Good for her, I thought on the way home. Eva always knew how to take care of herself. Tatum was in for a fight, and he would lose.

Back at the loft, Big Boy greeted me. A note from Summer was stuck to the refrigerator:

"Beer and leftover cheese pizza in the fridge. Please rest."

After a couple of slices and a cold beer I took Big Boy for a short walk and sent a few text messages.

I asked Harden to check into a filmmaker, first name Cecil, and find out what type of film company he ran. I also texted Tyndall to see if he could meet on Monday.

They both replied, "K."

22

Sunday morning I walked Big Boy and picked up a copy of the *Pensacola Herald*. A huge photo of Amos Frost in his dress uniform was on the front page. The article made it seem as if he had died in the line of duty. There were photos of him leading a bible study at his church, coaching Little League, and on a SWAT call. The paper included quotes from his coworkers and friends, but oddly none from his ex-wives. The editorial proclaimed the need for more responsible journalism. It didn't mention my name or my newspaper, but it was about me.

I went over to Dare's for brunch. A light breeze off Pensacola Bay made it comfortable enough for us to sit outside.

Dare made a healthy version of eggs Benedict with her special hollandaise sauce, tomatoes, and turkey bacon. I brought champagne and fresh orange juice for the mimosas and sliced the fruit. A Preservation Hall album played while we cooked, and Dare shared her New York adventures. I filled her in on the last few days. Big Boy sat on the floor of the kitchen, happily eating strips of crispy bacon.

"How many battles can you fight at one time?" she asked as we sat down to eat on her back porch. In between the neighboring houses, we could see shrimpers trawling the bay.

I handed her a mimosa. "I'm about at my limit, but I have to see this through. You know that."

Dare smiled. "It seems you're always on some crusade, carrying the whole world on your shoulders." Taking a sip of mimosa, she added, "And the world doesn't care; some even resent you for it."

"I guess I'm a real jerk."

Big Boy was full and napped in the sun, soaking up rays. "Well I do worry about you," she said. "You have no social life other than drinking in bars with Gravy, your staff, or some news source. You don't go out on many dates. You're obsessed with a newspaper that's on constant life support. Seems like every time I see you someone has either beaten you up or threatened to shut you down."

Dare must have seen the surprise on my face. I hadn't mention Hop-jacks or Walnut Hill. I had combed my hair to hid the stitches and had tried hard not to show how badly my ribs ached.

She smiled. "What? You think you are the only one with sources?"

"I didn't want to bother you," I said. "The doctor said I'll be better in a week or so."

"Are you in pain?"

"Only when I exhale, but the mimosas are helping."

Dare asked, "Don't you ever get tired of pushing rope up a hill? You and I are outsiders. Pensacola tolerates us, but its patience with you may be wearing thin."

"Someone has to drag this place into the twenty-first century . . ."

"Even when it's completely against its will?" she interrupted.

"Yes." This conversation was one we had countless times. We touched our glasses and laughed. Big Boy looked over at us, sniffed loudly, and laid his head back down. He had heard it all before, too.

"I missed talking with you," I said.

"Me, too. You can be such a stubborn jackass."

I shrugged.

"You are a hard person to be friends with," Dare added.

"Yeah," I said, tossing the dog my last piece of bacon. He ignored it. I wasn't sure if it was because he was full or the scraps off my plate were beneath him.

"Dare, the handwriting analysis came in early this morning. The expert confirmed that Sue wrote the note."

"I knew it," she said as she got up to clear off the table. I let Dare soak in the news and waited for her to digest it.

Dare came back to the table and refilled our flutes. I asked her, "What lies do you think Sue was writing about in her note?"

She said, "On the flight, I tried to figure it out. Sue complained how secretive Bo had been the last year or so. At one time, she was convinced he was having an affair and hired your buddy Harden to tail Bo, but nothing came of it."

Harden had never mentioned working for Sue Hines.

"Having Julie and Jace in their home put a strain on her marriage," Dare said. "Jace only thinks of Jace and left his fifteen-year-old alone with Bo and Sue. Julie and Sue got along at first, but it didn't last long. Bo seemed to be the only who could connect with her."

"Have you had any luck talking with Julie since Sue's funeral?" I asked.

"Not yet, but we have a date for coffee on Friday," said Dare. "I did see on Facebook that she dyed her hair a ridiculous shade of red."

We sipped our mimosas. Something wasn't right.

I said, "I thought Bo and Jace hated each other."

"Jace and Bo were members of the same hunting club in Alabama. They had a falling out—as always happens in any relationship with Jace—but Sue kept them together." She added, "I had heard long ago it was some grudge over a girl they both dated, but like everything in this town that happened before 1990, nobody will ever share any details about it. The vagueness of these people slays me. Even Sue said she couldn't remember any details."

I said, "I wish Roger was still here. He would know."

We toasted her glasses to his memory. Dare said, "I miss him, too."

"Why does every fight around here always go back to high school?" I said, not expecting an answer. "In the Mississippi Delta, you trade punches, somebody pulls you off each other, and everyone goes for a drink. The dispute is settled."

"Not here," Dare said. "You have two problems: Frost and Jace. Sheriff Frost isn't going to let up, and he will impact your sales. A dead deputy is never well received by the community, and people will want an explanation."

"Or a scapegoat," I said.

She nodded. "Bo and Jace together can be formidable. Jace is shrewd enough to play up Amos Frost's suicide. You can expect him to come out swinging this week."

Dare always had the ability to push through the emotions and coldly assess the situation.

She asked, "What are you going to do with Sue's note?"

I said, "I'm going to publish it on the blog first thing in the morning."

"Is that smart? Why bring Sue's death into this mess? You've already been called a sleazy journalist. Won't the post feed into that?"

"The note is relevant," I said. "It's how we put the attention back where it needs to be. My spidey sense is saying there's more to all this than Bo Hines stealing a couple hundred thousand dollars. I've got to find out what before Frost, Hines, Wittman, and the bank take me down."

Dare asked, "You are talking with Gravy, aren't you? You can expect threats of lawsuits if you carry out this strategy."

"Yes, Dare. I'll be fine." I wish I felt as self-assured as my words sounded.

After we washed the dishes, I kissed Dare on the cheek and asked her to see if she could find out any more about the falling out between Hines and Wittman. Then Big Boy and I headed back to the loft.

As I got the dog settled and started to work on my draft on the blog post regarding the suicide note, I received a text from Alphonse Tyndall.

"Need to talk. Can you meet me today instead of tomorrow? Hopjacks at 3?"

An hour later when I walked into Hopjacks I spotted Tyndall in the corner of the bar nearest the front windows.

"What's up, Sheriff Razor?" I asked as I motioned to the waitress to bring me a Bud Light and sat down.

He smiled and said, "Thanks for seeing me on a Sunday afternoon, Mr. Publisher."

"I needed the break from writing," I said. "I don't like sitting with my back to the window. I'm trusting that you'll watch behind me."

"No problem, Walker." He paused as the beers were delivered. "I don't like how Sheriff Frost is going after you in the media."

I ordered some fries and made another mental note to eat healthier, just not on Sunday afternoons. Rain began to fall. The smokers at the tables on the sidewalk grabbed their beers and pizzas and scampered inside.

"I've dealt with this crap before," I replied, hoping the words sounded more confident than I felt. The bandages around my ribs itched, but I fought off the urge to scratch them.

"You have nothing to do with Amos Frost's death."

I said, "But it helps the sheriff to take the focus off him and his administration."

Tyndall put down his Guinness. "No, you're not listening. Your newspaper had nothing to do with his brother's suicide."

"What are you talking about?"

He said, "What do you know about Amos Frost?"

"Good lawman. Popular with the street cops. Sort of the opposite of his older brother. Deacon in his church. Little League coach." I took a swig of my beer and continued, "But his personal life may have been screwed up. Two ex-wives and working on a third. Possibly struggled with a 'young stripper habit.' That's all I have."

Tyndall nodded in approval. "Not bad. You do have pretty good sources, but there may be more. I suspect he was being blackmailed."

I didn't see that one coming. "Blackmailed? Fooling around with strippers isn't a crime."

Motioning for me to keep my voice down he said, "I didn't say he committed a crime. However, his face did pop up in one of the videos of the porn ring we talked about the other day."

If I could whistle, I would have. Instead, I signaled the waitress for another round of beers.

Tyndall explained that the film company had found a new revenue stream—letting members participate in its videos. For two hundred dollars, men and women could have sex with the "actors."

"You pay a membership fee. Once or twice a month you get a text to go to some place in the two-county area. Usually, they give you a mask. But Frost was too drunk or too high and didn't wear his."

Mentioning the three hundred pound Amos Frost having sex made me cringe.

Tyndall continued, "All the time we've worked on this investigation, we received little cooperation from the Escambia County Sheriff's Office. They didn't block us, just didn't seem interested. And they didn't lend us any resources that might have sped up the investigation."

I asked, "Was Lieutenant Amos Frost the problem?"

He nodded. "When I confronted him last week about it, he first denied knowing anything, but when I offered to show him the video, he confessed."

"Where does the blackmail come in?" I asked.

"The producer—"

I interjected, "Cecil."

Tyndall gave me a half smile. "Cecil Rantz had asked Amos Frost to notify him if any law enforcement began to investigate his operation. He promised Frost that he would never release the video and would give him the only copy when his crew left town."

"Did Frost tell Rantz about your investigation?"

"No, he was too good a cop to do that, but he made sure the sheriff's office didn't provide us resources. Lieutenant Frost admitted to me that he was trying to get the filmmakers to finish up here and move to some other location."

I said, "So you think he saw the roof caving in on him. That he was about to be exposed."

"Not sure. Maybe. We were supposed to meet Friday morning at Waffle House in the north end of the county. If he helped us and shared everything he knew, I would have tried to keep his name out of it. But there weren't any guarantees."

The summer rainstorm stopped, and the smokers migrated back outside where a waitress was wiping down the tables and chairs on the sidewalk.

"Why are you telling me all this?" I asked.

"The film scheme is part of a much bigger deal, an international deal," he said. "This week, we are going to round up all the ringleaders. We still don't know who is financing the operation. Amos Frost's suicide has pushed my bosses to pull the trigger and shut it down. Somebody will cut a deal." He took a big swig of his beer and smiled. "I thought you might be able to use what I gave you to get Sheriff Frost off your back."

We ordered one last round. The *Insider* traded ads with Hopjacks for free pizza, fries, and beer, so I used our trade to pick up the tab. Tyndall handled the tip.

As we finished our beers, I made the decision to share Bree's dilemma.

"Razor, you may want to check into Monte Tatum. My sources say he has been keeping company with Rantz, maybe invested in his operation."

"Tatum? The Green Olive owner?"

I nodded.

He said, "Monte Tatum. That makes some sense, but he doesn't have the kind of money it takes to run the operation we're closing down."

I said, "I can't tell you my source, so don't ask. He has invested at least twenty grand in Rantz's company. You need warrants for his offices in the SunTrust building, the club, and his house. I hear he may have videos at all three places."

"How reliable is your source?" he asked, looking me in the eye.

I stared back. "Very."

"Well, let me talk it over with my team," he said as he shook my hand and got up to leave. "Don't write anything until the sweep, and I'll keep you in the loop."

"It's a deal," I said.

23

Monday morning I decided to take Big Boy on a long walk. My ribs weren't aching, and the rain had cooled the morning temperature down to the high sixties.

We hiked to Roger Fairley's grave in St. John's Cemetery. The Masons had established Pensacola's second cemetery in 1876. I often teased Roger that his ancestors had helped to fund the purchase of the twenty-six acres only so the Fairleys could have the prime burial plot on the northern slope near a magnolia tree.

Pensacola was predominately a Roman Catholic town prior to the Civil War. As more Protestants began to migrate to the coastal town, tensions mounted between the Spaniards and their descendants and the new arrivals. The Masons, a secret society that the Catholic Church prohibited its faithful from joining, had gained a foothold in Pensacola when the British controlled the settlement in the late 1700s. Fearing the Catholics might refuse to let any more Protestants be buried in St. Michael's Cemetery, the Masons created their own cemetery.

From the cemetery's inception in 1876, the Masons were surprisingly more progressive than their Catholic counterparts and opened the cemetery to people of all religions and races, although the groups were separated and the areas for white people had much larger plots.

Roger was on the board of the St. John's Cemetery Foundation, as each generation of his family had been. He loved to brag about the cemetery's historical significance.

"St. John's contains the largest and most diverse number of gravestones and monuments in Northwest Florida," he would say over martinis, trying to persuade me to write a newspaper article on the cemetery. "It's where the leaders of Pensacola are buried."

He regaled me with the names of the more illustrious cemetery occupants. Dick Pace, born 1896, built Pensacola's first paper mill, Florida Pulp and Paper Company, which later merged with St. Regis Paper Company. He enticed Monsanto and Escambia Bay Chemical to locate plants in the area. I often reminded Roger that the corporations were three of the biggest polluters in Northwest Florida. Pace also founded the Pensacola Country Club, Pensacola Yacht Club, and the Fiesta of Five Flags celebration—three of my least favorite Pensacola society fixtures.

Another historical figure buried there was O. J. Semmes, born in 1876, who was superintendent of the city's streetcar system, later founded the Semmes Coal and Ice Company, and chaired the Escambia County School Board for thirty-six years from 1921–1957. The board named an elementary school in his honor.

"And he ran one of the most segregated school systems in the country, one that wasn't integrated until a federal judge ordered it after Semmes' death," I would chime in.

Roger would get the point and drop the subject.

Big Boy and I walked into the cemetery through its G Street entrance, a gatehouse constructed in 1908. On one side of the structure was a chapel that hadn't been used in decades. The other side had storage for lawn equipment.

A fish fountain near the gate had some rainwater in it. Big Boy lapped up a little before we trekked over to the bench by Roger's grave.

"Hi, Roger," I said. Big Boy laid down near the stone marker. Clearly he still pined for his former master.

The doctors had allowed the dog to stay in the hospital room with Roger up until he passed. Big Boy attended the graveside service with me. His first week at the loft he had run away a half dozen times. I would find him either on the deck at Roger's house or at St. John's Cemetery.

"We miss you, buddy," I said. "The wagons are circled around me, and all the guns are aimed in my direction. You always said I had a 'justice gene' that made me pick fights against impossible odds and that it would be my ruin one day. That day keeps getting closer."

Big Boy raised his head. Some squirrels were playing on a gate about twenty yards away. He ran over to bother them, bored with my monologue.

I sat and tried to make sense of the thoughts running through my head. I still needed more information. The pieces didn't quite fit together, but I was pretty sure they should.

As we walked back to the loft, my post on the suicide note went live. I resisted the urge to immediately check the readers' responses. I powered on my computer only after I showered and fed Big Boy.

The blog already had thirty-five comments on the post about the suicide note—none flattering. It was worse on the *Herald* website where they had posted a brief blurb about the note. Most hoped Hines would sue me. Some asserted the note was a fake. A few claimed Kettler put me up to it to discredit Wittman. The internet trolls ripped to shreds anyone defending me.

Assistant State Attorney Clark Spencer called. "My boss wants to know who gave you the suicide note."

"Someone fat," I said.

"Holmes, this is serious. The cops didn't find any note at the scene. Then you publish one a week after Bo Hines attacks you in the newspaper and after Sheriff Frost goes after your journalism ethics. You have to admit it looks bad."

"I know, I know, but even if I knew who gave it to me, I couldn't tell you without their permission. I will have Gravy drop it off with the handwriting analysis we had done on it. Just check it out, Spencer."

Spencer said, "Get us the note immediately. We will do our own analysis, but I can tell you unless you can come up with more on how you got the note, you can expect a subpoena, maybe even a search warrant."

"Do whatever you have to do."

Gravy didn't pick up his cell phone when I called. I tried his office and was told that he was in court, but he would return my call when he got out.

We held the *Insider* staff meeting. The excitement of last Thursday had evaporated. The talk they heard over the weekend hadn't been positive.

"I'm dreading the phone today," said Roxie. "Sheriff Frost has gotten people riled against us. The last phone call businesses want to receive is one from us asking for money."

"This will die down," I said. "There are some things in the works that will undermine Frost's venom. Our readers trust us to find the truth."

Roxie stared back but didn't say a word. I hadn't convinced her, but she was willing to wait a day or so.

I added, "It's probably a good idea to take a break from sales calls the next few days. But I promise people's attitudes towards us are going to change."

Jeremy said, "Tell us about the suicide note. Why did you hide it from us?"

I told them how I had obtained the note. "Before I did anything with it or got you all excited about it, I wanted to verify the handwriting. I didn't get verification until Sunday morning."

Mal said, "What does 'no more lies' mean? How does it change anything?"

"That's where good investigative journalism comes in. We have to find Pandora Childs. We need more information about the pasts of both Hines and Wittman."

I looked directly at Doug. "You need to nail your Save Our Pensacola story to set up my follow-up that will run next week and tie it all together."

He said, "I'll have my final draft to Roxie by noon."

Mal snickered and mumbled, "Sure you will. Last staff meeting you said it would be finished by 10:00 a.m. that day."

"Doug, make it happen," I said. "I need you to do some legwork for the follow-up story. Also, there may be a big police bust this week. You need to be ready to pounce on it."

Jeremy quipped, "We aren't the ones being busted, are we?"

I laughed and so did everyone else. Then we headed back to our desks to take on the world.

Gravy called. "What kind of shit storm have you started?" he asked. "The state attorney's office has called three times demanding the suicide note and handwriting analysis. I assume you told them I had them."

"Guilty," I said. "Deliver the information to them, but drag your feet. Maybe have a carrier make it her last drop of the day."

Gravy said, "Walker, I don't need the state attorney on my ass. You already have Frost watching me closely. Don't bring me into your shit."

"You're already in my shit," I replied, keeping my voice calm. "I'm the client. Just do as I ask, please."

"A pro bono client," he said. "What will I say if Spencer calls again?"

"Tell him I have the documents and you're waiting on them."

Gravy said, "I need better clients." Then he hung up.

My cell phone vibrated. A reporter from a Mobile television station wanted to know if I would be going to the press conference that afternoon and if I'd be available for comments afterward.

"What press conference? Why would I want to comment?"

The reporter said, "Bowman Hines and Jake Wittman are holding a press conference today at 4:00 p.m. on the courthouse steps. They tell us their attorneys will attend, and they will expose you for the tabloid hack writer that you are."

I told Doug to finish his story on time so that he could cover the press conference. I played briefly with the idea of sitting it out but knew I wouldn't.

My cell phone vibrated again.

"I've never known a man so determined to get his butt kicked," Dare said when I answered. I couldn't tell if she was angry or teasing. "I hope you know what you're doing."

"Dare, stay with me on this," I replied. "You've got to trust me. We will find the truth."

"I'm in your corner, regardless of how difficult you make it at times," she said. "I know you had to publish the note. What's the feedback so far?"

I walked out to the stairwell so the staff couldn't hear how bad it was.

"Spencer demands to know how I got the note. Jace and Bo have called a press conference this afternoon to blast me. I'm sure his attorneys are fired up to come after me. My checking account has $104 in it. And my dog smells like the bathroom of a truck stop."

"What will you do?"

"Take them all down. What other choice do I have?" I added, feeling my cockiness didn't ring true.

I checked my email when I walked back into the office. There was one from Clark Spencer that contained the official statement from the state attorney's office on the suicide note. It stated they would analyze the handwritten document and release a report as soon as it was available, probably in two days.

My name wasn't mentioned in the press release.

Roxie yelled at me, "The marketing director for Evans Land just called. They bought eight full-page ads. The first one will run next week."

I smiled.

Roxie said, "They're prepaying and will drop off the check before 2:00 p.m."

Dare had come to my rescue yet again.

I needed to work, but if I sat in the office, all I would do was check comments on the blog and worry about the upcoming press conference. I decided to drive my 1995 Jeep Grand Cherokee to The Green Olive. Maybe Tatum would be around.

As I walked out the door, Roxie said, "The marketing director also said Dare would have a package for you to pick up later this afternoon. Do you want me to get it?"

"No, I'll handle it."

24

One o'clock in the afternoon drinking in Pensacola was an art. The predictable cast of characters at The Green Olive included a chain-smoking hipster attorney in a charcoal gray flannel suit chatting up a secretary while hiding out from his bosses, a drunken former city councilman lamenting how the voters didn't appreciate him, two city road workers on a "lunch break," and a cadre of college kids either coming or going from Pensacola Beach.

More memorabilia than the TGI Friday's backroom crammed the walls of the dimly lit shit hole. The ancient sound system was either playing Aerosmith or Def Leppard. I couldn't quite tell. The place seemed dirty, but it was too dark to know for sure.

In the corner sat Monte Tatum. It wasn't hard to spot his gold chain and hairy chest peeking out of a too-tight, open-collared shirt. He had dropped his professional business attire for the day. He looked a little stressed and strung out. Maybe he hadn't been sleeping so well. Eva had told me her attorney had scheduled his deposition for the following week.

Tatum was ignoring a young, skinny, blond waitress who was trying to convince him breast enhancement would be good for his business.

"If I had new boobs, they'd make my job so much easier," she said leaning into Tatum. "Like, I won't have to talk as much, because they'd do all the talking. The bigger, the better!"

Tatum eyed her chest and licked his lips, but he didn't say anything to her as I approached his table. He didn't know what I had heard.

"Well, if it isn't Walker Holmes," he said, reaching out to shake my hand while dismissing the waitress with his other hand. "What brings you to The Green Olive?"

"I'm working on my Yelp review of your fine establishment," I said as the bartender brought me a Bud Light with a lime.

Tatum grunted, maybe it was his version of a chuckle. His skin glistened with sweat, and his pupils were dilated.

"Over the past year I've begged you to come to my bar so we could get to know each other better, and finally you show up at one in the afternoon," he said. "Who are you hiding from? The guys who whipped your ass at Hops?"

"Screw you," I said, as I sat down across from him. "You're the one dressing down today. Your Brooks Brothers suit at the cleaners?"

"I've been a little under the weather," Tatum replied. "I stopped here to check on things before I go back to bed." He looked over at his bartender. "They'll steal you blind if you don't check on them every day."

"Maybe you should talk with your HR department about the screening process for new employees," I suggested.

He grunted another chuckle. Sitting up a little straighter, he pulled his shirt collar together and fastened a button to cover up the black fur on his chest.

"Holmes, I'm running for the county commission again in two years," he said. "I want your support."

I shook my head. "Too early for endorsements."

"I'll start placing ads for the bar in your newspaper. We'll prepay at the first of each month."

"The answer is still no. We will wait until we know who is in the race."

Tatum said, "I hear you need the cash. Let me help."

"In the last race, you had a chain of dry cleaners and ran as a successful small business owner," I replied. "How do you think this place will improve your chances next time?"

"This's an iconic place. Getting a first drink at the Olive is a rite of passage for most of this town."

Tatum took a sip of his vodka and soda and leaned towards me. "Besides," he added, "you blasted me for owning those cleaners."

I shrugged. He had a point. We had reported on his EPA violations. His operations used perchloroethylene, commonly called "perc," to clean clothes. Perc was a suspected carcinogen that could also cause short-term health effects such as respiratory distress and sore throats. Dry cleaners were required to inspect equipment regularly to look for and repair leaks and keep records of the inspections and the amount of perc purchased each year. Tatum did not.

I said, "And you filed a bullshit defamation lawsuit against the *Insider* after the election that cost me ten grand in legal fees to defend."

Tatum had found a Tallahassee firm to demand a retraction of our reporting on the dry cleaners. I refused, and the firm filed a defamation lawsuit. Gravy passed me off to a constitutional law attorney who skewered Tatum's allegations. The judge granted us summary judgment, but not attorney fees. I was still paying off the legal bills in five hundred dollar monthly increments.

Tatum sat back up and bowed his back. "You cost me that fucking election."

"Not my problem," I said. "Your shady business practices hurt you, not our reporting."

"Screw you, Holmes. Remember I tried to be nice and make peace," he said as he got up from the table, gathering his cell phone, wallet, and BMW keys. "I'd have someone kick your ass, but somebody already beat me to it."

He yelled to the bartender, "Whatever this asshole orders is on my tab." Then he left.

The waitress who wanted the breast augmentation brought me another Bud Light. She said, "Wow, you set the Olympic record for getting under his skin."

"It's my superpower."

She smiled. "You're Walker Holmes."

"Guilty," I said as I squeezed the lime into the bottle and took a big swallow.

"You spoke to my communications class at UWF last year."

"How did I do?"

She said, "It was the most interesting class we had all year. You didn't hold back. It got me reading your blog."

She sat down at the table. No one seemed to notice. The bartender was on his cell phone. Everyone else couldn't see past their half-full glasses.

"Have you graduated?" I asked.

She shook her head. "Ran out of money, but I will finish."

Sure she would, I thought, but there was no harm in pretending otherwise. I noticed the cameras in the bar weren't pointed at Tatum's table. This girl wasn't as stupid as she wanted others to believe. Her boss wouldn't catch her on video talking to me. Maybe she actually would go back to college.

I asked, "What's going on here? Who hangs out at The Green Olive?"

"Drunks and guys hiding out from their wives and bosses fill this shift," she said as she surveyed the room. "Attorneys, reporters, aging players, and more hipsters come in later."

Pointing to a television behind the bar, she added, "Like that guy."

I turned to see Sheriff Frost being interviewed by a reporter. "The sheriff?"

"No, no," she said shaking her head. "The tall, good-looking man behind him."

It was Bo Hines talking to Peck in the background of the shot.

"Bo Hines?" I asked.

"I don't know his name. For a while he was coming in here two or three times a week, but he hasn't been around the past two months."

"Was he alone?"

She said, "No, he usually had a woman with him. She had a hippie vibe, somewhat attractive, always ordered apple martinis."

It sounded like Pandora Childs.

The waitress continued. "They would sit over there." She pointed to a dark corner away from the pool and foosball tables. "He couldn't keep his hands off her."

"Did they stay long?"

"Four or five drinks, but usually they left in separate cars by 6:30."

I asked, "Do you ever work the late-night shift?"

"That's what Tatum calls 'looking for ass time,'" she said with a smirk. "Girls, boys, drunk, high, it doesn't matter. Most everybody wants to score. The tips are good, but I just try to get out in one piece."

"Drugs?"

She said, "Listen, I'm not looking for trouble. What they do is their business."

So, the answer was yes.

"What about the cops?"

"The precinct is only a few blocks away. They are the biggest partiers, and the boss says they don't pay for anything."

The bartender yelled her name. As she got up, I handed her my business card and a twenty.

"What's your name?" I asked.

"Sally," she said with a smile. "Sally Mitten."

"Call if you ever have a news tip, Sally Mitten," I said.

She took the tip and card and tucked them in her soon-to-be-expanded bosom.

I walked out into the hot, bright afternoon sun, jotted down a few notes, and made my way to the courthouse.

The press conference was high theater, even the television stations from Mobile had camera crews on the courthouse steps. A dozen or so Save Our Pensacola followers stood in the shadow of the building as well as several city council members.

Jace Wittman began by saying that he had called the press conference to give an update on the petition drive and to speak out in defense of his deceased sister, who couldn't defend her reputation against the inflammatory writing of "a yellow, tabloid, so-called journalist who wanted to get more hits on his blog."

I think he meant me. Wittman didn't look my way, but I felt everyone else's eyes on me. I didn't take my eyes off him.

Bo Hines stood behind Wittman dressed in jeans and a Hines Paving Company gray work shirt with his last name under the company's logo. He wanted to appear as though he had been driving one of his trucks all day, something he hadn't done in twenty years. Julie Wittman was MIA.

"We have been inundated with people wanting to sign petitions since this morning's article in the *Pensacola Herald*," Wittman said. "Thanks to my brother-in-law's donation, we have hired people to man the phones at my real estate office and drum up more signatures for the petition."

He continued, "A. J. Kettler, Stan Daniels, the Pensacola City Council, and the *Insider* have tried to manipulate this so-called public-private project from the beginning. They will do anything to steal this land from the people of Pensacola, land that should be preserved for our children and grandchildren."

Wittman went on to complain, as he had done since the project was first proposed, that the city had never sought requests for proposals from other potential development groups.

"Daniels made sure his client, Kettler, got his ballpark," Wittman said. "This was not a citizen-driven process. The promoters manipulated it for their personal gain. We will defeat the project, and then the people, not the carpetbaggers, will decide what's best for Pensacola. Kettler can build his ballpark somewhere else."

Wittman added that his brother-in-law wouldn't be speaking today, but he had a statement prepared by Hines' attorneys to read.

"The Hines family wants to reiterate its support for Save Our Pensacola," he read. "It will contribute whatever funds it takes to stop the construction of the maritime park with its ballpark."

Wittman continued, "We were distressed today to learn those supporting the ballpark have attacked the memory of Sue Hines in order to defeat our grassroots petition drive. Our attorneys will seek every legal means possible to punish those who have so heartlessly tried to damage the reputation of a beloved woman of this community. We will continue to cooperate with the authorities, but we will not let the legacy of someone so dear to all of us be tarnished."

I kept my chin up, arms folded, and looked ahead. Inside I wanted to whip my own ass for posting the suicide note.

A television reporter asked Wittman about the note. "I can tell you that was no suicide note. As I said earlier, Mr. Hines isn't going to comment, but that note was written weeks ago and had nothing to do with her death. My sister often wrote notes to Bo and me when she was upset with us."

The reporter asked, "What lies is she talking about?"

Wittman said, "Who knows? Probably referring to a hunting trip we took when she thought we were in Tallahassee."

Puff! And my "smoking gun" vanished.

The reporters cornered me after the press conference. I hated being part of the news, but there was no dodging the scrutiny.

"The note we published today was written by Sue Hines," I said. "Our expert confirmed it. And, yes, it clearly is a suicide note. Mrs. Hines was fed up with the lies concerning the missing Arts Council funds and whatever else her husband has covered up."

I continued, "The public has a right to know the truth, regardless where it leads. Kettler, Daniels, and the city had no warning of my publishing the note. Any such allegation is ridiculous."

I told the reporters that I stood by what I wrote and threats would not deter my paper from reporting the truth. "I regret any pain this may cause the Hines family, but the news needed to be reported."

Over the reporters' shoulders, I saw Bo Hines wiping his eyes with a handkerchief. Surely a photographer caught it. I stayed long enough to make sure I answered all questions. I wanted Wittman, Hines, and the Save Our Pensacola folks to leave first. I stood my ground.

I waved Yoste over and told him to type up his notes and email them to me. I would post them on the blog tonight. He moved away from me as quickly as possible, making sure no one thought he was with me.

My cell phone vibrated.

"Well, how did it go?" Gravy asked. "You did go, didn't you?"

"It was just short of a public hanging," I said.

He laughed. "I expect nothing less from the fearless Walker Holmes."

"I'm walking over to Dare's office. Let's meet at Hopjacks for beers in an hour."

When I got to Jackson Tower, Dare was out, but her secretary handed me two large books bound together with a rubber band. The yellow Post-it note under the band said, "Here are Bo and Jace's high school yearbooks from Pensacola Catholic High. Check out the prom photos."

I left Dare a thank-you note and said I would catch up with her later. When I got back to the office, I opened the two yearbooks. I saw that Wittman and Hines had the same senior prom date—Celeste Daniels, Stan's little sister.

Two weeks after the Pensacola Catholic and Booker T. Washington proms the fifteen-year-old went missing and never returned home.

25

The *Pensacola Insider* once included the disappearance of Celeste Daniels in a cover story on cold cases involving missing person reports.

The article said that according to police reports she was last seen on May 14, 1973, leaving Pensacola Catholic High School. Celeste stood five foot three and weighed a hundred and five pounds. She had worn a yellow tank top and hip hugger slacks with a floral print when she left school that day.

Her big brother Stan was supposed to give her a ride home, but ended up having to stay late for a student council meeting. No one could remember seeing anyone pick her up from school that day or seeing her walking home. Police never found her body.

The police reports gave us little more information than that. In the seventies, Pensacola probably only had one or two missing persons cases a year. The officers weren't the most literate people in town, mostly high school graduates and guys with GEDs. Stan refused to cooperate with our reporter, saying he didn't want to dredge up the past. Their parents had been dead for decades. Celeste Daniels' story was a minor part of the cold cases article.

I texted Daniels, and he agreed to meet me for coffee Wednesday morning in my office before eight. With Hines and Wittman trying to derail the park, maybe he would be more cooperative with me. The old families of Pensacola only want to talk about their accomplishments and avoided discussions of the blemishes in their pasts. Kettler's need for the petition drive to fail might be the impetus to get Daniels to share what he remembers about his sister's disappearance and her relationships with Hines and Wittman. If not, then it was another dead end.

After taking Big Boy for his afternoon constitutional, I headed out to find Gravy and beer, and not necessarily in that order. Before I left, I posted Yoste's notes on the Wittman-Hines press conference to the blog with some additional commentary about the questions the reporters asked me. Feeding the blog was almost as important as feeding the dog.

At Hopjacks, Gravy asked for the details of the press conference.

"It was a disaster," I said. "They are trying to pass off the note as some earlier tiff between Bo and Sue, and the media is lapping it up."

While he ordered a Dead Guy ale and my Bud Light, Gravy said, "Remember what Oscar Wilde said, 'There is only one thing in the world worse than being talked about, and that is not being talked about.'"

I said, "Spoken like a true trial attorney."

Over beers, Gravy told me his courier had delivered Sue Hines' note and the analysis report to Spencer. Gravy had caught a few minutes of the press conference on the six o'clock news. The camera zoomed in on Bo crying in the background. They didn't show me on camera and merely said the publisher of a local weekly newspaper stood behind his reporting and denied any connection with the park developers.

"The buzz around town isn't too favorable for you," Gravy said while eating a slice of what Hopjacks called its "Butcher Block" pizza, which fittingly had more meat than tomato sauce and cheese.

He continued, "The hospitals and banks are being pressured to pull their advertising from the paper, and the sales staffs at the *Herald* and the TV stations smell blood in the water."

"I just got a new set of credit card checks, screw 'em," I said. "There is more to all this. The Arts Council embezzlement, Sue's suicide, the petition drive. They are all related somehow. I can feel it."

Gravy shook his head. "You are stretching this. Maybe you need to back off some. Surely there is some environmental or public education issue you can investigate."

He wasn't smiling. "The state attorney's office wants you to come in for questioning. They threatened to file obstruction of justice charges against you, but I told them that was bullshit and you did their work for them finding the note."

"The note is real," I said. "It is a suicide note. I don't know who wanted me to have it. The bartender at New World Landing can verify that he handed it to me. Hell, I'll take a lie detector."

"Doesn't matter," Gravy said. "You embarrassed the state attorney when you published the note without forewarning him. People are pressuring him to not cut Hines any deals so he's looking for any excuse to put your ass in a jail cell. Remember the scathing column you wrote about what you called his 'selective' prosecution of cases. You can't count on his coaching memories to rescue you. You burned that bridge."

He paused to watch a brunette walk by in a little red dress. "The state attorney and the judges have been waiting for you to slip. If you don't come in voluntarily, he will issue a subpoena forcing you to appear. If you fail to appear, he will have you arrested for contempt. This could move very fast. In the next forty-eight hours, this could all explode in your face."

I didn't say a word. Just sat and drank my beer. Gravy gave me time to let it all soak in, but I had no intention of backing down. The "justice gene" wouldn't allow it.

"Tell me about Stan Daniels," I said.

"Daniels is Mr. Pensacola, former United Way chairman, former chairman of the Pensacola Bay Area Chamber of Commerce. Hell, Stan Daniels is the former chairman of everything," Gravy started. "His firm does defense work representing corporations against guys like me."

He grabbed another slice of pizza and said, "I don't think he has been in the courtroom in over thirty years, but he doesn't need to go to court. His minions handle the dirty work."

I asked, "What do you know about his sister Celeste and her disappearance?"

"I wasn't even born until a year after Celeste Daniels went missing," said Gravy as he waved to the waitress for another round. "The nuns at Catholic High used her disappearance as a warning for how dangerous the world can be for teenage girls. Everyone assumed she was killed by some drifter. Why?"

"Bo Hines and Jace Wittman both dated her."

"So?" he asked.

"Hell if I know what it means but I will soon."

Another short skirt walked by the table. Gravy was becoming too easily distracted. Too much competition. I needed him to stay focused.

I said, "I stopped by The Green Olive before the press conference."

"What?" Gravy asked turning away from eyeing the bar crowd. "You didn't mention Eva Johnson, did you? Her attorney will kill me if you messed up their lawsuit."

"No. I did have a brief conversation with Tatum, but Eva's name was never mentioned," I said. "But the most interesting tidbit I got was from a waitress. Bo Hines and Pandora Childs were regulars at The Green Olive."

Gravy put down his pizza slice. I relayed what the waitress had shared.

He said, "Hines may have been cheating on his wife. So what?"

"I don't know," I said. "What I do know is we've got to make sure Hines' trial happens. Maybe the affair was the secret."

"Maybe, but still a stretch," Gravy reasoned.

"Yeah, that's right. Maybe Harden didn't look in the right places or Hines and Childs hadn't hooked up yet. I don't know."

"Without testimony from Childs, Sue's note won't have the impact you thought," said Gravy.

"No shit. I feel like we have all these puzzle pieces," I said. "But I don't know for sure if they are part of the same puzzle."

I took a long sip of beer and continued, "My sources tell me the shit is hitting the fan this week. It involves porn, the dark web—whatever the hell that is—underage girls, and maybe Monte Tatum."

"Damn, Walker, the hits keep coming," said Gravy. "Did Eva Johnson give you any worthwhile information?"

"She was very helpful. Tatum is a slimeball. How big of one? Yet to be determined."

He took a bite of the pizza, wiped the sauce off his chin. Only Gravy would find sauce in an almost sauceless pizza. I drank my Bud Light. The staff gave us extra attention, wanting to make up for the fight last week. New beers appeared before we finished the ones on the table.

"Are you going to be able to help Bree?"

I shook my head. "Too early to tell for sure. I haven't quite found the right pressure point, but we need to see how this week plays out."

Gravy said, "Remember, Tatum's a vindictive bastard. He backed off after his lawsuit was thrown out by the judge. If you take him on again, you could be creating another lifelong enemy, something you don't need."

"He'll have to get in line."

When I got back to the loft, someone had painted in blood red on the gray metal door, "Murderer." Living downtown, doors and walls were regularly tagged. I got out the gray paint, and Big Boy watched me repaint the door. No need for the staff to see this kind of crap.

The dog stood guard while I worked. Maybe he was getting a little worried, too.

26

At 4:00 a.m. my cell phone rang. Alphonse Tyndall said, "It's going down now. Might want to have someone outside Central Booking."

I called and woke up Teddy. "Ted, I hate to ask, but the cops are busting a big porn ring. Need you over at Central Booking. Get photos of everybody going in."

I could hear Mal in the background asking what was happening. Teddy shushed her before agreeing to go.

Bleary eyed, Teddy came into the office at 7:00 a.m. with Mal in tow. I had coffee and bagels on the counter.

"They arrested about a dozen people," said Mal. "A few faces you might recognize."

Teddy loaded the memory card from his camera on his Mac. Monte Tatum's disheveled mug was among the photos.

Mal said, "The deputies said that there would be a press conference at the county courthouse at 11:00 a.m."

I immediately wrote on the blog.

BUZZ: PORN RING BUSTED

Early this morning, law enforcement rounded up what may be a national pornography ring run out of the Pensacola area. Several people arrested, including at least one local bar owner. A press conference is scheduled for 11:00 a.m.

Teddy and Mal picked out the four best photos, and Teddy began to edit them for the paper. We still needed the week's issue completed and to the printer by 6:00 p.m. Fortunately, all the editorial had been copyedited and approved. Only two ads were outstanding.

At the staff meeting, we agreed to pull one news story, a profile of the new president of one of the hospitals. Instead, I would attend the press conference and complete an article by 2:00 p.m.

At the courthouse, the media gathered in Courtroom 601. Sheets covered two easels near the podium. Florida Department of Law Enforcement agents prevented us from peeking under them. Someone had tipped off CNN, and they had a crew from Atlanta in the room.

Florida Attorney General Charles Gore walked to the podium, flanked by State Attorney Newton, Sheriff Frost, Tyndall, and several law enforcement officers.

Tall, slim, gray-haired Gore said, "This morning we arrested thirteen men and women associated with a national pornography operation that generated millions of dollars exploiting women and children."

The FDLE agents pulled back the sheets, revealing poster boards with photographs of those arrested. Tatum's mug shot wasn't there. Good thing I didn't mention him in the blog post. At the top of the boards was written "Operation Cherry Bomb."

Gore explained Operation Cherry Bomb had begun a year ago when police in Miami found a large porn site, Deb's Playpen, populated with photos and videos of teenagers under the age of eighteen. Agent Alphonse Tyndall gained administrative access by anonymously posting photos with a computer code hidden in the file.

"It's really cutting-edge police work," said Gore. "Once he gained administrative access, Agent Tyndall attached the code to other photos on the site. Every time a website visitor clicked on an image, their computer also downloaded extra data that reported back to us the computer's true IP address and type of operating system."

Tyndall found that the Web server was physically located in a Pensacola-based hosting service, Lightning DNN. While the team had access to the website, they didn't know the identities of the users and their passwords.

With a judge's approval, the Child Predator Cybercrime Task Force staked out the home of one Lightning DNN employee, Wesley McKee, who was also tied to a film company that was secretly shooting porn videos in the area using amateurs. The film company uploaded the videos to Deb's Playpen.

"At five this morning, we picked up McKee, Cecil Rantz, the owner of Happy Cumings Films, and their accomplices," said Gore. "We have their computers, laptops, and portable hard drives. We also have what we believe is the master list of all 27,000 users of the site."

The reporters pelted Gore and Tyndall with questions. They didn't answer many of them, saying the investigation was still active. More documents would be released after the grand jury indicted the individuals and later at the trials.

I said, "Mr. Gore, Walker Holmes with *Pensacola Insider*. What has been the involvement of local law enforcement agencies?"

Sheriff Frost's face turned red. He stared at me, willing me to die. Not quite sure if I knew about his brother's secret.

"They have been very cooperative," said Gore. "Without their manpower, we couldn't have made all the arrests in less than three hours."

I said, "Our photographer was at Central Booking this morning. He took photos of people not included on your boards."

The attorney general looked a little flustered. He glanced at Newton, Frost, and Tyndall. I had mentioned something he didn't want to answer.

"Mr. Holmes," he replied, "the officers gathered up several people, not all were charged. A few were witnesses cooperating with our investigation. We ask that you use those photos very carefully."

I didn't let up. "Do you consider McKee and Rantz the leaders of this operation?"

"Yes, but we do expect more arrests in the upcoming days," said Gore. "We've only begun questioning the men and women arrested today."

The other reporters stared at me. I had made it clear I knew more than them about this. They didn't like being scooped. Tyndall wasn't happy either.

As I walked out, a Florida Department of Law Enforcement agent stopped me.

"Mr. Gore would like to meet with you tomorrow," he said as he handed me a business card. "He will be here the rest of the week."

"My attorney will contact his office," I said. Gravy wasn't going to like getting another phone call about me.

Frost pounced on me, dragging me into a hall away from everyone else. Towering over me, standing inches from my face, he whispered, "What the hell do you think you're doing?"

His breath smelled of cigarettes and coffee. I stepped into him, stood as tall as I could. "My job."

The sheriff stepped back. He looked like he wanted to throw a punch. I braced myself.

"You've blamed me for your brother's death," I said, matching his temper. "We know he was caught up in this porn mess. They were blackmailing him."

Frost grabbed my arm and pulled me into an empty office. "You print anything about Amos and this shit, and I'll sue you. I'll own your paper and your ass."

Slightly bigger than a closet, the room had a desk, phone, and two chairs. The court system probably used the windowless room for interviews or temporary workspace. If Frost wanted to pound me, no one would see it.

"Your brother came to you for help," I said. "You left him out to dry. You could have prevented the suicide, and you know it."

That took the air out of him. "You think you have it all figured out. You don't understand crap and can't prove anything."

I said, "Not yet, but somebody always talks."

"Not in this case," said Frost as he straightened his tie and smoothed the lapels of his jacket. His voice was calmer. "Besides, what purpose will it serve? Other than destroying the name of a good officer. My brother wasn't perfect, but he did a lot of good in this community. Anything you publish will hurt his wife and children, not me."

Words eluded me. No quick, snappy comebacks came to mind. I stood staring at the sheriff.

"Holmes, you are such a hard-ass. Your personal feuds are leaving a trail of dead bodies, and you stand there not giving a damn about anyone or anything other than your crappy little newspaper."

"There's nothing personal about any of this," I retorted. "It's about the truth."

"Keep telling yourself that," said Frost. "Repeat it in front of a mirror over and over again, and maybe you will start to sound convincing."

I began, "You—"

But Frost cut me off and jabbed his bony finger into my chest. "Tell it to Amos's wife and sons. Tell it to Bo Hines. You aren't from here. You don't understand how things work in Pensacola, and you have to be stopped. There have been too many casualties."

I knocked the sheriff's hand away. "We will continue to report the news."

"Not for much longer," said Frost as he headed out of the room.

I sat down in the chair and stared at the drab gray walls. Had I fallen into the Pensacola trap and let grudges drive my reporting? Was I any better than Frost, Wittman, or Tatum?

As I walked back to the *Insider* office, Bree called.

27

"Walker, Mal told me that** Monte Tatum had been arrested for child porn," she said. "Is it true?"

This wasn't a conversation I needed right then. We had a paper to get out. "Tatum wasn't included in the press conference, even though Ted and Mal saw him at Central Booking this morning."

Bree's voice trembled. She was about to cry. "What does that mean? The bastard gets off free?"

"I don't know, Bree. Give me a couple of hours to get my paper out and sort through this. You around tonight?"

"Yes, I'm going to a lecture at the library. Should be free about eight."

"Text me when it's over. We can meet at Hops or Intermission."

Back at the office, I called a quick staff meeting to fill them in on the specifics. The absence of Tatum's name on the arrest list surprised Mal and Teddy. Mal's face showed that she felt a little guilty that she had said anything to Bree.

"You saw the photos," she said. "They perp-walked Tatum."

"Yeah, but we don't know for what," I said. "Listen, we will hold Tatum's photo. We'll get answers soon. First, I need to finish the article."

Mal said, "That's the only piece we're waiting on. Once I send the pages to the printer, Teddy and I are going to bug out. Our day started early."

"No problem."

The article on Operation Cherry Bomb went smoothly. I put on my headphones and listened to Norwegian composer Edvard Grieg's piano concertos. I didn't need any more words in my head.

Once Mal sent off all the pages to the printer, she and Teddy left. I texted Tyndall to see if he could meet for drinks. We agreed to meet away from downtown. Tyndall suggested Satchmo's, an old club on the west side that opened at four o'clock but didn't have many customers until seven.

Satchmo's had been around since World War II. It's where the African-American veterans congregated when they came home to a segregated Pensacola and had evolved into the unofficial American Legion hall for the black community.

The blue cinder block building had no windows and a purple door. I wasn't sure it even had a back door. The only light inside came from the neon beer company signs and the bathroom lights when the doors opened. The jukebox played only Nat King Cole, Louis Armstrong, Billie Holiday, Charlie Parker, Jelly Roll Morton, and other artists from that era.

Erlene was tending the bar, and Alphonse sat at a table by the jukebox. Satchmo's carried only Budweiser, Bud Light, Miller, Miller Lite, Colt 45, and Heineken. All bottles, nothing on draft. I ordered a Miller Lite.

Alphonse was nearly invisible in the dark room, except for his white shirt.

I said, "Nice show today. You came off the hero. Not a bad start to your sheriff's campaign."

"You almost blew it with your questions," he said over Charlie Parker's "Embraceable You." "My boss called a meeting and dressed us all down about leaking information to the media."

"Does he suspect you?"

"No, Gore doesn't understand my roots in the community. He thinks the leak came from the state attorney's office."

"If he only knew I'm on their shit list, too," I said laughing. "I was surprised Gore gave so much detail on the investigation. He made you look good, but did he go a little too far?"

"Gore wants to run for governor in four years," said Tyndall. "He likes these theatrical presentations. You can expect more of them around the state."

The bar was empty. Erlene was setting up for the day, but kept an eye on our beers.

Alphonse asked, "What is your deal with Monte Tatum? My aunt told me that when you are on someone's ass, you don't let go. She said you wouldn't let the officer off the hook for killing my cousin, even though there was no money in it for you."

"It's my 'justice' gene."

"What?"

"Never mind." I walked over to the bar, put ten dollars on the counter, and Erlene handed me a Heineken for Tyndall and another Miller Lite. She kept the change without asking.

"At your suggestion, I looked into Tatum," Alphonse said, nodding thanks for the beer. "Our agents had seen the two together several times. Money exchanged hands. We included him in the bust."

"Why wasn't he arrested?" I asked.

Alphonse said, "His lawyer got to the attorney general before we processed him at Central Booking. We were told not to book him, only hold him."

"He cut a deal?"

"Sort of," he said. "Tatum really wasn't part of the operation, but Rantz hooked him on the idea of producing porn being an investment. He gave us some very valuable information on Rantz."

"I needed him taken out, Razor," I said. "He's a sleaze that preys on girls when he gets them high or drunk. He films having sex with them and lords it over them later."

"Shit," said Tyndall. "Definitely sleazy, but not necessarily illegal, especially if the girls don't want to go to court."

"Yep, there's one girl that's worried a video might pop up on the web and ruin her career," I said. "I offered to help."

We drank our beers, listening to Nat King Cole's "Mona Lisa."

Alphonse smiled. "We seized all Tatum's computers, his tablet, and his cell phone. Heck, he handed over hard drives we didn't find in the initial search, anything to avoid time in a jail cell."

"What about his CDs and any videotapes?"

"None. Told us he digitalized them all. Kept them on a portable hard drive that he delivered to us. He hasn't asked for any of it back."

"Probably relieved that his name didn't pop up at the press conference."

He nodded. "They are evidence. We may not ever go through them, but the attorney general won't be giving the hard drives back to him."

I chuckled. "This could be the beginning of a wonderful friendship."

Bree and I met at Hopjacks. Neither of us had eaten so we ordered hummus and a pepperoni pizza. The bar hosted trivia night on Tuesdays, which gave us about two hours before the purple-haired waitress began shouting questions on the sound system.

"Anyone beat you up today?" asked the waiter

I laughed. "Not yet, but the day's not over."

"I'll keep an eye on the room for you," he said.

"Thanks," I replied, realizing that he was serious.

Bree said, "How are your head and ribs?"

She sat close to me so that we didn't have to shout over the music. Her perfume smelled of jasmine. I hoped I didn't reek of Satchmo's.

"Healing," I reassured her.

"I know you are too busy to deal with my petty stuff. I so hoped the cops had arrested Tatum today. I apologize for crying on the phone."

"Bree, I don't think you have to worry about Tatum."

She grabbed my arm. Confusion showed on her face; she didn't want to get her hopes up again. "What do you mean?"

"Law enforcement confiscated all of Tatum's electronics and files in the raid . . ."

She interrupted, not realizing she was squeezing my arm tighter. "But he wasn't arrested. He's sitting at his table at The Green Olive right now."

I said, "Yes, because he agreed to testify against the leaders of the operation. He won't get his files back."

Still not believing me, she let go, took a swallow of her beer and said, "It's only a temporary fix."

I shook my head. "No, those files will never reappear."

Bree looked me in the eyes. She was trying to read me. "Promise?"

"You have my word," I said, crossing my heart.

She hugged and kissed me. "Thank you, thank you."

I may have held the hug too long, but Bree didn't seem to mind.

"I feel like I've been unshackled and a huge weight lifted off my back," she said, glowing. She was beautiful, I thought.

The waiter delivered the pizza and more beers. Bree asked, "How did you do it?"

I said, between bites, "You don't want to know. I'd have to kill you."

She laughed, "Like a Navy Seal?"

I figured Bree had dated more than her fair share of Navy Seals. We talked about the newspaper. I told her about not only the Operation Cherry Bomb press conference but also the Wittman-Hines presser on Monday. She seemed genuinely interested, and it felt good to let down my guard a little.

Whether it was the beers or her perfume, I found myself touching her more and more as I shared my stories. She laughed at my jokes, and Bree had a great laugh.

She told me about her freelance design work. Pulling her tablet from her bag, Bree showed me some of the posters and brochures she had designed. She was very talented, and I told her so.

The beers piled up. The trivia nuts staked out their territories in the bar. The decision time approached. Would we continue drinking else-where or end the night here?

"Where did you park?" I asked.

"I'm behind Jackson Tower."

We walked together down Palafox, delaying the decision a couple of blocks. Bree held my hand. I squeezed, she squeezed back. I debated asking her to grab one more drink at Intermission when I heard glass break, tires squeal, and Big Boy barking. I ran toward the office, wor-ried someone had harmed the dog.

A brick had shattered an office window. He had to have a pretty strong arm to reach the second story. Big Boy barked and peered out the broken window. A crowd from Blazzues gathered in the street pointing at the window.

Bree came up behind me. She ran a little slower in her heels.

"Angry reader?" she asked.

"Must have missed my fan club meeting."

Bree waited with me for the police. She took Big Boy for a walk while I dealt with the officers. Then she later helped me clean up and place a sheet over the window.

"Well, thank you for a wonderful evening," she said as the clock at the courthouse struck eleven o'clock. "I'm opening the café in the morning, so I better get to bed."

I said, "I really enjoyed the conversation."

"Me, too," she said and kissed me deeply before she left.

28

The next day's headline of the *Pensacola Herald* read, "Sheriff Calls Out Tabloid." While I was dining with Bree, Sheriff Frost had attended a Save Our Pensacola rally. While he didn't come out and fully endorse the petition drive, the sheriff did target me.

"Walker Holmes, the *Insider,* and his blog are cancers in this community, dragging people through the mud for the publisher's twisted pleasure," said Frost. "He claims that he cares about this community while he destroys families like Mr. Hines' and my brother's."

According to the article, the sheriff asked Bo Hines to stand with him. He continued, "Mr. Hines has shared with me today that Holmes had told him that the *Insider's* reports on his alleged theft of Arts Council funds never would have been published if Hines had agreed to buy ads in the paper."

Bullshit, I thought.

Frost said, "That might not fit the legal definition of extortion, but it shows what kind of snake we have in this community. No more. No more fake news. No more deaths. No more *Insider.*"

The *Herald* reported that the crowd picked up the chant and repeated the "no more" mantra with Frost, Hines, and Wittman leading them. Wittman reportedly urged people to boycott businesses that advertise in our paper.

"The publisher of the *Insider* is an outsider," said Wittman. "He has no roots here. It's time he left. I'll pay for the moving van."

The person who threw the brick through my window last night was probably someone who attended that rally, I thought as I poured myself another cup of coffee. Big Boy had slept in.

But the *Herald* wasn't finished with me. The daily newspaper's editorial blasted me for being unprofessional and biased in my coverage of Sheriff Ron Frost, Sue Hines' death, the upcoming trial of her husband, and the Save Our Pensacola petition drive. They said I had falsely claimed Sue Hines' note was a suicide note. They blamed my irresponsible reporting for the death of Lieutenant Amos Frost and alleged our newspaper had nearly blown Operation Cherry Bomb by staking out Central Booking and reporting on the sweep before the press conference.

"Clearly Walker Holmes has personal grudges against Bowman Hines, Jace Wittman, and Sheriff Ron Frost, and he hasn't hesitated to use his tabloid and blog to torment and punish his foes."

Someone began banging on the door at the foot of the stairs. It was Tiny.

"Mr. Holmes, I heard you had some trouble last night," he said, walking past me and up the stairs. He petted Big Boy, who had finally climbed out of bed to see what was happening. "Let me clean up for you."

"Thanks, but I took care of it," I said following him up the stairs.

He laughed. "Your cleaning and my cleaning are different things. Let the professional do the job. Where's your broom?"

Tiny spent the next twenty minutes carefully removing every last pieces of glass. He swept the floor, humming to himself the entire time. Big Boy and I stayed out of his way and sat on the couch.

"There," he said. "Now you can walk with bare feet and not worry about anything."

I fished for a twenty in my pocket. "Tiny, thank you . . ."

He said, "Put your money away. I'll take the dog for a walk while you write."

Big Boy heard the word "walk" and ran to get his leash. The pair left. I could hear Tiny whistling as they traveled down Palafox.

The morning heat and humidity seeped through the open window into the room. When placed in a fight or flight situation, I'd always fought. I would fight this, but I needed to change my strategy. Waiting for the trial to redeem me wasn't working.

I was tired of the beatings, threats, and broken windows. A man like me, destined to lose everything—and on the verge of doing so before we published the next issue—could be a dangerous man. I needed to stop being reactive and become more proactive. If this was the end of Walker Holmes, how many bad guys could I take down with me?

We needed the Hines trial to happen. Locating Pandora Childs and maybe finding others who might talk would ensure the state attorney followed through on the prosecution. Sitting on the windowsill from which Tiny had cleared of all the broken glass, I outlined a series of posts that I'd schedule to go live on my blog at regular intervals over the next two days. I would augment them with a running commentary on my interviews, meetings, and conversations over the same period.

I needed to create a sense that I was closing in on Hines. Maybe the other media would start asking questions of him, too. The key would be to get inside Hines' head and force him to react. And maybe, just maybe, someone would come forward with helpful information.

Meanwhile, I should expect the state attorney to come after me more aggressively. Hines' attorneys had probably already begun drafting the civil lawsuit against me.

One thing that worked in my favor was the *Herald's* front-page coverage and editorial would drive readers to my blog. Pensacola would want to see how I responded to Frost, Hines, and Wittman and their assaults on my newspaper and my character.

Before Daniels arrived, I emailed a public record request to the City of Pensacola to review all the proposals for the site work at the maritime park and any emails or memos regarding the bid. If Hines and Wittman had a source inside city hall, they would get phone calls.

By the time Stan Daniels walked into my office at 7:20 a.m. I was ready for him. He looked like old money when he sat down in my conference room. His suit cost more than four full-page ads in my paper. Hell, his Rolex might buy an entire issue. His smile and handshake were warm. Before he sat, he took his jacket off and hung it on the back of the chair.

It was time I rattled his cage.

"We're doing a story on your sister's disappearance," I said. "I need you to tell me what you remember."

Ever so slightly, Daniels stiffened. The smile in his eyes disappeared, replaced with something hard and ice-cold. He ignored my question.

"Walker, it's old news that no one cares to read," he said. "Aren't your hands full with more urgent matters?"

I pressed him. "I'm tired of how this town covers up its past. What you remember might help defeat the petition effort."

"How could it possibly help?" Daniels asked.

I opened to the prom pictures in the two yearbooks. Two very different proms. One photograph, just for the parents, had Celeste with four other girls in candy-colored dresses; the other prom photo was, "Let's have our picture taken before we get drunk and end up in a pile on the beach." With her golden hair piled up high and a violet, backless gown that matched her eyes, Celeste stood out in both photos.

I said, "Celeste went to both school's senior proms—one with Hines, the other with Wittman. A freshman dating two popular seniors is unusual. I need to know more about her, Stan."

"So you can drag another dead woman's reputation through the mud?" Daniels asked. His cheeks reddened. I'd struck a nerve in the unflappable attorney.

"No, I believe we can find out what happened to her, but I need more information. Trust me. Someone out there knows the truth about her disappearance."

Daniels slumped in his chair. "Don't you think I've tried? After my legal career took off, I had private investigators dig, posted pictures in newspapers all over the country, even offered a $25,000 reward. Nothing."

"What kind of person was she?"

"Beautiful, bright, full of life, and a wild force of nature. When she turned fifteen, she thought she could do anything she wanted, which drove my parents and the Sisters of Mercy crazy."

Daniels got up and stood by the window, staring out, tapping into the buried memories of his kid sister. His aura of self-confidence had dissolved.

"It was a different era and mindset. The Vietnam War was winding down. People were so full of passion and rebellion and had the desire to change this city and make things better. Women were claiming their sexual freedom and demanding more than marriage and kids. And Celeste was ahead of her time."

He sat back down and took a long sip of his coffee. I didn't say a thing. Daniels had been transported to another time, a time before Rolexes and custom-tailored suits were a part of his life.

"She wore her dates with Bo and Jace like badges of honor. She wasn't like other freshman girls who sat home watching David Cassidy in *The Partridge Family* on Friday nights. Celeste enjoyed going to the Firehouse Drive-In with upper classmen and was proud to be asked to both proms."

Daniels turned and faced me. His face had softened.

"Bo was the sought-after football star at Washington High. He had already been awarded a college football scholarship to Florida State. Jace wasn't a bad athlete either and was debating several college offers. Celeste enjoyed pitting them against each other and teased me about it. She loved how it put her on my level."

Daniels seemed to like saying her name, something he might not have done for years.

He paused, picked up the Catholic High yearbook and thumbed through the pages, stopping every few pages. I left the conference room and him with his memories while I poured both of us more coffee.

I imagined his mind was tumbling with images . . . of the beach in early spring before tourist season when it was quiet . . . of a girl in bell-bottom jeans, laughing wildly like nothing bad was ever going to happen to her. . . . How could it ever? She was so full of life. Wild with the beach wind in her hair, driving down Pensacola Beach far too fast.

When I returned, Daniels seemed to have aged ten years. He said, "I went to both Bo and Jace when Celeste went missing. They knew nothing. Bo helped me search all over town for her. Jace seemed frantic when I told him she had disappeared."

I said, "We didn't see either of their names in the police report."

"Bo's grandfather made sure they didn't appear anywhere," he said. "My parents didn't believe the boys had anything to do with it. They came from fine families. There was no need to drag their names into it."

"Who can I talk to that remembers those high school days?" I asked. "Are there any teachers still around?"

"Jacob Solomon. He taught Latin at both Catholic and Washington high schools back then," Daniels said after pondering my question for a few minutes. "He's in his nineties, but still sends me newspaper clippings and notes of congratulations. He's invited me over for tea several times, but I never can find the time."

"Stan, what do you think really happened?" I asked.

Stan took a deep breath. His eyes flirted with something in the distance and then settled again, cold and dark, on the floor.

"She's dead," he said. "There is no way Celeste would run away and not contact us. Her disappearance killed the souls of my parents, completely drained their marriage and faith. Every time the phone rang, they expected it to be her. My mother refused to leave the house, not wanting to miss a phone call. My parents didn't attend my high school graduation, never went to one of my college football games. Both died before I graduated from Florida, simply quit wanting to live."

He looked up at me and voiced the question I wanted to ask.

"How did I cope with it?" He took a deep breath. After all, he had told this part of the story before and was used to telling it. "I turned to alcohol. Avoided, by the grace of God, any DUIs but totaled two cars before I hit thirty. My wife stood by me. Eventually, I became a friend of Bill W."

I asked, "Bill?"

"A member of Alcoholics Anonymous. I'm a recovering alcoholic, haven't had a drink in twenty-seven years. Bill W. is Bill Wilson, one of the founding members of AA."

Stan Daniels was human after all. He put the yearbooks down, picked up his jacket and headed for the door.

"Where do you expect to take this?" Daniels said as he shook my hand, more perfunctory than warm this time. "Why dig up painful memories?"

I said, "I don't know if Hines and Wittman had anything to do with your sister's death, but I will talk to Mr. Solomon and see what he remembers about all three of them."

He stood there half silhouetted by the sun in the skylight and said, "I wonder what our world would be like . . . you know . . . if she were here."

Yeah, I thought, sometimes a person's absence goes on like a living thing, still affecting the living.

Daniels looked out the window down Palafox Street and continued, "Don't use my sister to save your hide."

"I won't," I said as he shut the door, knowing that was exactly what I had to do.

I am an ass, I thought.

29

After Daniels left, Big Boy sauntered downstairs, having had a nice rest after his walk with Tiny. He found a piece of donut in Jeremy's trashcan and began to eat it on the couch.

"You really are disgusting," I said. The dog ignored me and finished his treat. "Come on, I need the exercise."

We went out for a short walk. Since this was his second one of the morning, Big Boy wasn't in any hurry. Good thing, my head and ribs still couldn't handle even a light jog. The binding around my chest itched.

My first scheduled blog post went live at 8:30 a.m. as we were walking:

> **BUZZ: WHAT SECRET?**
>
> The suicide note believed to be from Sue Eaton Hines will be authenticated soon by the state attorney's forensic experts. Below is the handwriting report from our expert.
>
> The question on everyone's mind is what secret? And for whom was the note intended? Who is "Sweetie"?

Within five minutes my cell phone vibrated. It kept vibrating every few minutes. Big Boy and I were still a block away from Pensacola Bay. I didn't answer any of the calls but checked the caller ID. They were from Dare, Gravy, Clark Spencer, Jim Harden, and a number I didn't recognize. My head hurt too much to be yelled at before noon.

Gravy texted, "Where the hell are you? Both the attorney general and state attorney want you in their offices today."

A block away from the *Pensacola Insider* office, I spied a group of gray-haired retirees with posters. An empty donut box in a nearby trashcan indicated they were probably charged up on Krispy Kreme and coffee. The dress code for the men apparently was black socks with sandals. The women wore red, white, and blue tops over white shorts. The protestors blocked the entrance to my office.

Save Our Pensacola saw an opportunity to pile on the *Herald's* coverage and attract attention to their petition drive. The protest would bring free publicity and draw television crews. The signs read "No More Fake News," "Take a Walk, Walker," "Bought and Paid-For Reporting," and "Boycott the *Insider*." The protesters, about a dozen, give or take a walker or oxygen tank, shouted, "No more. No more fake news. No more deaths. No more *Insider*."

I took off Big Boy's leash, and he walked right past the picketers unscathed and unbothered by the commotion. He sat on the mat in front of the door. I swore he smiled at me, daring me to follow him. I hated that dog.

I saw one of my "shadows" from last week's meeting at New World Landing—crew cut, Hawaiian shirt, khaki shorts, and the prerequisite socks and sandals. Walking up to him, I asked if I could help him.

"We're shutting you down, Holmes," he said, not removing his aviator sunglasses. "Your bull crap must stop. Attacking the good name of a dead woman is low even for scum like you."

He jabbed me in the chest to punctuate his last sentence. I was getting tired of people doing that. I hoped I didn't wince because it felt like I had been stuck with a hot poker.

"Freedom of the press is a bitch," I replied.

Turning to all the picketers, I added, "If you need a bathroom, our office is on the second floor. Don't pet the dog. He has fleas."

Big Boy quit smiling. He was no longer amused. We went upstairs. I texted the staff to stay away and work from home. None of them needed to become targets, too. Then I called the window company to replace the glass.

After my shower, I listened to my voice messages and read my emails. Based on them, I was either a fool or a jackass. Jackass appeared to be in the lead. The unidentified number on my cell phone was one of Bo Hines' attorneys demanding I remove the blog post. I didn't return any of the calls and didn't delete any posts.

Instead, I turned on the coffee pot, got into comfortable khaki shorts, and gingerly sat in my worn leather chair with my laptop. My ribs weren't doing too well. I debated whether to take a pain pill and decided against it. I took a couple of aspirin.

I wrote up my interview with Stan Daniels and posted a teaser to the blog:

COLD CASE: CELESTE DANIELS

On May 14, 1973, Celeste Daniels, age fifteen, was seen leaving Catholic High School. Her family and friends never saw her again. The *Insider* reported on her disappearance in a 2008 cover story on cold cases. We believe that someone in Pensacola knows what happened to this high school freshman, and we are asking for them to come forward with any information they might have. Please email me at walker@ theinsider.net.

After two more cups of coffee, my head calmed down. My ribs were tender when I turned my torso, but otherwise I wasn't hurting too badly.

Outside, reporters interviewed the picketers. A TV camera crew taped them. Every negative story about me gave an opening to their sales reps to steal one of our advertisers. Dollars, not journalism, drove their Walker Holmes stories.

I took a photo of the protestors being interviewed and posted it on the blog to let readers know we were being picketed. Might as well get ahead of the other news outlets.

The office phone rang. Of course, it was Gravy.

"You won't answer your damn cell so I figured at least someone would pick up this line," he said. "You've really stepped into it this time. The attorney general wants you. The state attorney himself called. I think I've got both of them to hold off until tomorrow. Attorney general at 9:00 a.m. State attorney right after lunch."

"I'm not going."

"Walker, they will issue a warrant and have you arrested."

"Screw 'em. I have a plan," I said, trying to sound confident. "Buy me some time."

"I have nothing to offer them. Your best bet is to make yourself hard to find. I'll play dumb and try to get them to delay issuing any warrants." He added, "When you miss the appointments, they probably won't get one of the judges to issue a warrant until Monday, but a judge might make an exception for you."

Looking out my window, I saw the reporters and TV camera crews drive away. The picketers packed up, too. It must be time for *Matlock* or *Murder She Wrote* back at the retirement home. Crew-cut drove away in his lime green 1998 Lincoln Continental. It had a bumper sticker: "Fight Crime: Shoot Back!"

"Okay, that should work," I told Gravy. "They won't know I'm not cooperating until it's too late to stop me."

"Stop you from what?" Gravy sounded like he honestly wanted to know.

"It's best you not know."

My blog posts attracted dozens of comments. Not all of them attacked me. Hines was taking a few licks, too. The item about the "secret" mentioned in Sue's note drew several negative comments against Hines. Readers posted rumors of affairs, shady business dealings, and the Arts Council theft. Ever so slowly, Pensacola was beginning to call him out on the blog, something Hines and his attorneys wouldn't like.

The photo of the picket line drew more teasing of Save Our Pensacola than support, though a few readers agreed with Frost's comments published in the *Herald*.

In contrast to those comments, classmates of Celeste Daniels relished the opportunity to write about her. People still remembered her wit and laugh. No new revelations popped up, but readers loved adding comments to that post.

I added my own comment: "The yearbooks from Catholic and Washington show Celeste Daniels went to the junior-senior proms at both schools. Does anybody remember those dances? Please email me, walker@theinsider.net."

Thirty minutes later, my next scheduled blog post went live:

FRIEND CONFIRMS HANDWRITING

Dare Evans, a close friend of Sue Hines, confirmed the handwriting of the apparent suicide note matched the handwriting on letters she had received from the late Mrs. Hines, as does the stationery. State attorney expected to issue their report on Friday.

I knew Dare would be pissed that I'd dragged her into this, but she didn't hold grudges against me, at least not for long.

Summer came into the office. "Boss, I went by the post office and picked up the mail. We still need every deposit we can get."

Good old Summer. She wore an A-ha T-shirt with "Take On Me" across her chest.

"Thanks, Summer, but I told you to stay home."

"Yeah, I know, but someone must oversee the window being re-placed. You aren't going to do it."

Okay, she had me.

"Summer, go home as soon as the window's replaced," I said and went upstairs to work. The heat from outside made my work area un-bearable. Big Boy stayed with Summer, protecting her from any more flying bricks.

I found Jacob Solomon's phone number in an online directory. I called, and he agreed to see me. He invited me to have lunch at his house the next day. He sounded excited to have company.

I tried to put together an outline of next week's story. The article needed to explain the suicide note. Dammit, it was a suicide note. It must push the state attorney to prosecute Hines and derail the Hines-Wittman petition drive.

The problem was I still had more questions than answers.

Checking my email again, I found one from Jeremy. "Walker, I ran into someone who thought he knew where Pandora Childs might be.

He said she liked to sneak away to Pigeon Forge and stay in a friend's cabin. Childs recently texted him a selfie from there."

Jeremy had attached the photo to the email.

His cell phone went straight to voicemail when I called him. I called his landline, and after convincing his mother that I wasn't firing her son and to please let him come to the phone, Jeremy got on the line.

"Great job, Jeremy," I said.

"Thought the photo might help," he said. He was proud of himself.

"Any chance your friend would give you Childs' new cell phone number? Her old one went dead when she disappeared."

"No, he had saved the photo but deleted the text message," said Jeremy. "He probably has it somewhere in his phone but wasn't willing to share it."

Within minutes of hanging up with Jeremy, my cell rang. Harden said, "I know this may be a little late, but I've got info on Cecil Rantz's Happy Cumings Films."

"No, the timing couldn't be more perfect. Tell me what you have."

"He shot the videos in public places and houses around Pensacola," he said. "His team recruited waitresses, strippers, and college coeds to have sex on camera. He recorded the orgies, of course, and uploaded them to the website mentioned at the attorney general's press conference. Men paid two hundred dollars a month VIP membership dues to participate in the orgies or just to watch the people live. Some of the girls may have been minors. The production made money from people paying to log onto the websites that played the videos for its VIP members."

That explained a little more of how Amos Frost was pulled into the filming and matched what Tyndall had shared.

"Rantz sent text messages to guys, and sometimes couples, that gave away the place and time for the fun," said Harden. "Investigators are convinced some of the girls were underage. They have tried to catch them in the act and find out who funded the enterprise. The few girls they questioned refused to cooperate."

"Well, apparently it was much bigger than Rantz's videos," I said.

"Apparently. My sources only knew about the local sex scene."

"And Amos Frost was one of the participants," I added.

The other end of the phone went dead for a few seconds. "Holmes, I wasn't supposed to tell you that."

"You didn't," I said. "Don't worry. I'm not writing about Amos Frost."

"Good." Harden sounded relieved.

"My arts reporter may have located the missing Arts Council executive director," I said. "I'll send you a photo she recently took in Pigeon Forge, Tennessee. Do you have someone who can track her down?"

He said, "I have a friend in Knoxville who could drive down. It will cost two hundred dollars, plus mileage."

"What choice do I have?" I asked. "Okay, have your friend send me an invoice."

Harden said, "There's a lot of talk at the courthouse about you not cooperating with the state attorney and attorney general."

"Yeah, they aren't too happy with me."

"No shit," said Harden before he hung up.

I posted Harden's information on the sex club on the blog:

LOCAL SEX CLUB TIED TO PORN BUST

Among those busted yesterday in Operation Cherry Bomb was pornographer Cecil Rantz.

Sources told the *Insider* Rantz recruited waitresses, strippers, and college coeds to perform sex acts on camera for his Happy Cumings videos.

Locals paid to perform with the girls on camera but wore masks. They were texted a code for when and where the orgies would take place.

Who paid? They could be revealed in the court documents soon.

Agents are looking for the financial backer or backers of the international child porn network.

Stay tuned.

Sheriff Frost wouldn't be happy because he would think the post was about his brother. Tyndall's boss would be upset because media would bombard his office with questions about the videos. The reporters would also be pissed because I wrote about it first. A trifecta.

Big Boy came upstairs. I heard Summer shout something as she slammed and locked the outside door to the office. The fortress was secure.

I grabbed a bottled water from the refrigerator and walked down to the offices on the second floor. The afternoon sun was coming through the windows. The new window matched the others perfectly. Sitting at my desk, I watched minions head home or to happy hour as they left their jobs for the day.

Summer had left several yellow Post-it notes on my computer. She wanted me to return calls to Clark Spencer, the television reporter who covered the protest, someone in the attorney general's office, Sheriff Frost, and Monte Tatum.

"You sonnabitch, you set me up," shouted Tatum when I reached him on the phone.

I didn't take the bait. "What are you talking about, Monte?"

Sounding more than a little unhinged and high, he rattled off, "I read your blog. You came into my club to scope me out for the AG. I know you talked with that bitch Eva Johnson."

The louder he got, the calmer I became. "Why were you taken into custody and let go? What kind of deal did you cut?"

"None of your goddamn business," he said. "That bitch Johnson stole from me, I fired her, and she wants to ruin me. Don't believe a goddamn thing she says."

"I have no idea what you're talking about, Monte," I said, knowing that using his first name irritated him even more. "My sources are coming from elsewhere. People have been talking about your sleazy club for weeks. Rantz was a regular."

"Who told you that? I'll sue you for defamation and for trying to hurt my business." He sounded a little less confident, a little more worried.

"Monte, you tried that before. I'm not your problem," I said. "However, if there are any insights you can give into Rantz and Deb's Playpen, we would love to interview you."

"Fuck you," Tatum said as he ended the call.

Gravy texted to see if I wanted a beer. I passed. I called Dare and left her a voicemail thanking her for the prepaid ads.

I texted Bree hoping she might want a drink. No dice. She called to say that she had promised her aunt a date night. At least she sounded as if she might be open to the proposition in the future.

Big Boy and I ordered wings and fries, anything other than pizza. We went to sleep watching the Dodgers on the television. Tomorrow was going to be a busy day.

30

Gravy called in the morning while Big Boy and I were out strolling, dodging packs of runners. We stood under an awning waiting for a summer downpour to subside when I took his call.

"No more stalling. The state attorney has served me with a subpoena concerning you first thing this morning. Spencer followed up with a phone call. He wants you in his office by one this afternoon or, and I quote, 'they will issue a warrant for your ass,'" said Gravy. "Attorney General Gore wants to see you no later than three o'clock. No subpoena yet, but it's coming.

"That's a little quick," I replied.

"Yes, but you have been putting them off," said Gravy. "And they want you to know they're serious. Spencer told me he has got a judge ready to sign a warrant. No more delays, Walker."

He added, "What kind of idiot has the attorney general and state attorney on their ass at the same time? At least, Sheriff Frost stopped calling."

Big Boy lifted his leg on a *Pensacola Herald* newspaper box, then flopped down by my feet satisfied.

"Thank you for running interference for me, Gravy. Tell them I promise to see both before the day is over."

"Promise?"

"Scout's honor," I said, trying to sound sincere. "Tell Spencer I will stop by his office at 3:30 p.m. Gore, I will see at 4:45. He can work overtime."

"Don't screw with them. They are serious about sending law enforcement to bring you in if you don't show. If you are arrested, you'll sit in Frost's jail all weekend."

Not a pleasant option. "I'll make it, Gravy."

Gravy asked, "Do you want me there?"

"No, I've got it. Stop worrying."

At the morning meeting, I let the staff vent.

"What the hell is going on?" said Jeremy, holding his triple shot, peppermint latte in his left hand and waving his right. "Protesters, smashed windows, you getting beaten every other night. Are our lives at risk?"

Mal said, "Shut up, Jeremy. The only people wanting to kick your ass are the karaoke singers at The Red Garter that you trashed last week in your column."

"Well, how many times can anyone listen to 'Sweet Caroline,' 'It's Raining Men,' or 'Damn, I Wish I Was Your Lover' before they pull out a gun and shoot up the place?" he replied.

Jeremy had a point. I told the staff about how he might have helped us locate Pandora Childs to soften the blow of Mal's jab.

Roxie ignored the Mal-Jeremy exchange. She wanted to restart the Best of the Coast sales. Summer had completed the database of the contact information of all the winners.

"Summer and I plotted out who I will contact first," she said. "We will exceed last year's numbers by twenty grand."

Roxie had made a few sales calls yesterday from home and hadn't gotten much push back. She said, "The flak over Hines and Frost surprisingly hasn't hurt as much as I feared. People like our approach to reporting. We're winning fans."

Finally.

Yoste was missing, which made Mal furious. "He wrote his big cover story and has gone fishing."

I said, "I promised him he could take today off, but he needed to do a follow-up piece on Operation Cherry Bomb. He emailed me he has some interviews set up for later today."

Mal said, "You baby him. It's got to stop."

Jeremy grunted in agreement.

I outlined my cover story for them. Admittedly it had plenty of holes, but I promised them I would have it pulled together by Monday. As always, I sounded more self-assured than I felt.

At a little before noon, I grabbed my laptop and headed to visit the North Hill home of Jacob Solomon and learn more about Celeste Daniels.

When I had called to set up the interview, Mr. Solomon was more than happy to meet with me and talk about Celeste. After all, he was the one who gave Dare the yearbooks.

Jacob Solomon lived in a little gingerbread house on a narrow side street in North Hill. In front of his house, a historic marker declared this was the site of the Queen's Redoubt, a British fortification that the Spanish artillery blew up during the Battle of Pensacola in 1781. The Spanish rebuilt it and changed the name to Fort San Bernardo. When the United States government took over Pensacola in 1821, the British residents convinced Governor Andrew Jackson to allow the fort to deteriorate, out of pure spite. Nothing now remained of it, except the marker.

Jacob and Ruth Solomon raised two sons and a daughter in the three-bedroom, one-bath cottage. Ruth had passed away two years ago in her sleep. The two sons, both doctors, lived in Atlanta and Miami. The daughter, Sarah, lived in Pensacola and worked as an attorney for the American Civil Liberties Union.

I parked in the driveway under an enormous hundred-year-old oak. Before I began to follow the stepping-stones to the front door, Solomon opened a side door to wave me in.

"Mr. Holmes, it is such a privilege to have you in our home," said Mr. Solomon. "I told my older brother Caleb you were coming for lunch, and he was so jealous. We're big fans of yours. What is it about Mississippi that it produces such great writers? William Faulkner, Eudora Welty, Willie Morris, John Grisham, and you."

I wondered where the best place was to sit. Mr. Solomon motioned to a leather lounge chair by a bay window.

"Mr. Solomon, please call me Walker. I only know five hundred words, and my goal is to put them in a different order every week and somehow tell a story."

He laughed and excused himself to get the sandwiches and iced tea with fresh mint he had prepared. The room where I sat must have been his study. Books filled the room, not only in the bookcase that covered an entire wall but also on the tables and stacked on the floor. On top of the table beside the chair was a book of crossword puzzles written in German. Under it, I spied a well-worn copy of Caesar's *Commentaries*, written in Latin, of course.

I shut my eyes for a few minutes as I heard Mr. Solomon whistling in the kitchen. I felt the love in this place. I pictured Ruth and Jacob sitting here with classical music on the stereo, reading and sharing tales of their days. I liked this house. The books had actually been read. Glancing up at the collected works of Dickens and Balzac above me, I thought if I picked up one of them the book would fall open to his and Ruth's favorite sections. Generations had read these books and discussed them at dinner.

I could hear a beautiful woman in a simple floral print dress saying, "Father, I am going to go grab that book, because I just know you remember it wrong!"

The thought warmed me. A real library was haunted by the ghosts of everyone who cared for a book in it.

"I'm a writer, too," said Mr. Solomon as he returned, balancing a tray of tuna fish sandwiches and tea. Barrel-chested with shoulders even broader than mine, the past ninety years had stooped him over and shrunken him to less than five feet. But his walk still showed vitality, and his eyes sparkled. His voice, slow and richly deliberate, made every word seem important. It was not difficult imagining him as a teacher.

"Ruth and I traveled all over the South visiting the childhood homes of great Southern authors. We went to the homes of O'Connor, Williams, Welty, Faulkner, and even the Sayre house in Montgomery and wrote about them, and we were fortunate to have our book published."

"I would love to read it," I said, meaning it.

We took our time eating, as people of his generation used to do. He asked questions about some of my past articles: deaths in the county jail, relocation of the downtown sewage plant, and the maritime park. I asked about his children, who were close to my age. He brought me a photo album of his grandchildren. He sighed when he saw a picture of his Ruth holding one of his daughter's babies.

After we rinsed the dishes, we talked about Celeste Daniels.

"A gifted student, Celeste Daniels was in my first-year Latin class," he said. "Smart and unafraid to show it. She reminded me of Katherine Hepburn—very athletic, sort of a tomboy, but still the boys were attracted to her. She bedeviled them on a regular basis though quite unintentionally."

Solomon had taught both at Catholic and Booker T. Washington. Later he became the dean of students at Washington, before becoming the principal of the school. But in the early 1970s he worked part-time at both schools. When Dare called him about Bo Hines, Mr. Solomon remembered a link between Hines and Wittman that predated Bo marrying Sue.

"Celeste liked both boys. I think she was drawn to athletes like herself," he said. "I taught both Bo and Jace. Neither of them was as good a student as Celeste. Bo worked hard but didn't have the brain power. Jace had the brains but was too spoiled and lazy."

"Did she date both at the same time?"

"Yes, sort of." He paused for a second, trying to remember something. With his eyes still shut, he said, "Ruth and I chaperoned the proms for both schools. Usually freshmen didn't go to those dances, at least not back then. Ruth felt Celeste did it to show off to her older brother and classmates. It was like winning a trophy for Celeste, or so my wife believed."

"How did Stan Daniels react to his baby sister dancing with his rival, Jace Wittman?"

"Stan Daniels had no rivals. He operated on a different level than everyone else, but he watched Hines and Wittman like a hawk, never letting Celeste out of his sight at either dance. Pretty and popular, she would have gone to both dances, even if Bo and Jace hadn't asked her. And, yes, Stan was so popular he had invitations to both dances, too."

I leaned over in the stiff chair, and it creaked. "Tell me about the day Celeste Daniels disappeared."

Mr. Solomon got up and walked over to the big bay window that overlooked his rose garden. I didn't want to rush him. Like the years and ghosts in his library, he would speak when he was ready. He touched a framed picture of Ruth in her wedding dress; she was smiling and radiant.

When he turned to face me, he said, "Ruth and I talked about that day often. Celeste had been distressed all week, asked to leave class several times. When she came back to the classroom, she had been crying. Something was wrong."

He paused and shut his eyes. "When she first disappeared, I thought she might have run off to get away from her overly protective mother. Ruth and I believed she would show back up in a few days with tales of a road trip to Panama City, Mobile, or Biloxi. There was even a report that she had been seen hitchhiking, but that later proved to not be true."

"How did Bo and Jace react?" I asked Mr. Solomon, who looked even smaller than when I first walked into his house.

He said, "Bo and his friends helped Stan and the Catholic High boys search for her. Jace walked around in a daze for a few days."

"Did you ever find out what was bothering her the week before she disappeared?"

He shook his head. "No, we talked about it some in the teachers' lounge, but we had no clue. The kids were pretty tight-lipped and didn't seem to know either."

"Did you talk with Mr. or Mrs. Daniels about Celeste?"

"I went to the principal, Sister Mary Thaddeus," he recalled. "She thought it best if we left the family alone and let the authorities deal with the matter. I think she worried it might reflect badly on Catholic High and hurt enrollment."

He walked around the library, glancing at the books, then stopped at the window. Outside, the day was bright and young and a tabby cat chased butterflies along the stone walk. His eyes filled with tears.

"The Daniels family fell apart when Celeste disappeared," he said. "Stan went to college and became a successful lawyer, but his parents were never the same. I left Catholic the following year. The tragedy had taken away from me the joy of teaching there. I dreaded walking the halls."

"But you remained a teacher," I said.

"I took a break and enrolled in the Masters in Educational Leadership program at the University of West Florida," he said. "Ruth's parents helped us make ends meet, and I worked part-time at the campus library."

He pointed to his framed diploma on a stand in the bookcase. "When I graduated, the Escambia County School District hired me as a dean at Booker T. Washington, which put me on the track to be the school's principal. I never taught in the classroom again."

Celeste Daniels's disappearance clearly ate at him, like it did her brother, Stan. Did it bother Hines and Wittman? The tabby cat pounced on the butterfly, crushing it. Mr. Solomon winced.

Thanking him for the lunch and the interview, I headed for the door.

"Would you ever be available to come speak to our book club?" asked Mr. Solomon as he shook my hand. "Caleb would be so happy to meet you. You can talk about whatever you like."

"Sure, it would be an honor," I replied, thinking, *if I'm not in jail.*

31

While I visited with Mr. Solomon, a scheduled blog post went live:

BUZZ: HINES CASE TO GO TO TRIAL

Sources inside the courthouse tell the *Insider* the embezzlement trial of road contractor Bowman Hines is back on track, and the state attorney will be ready for trial in two weeks, despite earlier rumors it would be delayed for Hines to work out a plea agreement.

Assistant State Attorney Spencer wouldn't be happy. Neither would Hines. I should be in Bo's head right about now, which was exactly where I wanted to be.

I had left my cell phone in the car and missed another dozen calls from the usual cast: Dare, Gravy, Spencer, Hines' attorney, and a few numbers I didn't recognize. Several left voice messages, which I never intended to listen to.

I called Harden about Childs. He said, "My buddy found her early this morning in a coffee shop. When she heard that Hines was blaming her for the missing funds, she agreed to come meet with you. She should be on the road now and will be in Pensacola tonight."

"Where do I meet her?"

"O'Riley's on Creighton Road about nine o'clock," said Harden. "Do you want me to go with you?"

"I've got it. Thanks."

I checked my emails and saw the city clerk had the documents regarding the site work for the maritime park. That would be my next stop after I typed up my notes on meeting with Jacob Solomon.

Finding a table at the Whataburger near the Pensacola Bay Center, I wrote up what I recalled from the conversation. Remembering what I heard was never the issue, but not letting my slow typing skills hamper the flow of words and thoughts was often a problem.

Accessing the diner's Wi-Fi, I made another post to the blog, one that would further push my insane plan:

WHAT TROUBLED CELESTE DANIELS?

Friends of Celeste Daniels, who has been missing since 1973 and presumed dead, tell the *Insider* the teen was very upset in the days leading up to her disappearance. Why? No one has come forward with that information . . . yet.

At Pensacola City Hall, my reception was formal but not hostile. Florida had one of the most liberal public records laws in the country. All state, county, and municipal records were open for personal inspection and copying by any person. Some officials, like Sheriff Frost, tried to play games in releasing information, but in the end, they released just about anything you requested.

The bored security guard always enjoyed my visits. I broke up his day of leaning over the desk and flirting with the secretaries.

A secretary escorted me to a conference room where the proposals for the park project were stacked in neat piles, each about two inches thick. The only documents I wanted to read were those concerning Bo Hines' portion of the original bid. I found the scoring sheet on which the staff had given Hines high marks for his company's site preparation and infrastructure plan for the park. I reviewed the amendment from the development team dropping Hines Paving Company from their group after his arrest.

Since the maritime park site was on Pensacola Bay where a fuel storage facility once stood, the land had some serious environmental "challenges." The naysayers also complained about it being in the flood plain where it would be susceptible to hurricanes, so dirt had to be trucked in to raise the site fifteen feet. Those issues meant the site work was worth $9.5 million to Hines.

All the bidders listed their subcontractors. Reading through Hines' portion of the original proposal, I found $200,000 for JW Safety Consultants. I had never heard of the company. The bid gave a Pensacola post office box as the subcontractor's address. I paid for copies of the pages referring to Hines Paving Company and went to find a place to hide out until my meeting with Pandora Childs.

It was 3:58 p.m. The state attorney would figure out in a few minutes I was a no-show. He would have sheriff's deputies look for me downtown. My hideout needed to be in the open but away from the happy hour crowds.

I had a place for this: Five Sisters Blues Café.

Five Sisters sat in the old "colored downtown." The Jim Crow laws forced African American businesses and customers off Palafox Street to West Hill, which eventually became known as Belmont-DeVilliers.

The neighborhood's heyday was in the late 1920s and early 1930s during Prohibition when restaurants, stores, and pawnshops lined the streets and hot music thrived alongside the gambling, drinking, and prostitution. Whites mixed with blacks once the sun set, and the cops looked the other way as long as the payoffs were made.

Five Sisters Blues Café opened during the roaring twenties and had survived recessions, depressions, the Klan, Baptist churches, and the new wave of street thugs. The youngest sister's great grandson, Theodore Ware, had taken over the café around the time when I started the *Insider*. Theodore was so tall he had to duck through every doorway he entered. His callused hands swallowed up mine when we shook hands. His face always had a smile. When he wasn't smiling, you ran.

Theodore and I became friends when a deputy killed his uncle, Jericho Ware, in 2006 during a traffic stop. I refused to let the death go unnoticed. After a few more busted ribs, I exposed the bad guys. The deputy got off, but Theodore appreciated the effort.

I didn't visit Theodore at Five Sisters much because he wouldn't let me pay for anything. Today I needed to be in a place outside my regular hangouts that had an electrical outlet for my laptop and wireless internet service. Theodore would take care of me.

Five Sisters was slow on Thursday afternoons. An elderly black couple ate fried chicken, collard greens, black-eyed peas, and cornbread at a table by the door. Two well-dressed young white women drank white wine at the bar and texted on their cell phones more than they talked.

Every three minutes they shared their screens with each other, giggled, and sipped their wine. Joan Armatrading's "Love and Affection" filled the room.

Theodore was out, but his niece Maya put me at a corner table near the bar so I could keep an eye on the room. She brought me a bucket of four longneck Buds in ice and a basket of sweet potato chips.

"Uncle Theo says you don't pay, and I'm to keep the bucket full until you say otherwise," she said.

"No, I'll pay," I said, pulling a worn twenty out of my khakis.

"Put it away. My uncle won't even let us take a tip from you, Mr. Holmes." She spoke matter-of-factly without anger or rudeness. Her nails were painted pink with zebra stripes.

"Let me know if you want to eat," she added. "Fried chicken is the special."

Many people stopped by the Five Sisters just to pass the time. They asked Maya about her momma or her aunts. They would see them all in church on Sunday, but life never got so busy they couldn't inquire as to their daily welfare. It had always been this way in Belmont-DeVilliers.

Firing up my laptop, I checked my blog. The comments had piled up, awaiting moderation. I approved them all, even one from Hines' attorney stating he planned to file a lawsuit against me for defamation, libel, and anything else he could think up. My cell phone continued to vibrate in my pocket every few minutes. I ignored it.

The flat-screen TV over the bar broadcasted the local news without sound. Nobody paid attention—a good thing since the video showed the Save Our Pensacola protesters marching outside my office.

Assistant State Attorney Spencer was interviewed, too. The station displayed my photo in a small box in the upper right-hand corner. It was an old picture. I don't think they were announcing I had won a Pulitzer.

When I looked back to my laptop, a shadow crossed my table and Theodore Ware sat down across from me.

"Mr. Walker, did my niece take good care of you?" he inquired in a deep and gravelly voice, folding his huge hands on the table.

"Yes, Maya has given me everything I need," I said pointing to the half empty bucket of beer. "Please drop the mister and let me pay for the beer."

He ignored my request. "I saw the news report on the television in the kitchen."

I shrugged my shoulders. "Nothing I haven't handled before."

He affected a good-natured laugh, but it was affected. A huge man, with a gray beard and a weather-beaten brow, Theodore didn't smile. He asked, "Who cracked your skull?"

"Unhappy readers."

Theodore smiled finally. Shaking his massive head, he said, "You just can't stay out of trouble."

"Life isn't a popularity contest," I replied. "I'll be fine, just need some time to collect my thoughts before my next interview."

"And you need somewhere to hide out for a couple hours," he said as he waved for Maya to refill my bucket. Then he added to her, "Have the cook fix a big bowl of red beans and rice for Mr. Walker. Bring him a plate of collards and cornbread, too."

"Maya, I better switch to tea," I said. "I've got an important interview later."

Theodore nodded his approval. After Maya walked away, he said, "No one will mess with you here. Give me your keys, and I'll move your ragged-ass jeep behind back."

He came from a way of life that was good-natured but had to be practical. History had proven that both a laughing nature and prudence were necessary for survival.

"Thanks." I fished out my keys, more than a little relieved.

"Let's move you to my office off the kitchen. You can stay there as long as you need."

For the next few hours, I wrote, monitored the blog, and ignored my cell phone that vibrated repeatedly. Of course, the food was fantastic. I even sampled the fried chicken and apple cobbler. To keep myself from falling asleep, I reread the bid Hines gave the city for the maritime park.

I started searching on the internet for JW Safety Consultants. Nothing. None of the other proposals had listed a safety consultant. I googled the post office box and zip code. They were the same as the post office box used by Jace Wittman's real estate company. "JW" stood for Jace Wittman.

In Theodore's kitchen office, another huge flat-screen monitor hung on the wall. The screen displayed six boxes that showed different views of inside and outside of Five Sisters taken from the video surveillance system. While working on my laptop, I found myself occasionally glancing at the screen, checking on the parking lot, kitchen, dining area, the bar, hostess station, and cash register.

There was no sound. My phone vibrated. Gravy's number appeared on the screen. I didn't answer it. A few minutes later, Gravy texted.

"The state attorney has a warrant for your arrest," he wrote. "Where are you? I can come get you and maybe avoid you being booked if you come clean with them."

I replied, "I need until the morning. Tell Spencer I will call him later tonight."

"Too late for negotiations. Frost has the warrant and has men out looking for you. Being inside the city limits won't deter him."

Shit.

Gravy wrote, "Only if I can take you to Spencer within the hour do you have any chance."

I wrote, "I got this but thx."

I looked up to see two deputies walking into the restaurant. They appeared to be demanding to see Theodore. Their stances were combative and confrontational, which meant they must have found my car hidden behind the restaurant.

Outside, I saw another patrol car pull up, cutting off any chance of slipping out the back door. As I started to pack up my laptop, Maya rushed into the office.

"We need to get you in the tunnel," she said while pulling back a throw rug on the floor and opening a trapdoor that fit seamlessly into the wood floor. "Here's a flashlight. This leads to Miss Bonnie's house across the street. Uncle Theo wanted you to talk with her anyway about your story. She will let you use her car."

I didn't have any quips to fire back. All I could manage was a real "thank you" as she slammed the trapdoor behind me and I climbed down the ladder to the tunnel. I heard her moving chairs on top of the rug.

The tunnel was narrow, only about five feet wide. The floor was dirt and the walls cinder block. The flashlight shone just bright enough to see five yards in front of me. I expected a rat to run in front of me any minute. None did.

I had heard stories about how the Prohibition raids of Five Sisters seldom had any arrests of politicians. There were rumors of a tunnel, but I could never get Theo to admit to anything. He would only smile, grab me a beer, and ignore me like he never heard the question. I thought the tale was another Pensacola urban legend.

When I climbed up the ladder at the end of the tunnel and opened the trapdoor, I was in a food pantry. A little boy wearing a Lakers jersey sat at an island in the middle of the kitchen. He looked up from his bowl of tomato soup. Not saying a word, he motioned his head towards the living room.

A little woman sat on the edge of a worn couch. She wore a thin paisley robe over a white nightgown. Her skin was nearly translucent.

"Miss Bonnie, I'm Walker Holmes," I said awkwardly, as any man would do who had just walked out of a pantry. "Thank you for letting me use your tunnel."

"I know you." Waving a bony hand at me. "You're that crazy white man who owns that little paper that stirs up all that trouble," said Miss Bonnie. She gasped to catch her breath as she completed the sentence. "Don't ever smoke. I used my inhaler an hour ago and can't use it again for another two hours."

"Can I get you some water or anything?"

"You got a cigarette?" she cackled, coughed, and pointed for me to sit down in a worn armchair. "Nah! I'm just pulling your leg. That's Theo's grandson in the kitchen. His job is to make sure I don't smoke and only drink one glass of sherry before I go to bed. I pay the little hustler a dollar to get a second glass without him telling his grandfather. I think that boy has mo' money than any of us."

She sighed as she tried to get comfortable on the couch. "Don't ever get old, Mr. Holmes."

"Yes, ma'am," I said. Out her window, I saw the cruisers down the street. Checking my watch, I had a little less than an hour before I had to meet Pandora Childs.

"I'll let you use my car," she said. She'd caught her breath. Her voice steadied. "Theo thinks you're some kind of hero. Heroes are destroyed in this town. You know that, don't you?"

"Yes, ma'am."

She spoke her mind. She had earned the right. She shuffled on the sofa, looking around at first for something and then faced me.

"Why did they kill my baby?" she asked. I saw tears had run down her cheeks.

"Ma'am?"

"Why did they kill Sue, my baby?"

"Miss Bonnie, are you talking about Sue Hines?" I asked stunned.

She pulled out a crumpled tissue from the pocket of her robe and nodded her head as she wiped the tears.

"No one killed her, Miss Bonnie," I said, trying to be comforting.

"Those boys did it. As sure as you and I are sitting here, those boys killed my baby. I raised her from the crib until she married. Those boys might not have done the deed, but they drove her to it."

The "little hustler" peeked in from the kitchen. He brought her a box of Kleenex and some sherry in a juice glass.

I gave him a dollar as Miss Bonnie wanted me to do. He took it silently, expecting the bribe. I heard him turn on the television, the squeak of shoes and cheers from an NBA game came from the kitchen.

"My baby never forgot her Momma Bonnie. Bought me that TV in the other room. My Sue loved me."

"What boys are you talking about?" I tried not to sound too urgent. "Bo and Jace?"

She took a dainty sip of her sherry and savored it before she nodded her head.

"She was disgusted with both and that young girl. She didn't like Mr. Jace and Miss Julie moving into her home. The daddy ignored the girl, and she spent too much time with Mr. Bo," said Miss Bonnie.

After another sip, she said, "I'm thinking my Sue uncovered something, and the burden was too much for her to bear."

"What kind of something, Miss Bonnie?"

"I don't know." She shook her head. "My baby tried to love on the girl, but she wouldn't have none of it. Not healthy having a young girl running around the house dressed like they do now days."

"Ever see Mr. Hines do anything inappropriate?"

She shook her head. "I don't spend that much time in their house anymore. Mostly my Sue would stop by here every now and then."

"What do you know about Celeste Daniel?" I asked.

"White girl that died when them boys were in high school?"

It was my turn to nod.

"Oh. That was a bad time. Jace went off to live with some relative for the summer before he started college. Bo went to Europe with his grandparents. Germany, France, Spain, and other places I can't remember. Nobody ever wanted to talk about the Daniels girl."

Miss Bonnie finished her sherry. "It's time for me to sleep. The keys are by the back door. Don't race the engine. My fool nephew did that and flooded it. It's an old girl too, you know."

And with that, Miss Bonnie shut her eyes. I'd been dismissed.

When I got to O'Riley's Pub, Navy and Marine pilots packed the place, attracting an assortment of women trying to attract their attention. Half a dozen or so University of West Florida coeds were celebrating a friend's acceptance into graduate school. Their designated driver, a freshman in their sorority, sipped a coke through a straw. Two Marines were begging them to try Fireball shots.

A few older women, most likely nurses from nearby West Florida Hospital, were dressed in jeans and tight tops and drank bourbon and cokes at the bar. They toasted their babysitters and shouted to the Marines that they liked Fireballs.

It was karaoke night and a DJ was passing out black binders to the tables. I already knew what to expect. Most of the guys would pick country songs because they could kind of talk their way through them. I knew I would hear Garth Brooks' "The Dance" at least seven times in the next two hours if I hung around the place. The women would choose Pink or Miranda Lambert. When they got really drunk, it would be "Wild Thang."

I ordered a Bud Light to be sociable, kept an eye on the door, and fought off the urge to drive my pen through my eardrums. While nursing my beer and listening to a sailor do Johnny Cash's "I Walked the Line," a text came across my phone: "This is Pandora. Come out to the parking lot."

She must have been spooked. Either that or she hated Garth Brooks. When I walked out, a set of car lights flashed near the edge of the parking lot. I saw her silhouette in the front seat. This was getting a little ridiculous, I thought as I headed her way.

My cell vibrated again. This time Jim Harden texted, "Childs found dead this morning in Tenn. Condo owned by Hines."

I felt a thud on my skull. As I passed out, I thought, *There went my stitches.*

32

Slap. "Wake up."
        Slap. "Wake up."
    Slap.

A male voice crept into my head, vaguely familiar, but I couldn't focus enough to connect a name to it. Each hit was a little harder. Trying to will my eyes open, I braced myself for the big one. He didn't disappoint me.

Shaking my head, I opened my eyes to find Jace Wittman looming over me, all sixty-six inches. He didn't put his weight behind the slaps, thank God. To him, they were light taps, but my head begged to differ. I caught a whiff of diesel fuel. The room swayed as it came into focus. I was on a boat.

Ropes bound me to a metal chair in the middle of a cabin on Hines' Sea Ray Sundancer 400, on which we had celebrated his Patron of Florida Culture award six months earlier. My chest, arms, and legs were strapped tightly. My ribs screamed for relief. I couldn't clear my head.

A small female form sat on a white row of cushions to my left near the glass door that opened to the stern. By her sat a man with a tall glass in his right hand and his left arm around the girl.

"Please, that's enough, Daddy," said a young voice coming from the couch. Julie Wittman's bright red hair came into focus. Neither alarmed or frightened, she sounded very unemotional. Was she medicated or drunk?

"Yeah, Jace, I think you have Mr. Holmes attention," said Bo.

The boat rocked, forcing me to swallow Five Sisters' red beans and rice that wanted desperately to reappear. The bile burned my throat.

"You don't look so good," said Jace chuckling. With his face inches from mine, I smelled bourbon on his breath. Fighting the urge to vomit and still trying to clear my head, I assessed my predicament. The boat was drifting. We were the only four people on it. Hines had a pistol on his lap. I steeled myself and looked into Wittman's eyes.

I smiled and said, "Beep."

He backhanded me, toppling the chair. I hadn't moved my head quick enough to dodge the blow. I felt his ring rip my cheek and saw stars and maybe a few planets. He said, "You think this is funny, you son of a bitch?"

Blood ran down my cheek. My eyes teared from the pain. I didn't say a word, not sure how my voice would sound.

Bo handed Julie the handgun and helped his brother-in-law right the chair. I smiled again.

"Jace, calm down. Mr. Holmes wants to get your goat," Bo said. "We have things to discuss with him."

Red-faced, Wittman jabbed a finger in my chest. I couldn't avoid wincing.

"I hate this prick," he said. "He never lets up."

"That's what you like to hear, isn't it, Walker?" said Bo as Jace retrieved his drink from somewhere behind me. "You love being in people's heads, don't you?"

"I wrote with no malice towards you or your brother-in-law," I said, hoping my voice sounded steady. My Mississippi drawl became more pronounced when under pressure, which gave each word an extra syllable. "I hate his politics, not him."

"I am my politics," Wittman yelled. "Dammit, don't you understand anything?"

"Why are we here?" I said, looking at my bonds. "Isn't this a little overkill, Bo?"

He shrugged his shoulders. "Maybe."

"What is this about?" I said.

Jace moved to sit on the white couch on my right. I was positioned on the wooden deck between them. The moon reflected on the Gulf in the row of windows behind his head. Wittman's belligerence had waned, replaced with smugness.

He said, "Your newspaper is sinking fast. Your advertisers are bailing. You've bounced checks with your staff and vendors. Your shareholders are ready to cut their losses. Next week, your bank is going to call in your loan."

"Nothing new, been there before," I said, not sure how confident I sounded.

"We can make it all go away."

"How?"

Hines said, "You move on to another story. Let the petition drive run its course without any interference—"

Jace added, "Who gives a shit about a Yankee and his baseball team?"

They were tag-teaming me, forcing me to turn my head back and forth as if I was watching a tennis match. I heard my brain rattle with each swivel.

Stringing them along, I said, "What's in it for me?"

Hines flashed his winning smile and said, "New advertisers and money to pay off your vendors and the bank. Consider it a gift that the IRS won't ever discover."

Maybe I should have told them that I needed time to think about their offer, but I couldn't avoid asking, "What about the Arts Council trial?"

Hines' smile froze. "My lawyers are cutting a deal with the state attorney. I'm providing testimony against Pandora Childs, the real thief."

"But Childs is dead," I said.

His eyes bore down on me, willing me to shut up.

"What?" asked Wittman. "When? Where? We had no idea where the bitch was hiding."

"No details. You slugged me before I could follow up on a text."

Wittman pulled my phone out of his windbreaker. "What's your password?"

I gave him the password. It wasn't the time to worry about my privacy.

When I did, Jace read Harden's text and put the phone back in his pocket. He took a big swallow of his drink. "Bo, you said she probably was hiding out in the Bahamas or some other Caribbean island."

He slurred the word "Caribbean."

I said, "Not hardly."

"Shut up!" said Hines, backhanding me. Somehow the chair didn't topple over. Through sheer will power, I kept it upright.

He said to his brother-in-law, "He's lying, Jace. Trying to pit us against each other."

Wiping his eyes and running his hands through his thick hair, Wittman said, "The bastard is just screwing with us. Right, Bo?"

I tasted the blood running from my nose. The metallic flavor pushed me to continue. I spit it out.

"Jace, why do you think I was at O'Riley's?" I asked. "I was there to meet Childs. I got a text from—"

"I said shut up!" shouted Hines. He hit me with his fist, knocking the chair over. I lost consciousness.

When I awoke, I was on my side still tied to the damn chair. I heard Hines and Wittman yelling at each other outside. Their words were indecipherable through the glass door.

Julie Wittman sat on the couch. The gun was lying in the fifteen-year-old's lap.

"Help me," I whispered. "Untie these ropes."

At first, she pretended not to hear me, but I kept repeating, "Help me."

Julie stared ahead, looking over me out the windows, not at me. She mumbled something.

"What?" I asked. "Please help me."

"Bo would be mad at me," she said.

"Your Uncle Bo and father are in big trouble," I said. "I can save them from themselves before it's too late."

She looked at me, waved the gun in my direction. "Bo would be mad at me."

I tried to scoot across the floor and maybe loosen the ropes. They began to give a little. Hines and Wittman entered the cabin as I almost freed my left hand.

Laughing Hines said, "Well, what do we have here? Trying to escape, Holmes?"

"Uncle Bo, he asked me to untie his ropes," said Julie.

"Good girl," he said and kicked the back of my chair. A wave of pain racked my chest.

Jace straightened the chair and untied the ropes. Bo took the gun from Julie and pointed it at me. I rubbed my wrists, coaxing the circulation back into my hands. I reached up and felt the stitches on my head. Thankfully they were still intact. I wiped the blood off my cheek, nose, and lips with my sleeve. Then I looked at the scarlet streaks on my white shirt.

I smiled again. The hell with these beatings.

"Julie, bring Mr. Holmes a washcloth with some ice," said Hines. "We're not savages, Walker. All of this is a misunderstanding."

Bo matched my smile, but his didn't reach his eyes. They were reptilian. He wanted me to think that he would let me go soon. Maybe he even convinced Jace that was what he would do.

When she returned with ice wrapped in the washcloth, I applied it to my nose and upper lip. Jace sat quietly, drinking his bourbon with a blank stare. Again, I was caught between them. Other than the moon's reflection, I could see no other lights outside.

Bo began to spin his tale. "Sue and I gave Pandora keys to our condo months ago. She wanted to take her nephews to Dollywood. She must have made copies before she returned them."

"What about her meeting me at O'Riley's?" I asked.

Jace said, "We don't know anything about that. Bo said you hung around O'Riley's on Friday nights. We sent Julie inside. When she spotted you, Bo texted you. I hit you when you came out."

I bit my tongue, seeing the glaring hole in the story. How did Bo Hines obtain Childs' cell phone? Wittman was too smart not to see it, but he was drunk. I needed to keep Jace engaged in conversation and keep him from passing out if I was to have any chance. He wouldn't want his daughter to witness a murder. Hines didn't seem to care.

"Why kidnap me?"

Wittman couldn't remember. He looked at his brother-in-law.

"We haven't kidnapped you," Bo said smiling again. "We needed your undivided attention so you would understand our offer."

"Why tie me up? Why the beatings?"

Jace said, "Tying you up was Bo's idea. You provoked the beatings. Those are on you."

My nose had stopped bleeding. I had to keep them talking.

"How about a drink of water?" I asked.

Bo said, "Julie, bring Mr. Holmes a glass of water."

After she left the room, I said, "Jace, you don't want her to see all this. Do you?"

Bo answered before his brother-in-law. "My niece knows how to keep her mouth shut. She needs to learn how the business world works, how deals are negotiated."

After Julie handed me the glass, Hines squeezed her leg as she sat down beside him. He still had the gun pointed at me.

I asked, "Why tonight? Why not wait until you finalized your deal with the state attorney?"

Jace found his voice again. The alcohol had dulled his cognitive abilities, but he was shaking it off, like a bear waking from hibernation.

"When the porn bust hit, Bo said it was the perfect time to grab you because everyone else would be distracted," he said. "If anything happened to you, people would think it was connected to your reporting on a child porn network."

I said, "But nothing is going to happen to me, right? You and Bo just want to talk to me."

"You always have to be prepared, Walker," said Bo as he got up and stood over me.

"We aren't going to start with the hitting again, are we?" I said. "As hard as it may be to believe, I'm not a fan of getting my ass kicked."

Julie giggled.

"This is all your fault," said Hines to me. His reptilian eyes had returned. The bourbon on his breath was overpowering. "You brought all this upon yourself."

He made two drinks and traded Julie a bourbon and Diet Coke for the gun. He put his arm around the teenager and kept the handgun on his lap. She didn't pull away, and Jace ignored them.

"Which one of you got Celeste Daniels pregnant?" I asked. It was a jump, but maybe it would buy me some time. The longer I dragged this out, the better my chances for survival.

Jace bolted up, spilled his drink, and rushed toward me. I grabbed his wrist before his punch connected with my chin. "I said no more hitting."

He wrestled his arm away, picked up his red Solo Cup, and went to the bar. I started to stand.

Bo said, "Sit back down, Walker. We're still negotiating."

He squeezed Julie. "You wouldn't want to deprive my niece of her education?"

I sat down, not taking my eyes off Hines.

"My guess, the baby was yours."

Wittman started laughing. "You really are clueless," he said. "Bo's impotent, shoots nothing but blanks."

Bo said, "Be quiet, Jace."

Jace continued to laugh. "He can't get anyone pregnant. Not Celeste, not Sue."

"Be quiet," Bo repeated.

I said, "So, you're the father?"

Jace stopped laughing. I had hit a tender wound. Instead of striking me, tears filled his eyes.

"Yes," Wittman said. "I loved her, really loved her. Everybody thought I dated her to hurt Stan, but she was special."

He continued, "We kept it from her family, but I couldn't keep secrets from my mother. She demanded Celeste get an abortion, even offered to pay for it. Celeste and I wanted to marry and move to Mobile or Birmingham."

Bo tried again to stop his brother-in-law. "Is this the kind of tale you need to discuss in front of your daughter?"

I needed Wittman to continue talking. I asked, "Why didn't you go ahead with your plans?"

With a tear running down his cheek, he said, "We were supposed to meet with her parents. We needed their permission to marry. I waited for her after school at the Burger King outside of Town and Country Plaza so we could rehearse our speeches, but she never showed."

I said, "Why didn't you tell this to the police?"

Wittman said, "I wanted to, but my mother told me to keep my mouth shut. It wouldn't have changed anything. I didn't know where Celeste was. The police would suspect I killed her and I would lose my college scholarship. I was a coward."

"That's enough ancient history," said Hines. "Jace, you're working yourself up. Let's review our offer to Mr. Holmes. He stops writing. Your petition halts the park, and he saves his newspaper. Win-win-win."

"How was she supposed to get to the mall?" I asked Wittman.

"Bo was supposed to give her a ride."

Hines said, "I waited outside Catholic High for about an hour. She never showed up. I assumed she had found another ride."

Jace said, "I went home, too afraid to call her house. I didn't learn she had disappeared until the next day."

Hines said, "We searched everywhere. Remember, Jace, how we talked to all her friends, visited her favorite spots. We got nowhere."

"Yeah, we did," said Jace.

Another thought popped into my head. "Jace, why did you start the petition? Was it because you needed the contract rebid so your consulting company would make money?"

"Walker, what's with all the questions?" asked Hines.

"Humor me. I'm a journalist." I said, finishing my glass of water. I tried to scan the room without being too obvious. The cabin was too clean, too tidy. Nothing to grab for a weapon.

Hines said, "I was going to make a lot of money on that maritime park. I cut Jace into the deal at Sue's suggestion to help him pay his late wife's remaining medical bills. She also wanted them out of the house."

Julie mumbled, "Aunt Sue never liked me."

"You fucked everything up with your Arts Council story," said Hines as his voice got louder with each word. He pointed the gun at my chest. "You wouldn't leave it alone. You had to take me down."

"You stole the money," I said staring down the barrel of the gun.

"Shit, I was going to pay it back once I could draw on the city contract," he said. "You had to hurt me. You were jealous of my success."

I shook my head. "Bo, people lost their jobs, paychecks bounced, and performances were cut because you stole the grant money."

He began to shake his head. "No, no."

I said, "You supported the petition drive because you wanted the city to cancel the construction contract and rebid the work. You didn't care about the maritime park, but you and Jace wanted the money."

"You can't prove it," Hines said. "You can't prove I stole from the Arts Council either. No one can."

I said, "No one can because you killed Pandora Childs."

At the corner of my eye, I noticed Wittman had raised his head. I had his attention.

"Again, no proof," Bo said, dismissing me with a wave of his hand.

I said, "There will be records, evidence tying you to the money and her death."

Laughing Hines said, "This ain't my first rodeo. You aren't that smart, Holmes."

Looking at Jace and then back to him, I asked, "What are you talking about? First rodeo? Have you killed before?"

Hines smiled and took a big sip of his drink.

Jace asked, "What are you talking about Bo?"

Hines said, "Shut up, Jace."

"He killed Celeste Daniels," I said and decided to push it. "He was jealous of your relationship with her. He couldn't stand Celeste loving someone else more than him."

Hines jumped up and pressed the gun against my chest. My ribs throbbed. I gasped and held back a scream.

"Enough of your shit," he said. "I could blow you away, dump your corpse into the Gulf. No one would ever miss you."

Gritting my teeth, I said, "My dog would."

Julie giggled again. I had forgotten she was in the room.

Hines shoved the gun into my rib cage one more time. The chair tilted back and my feet were off the floor. He liked to see me wince. Getting that pleasure satisfied his bloodlust for the moment. He went back to the couch, set down the gun between his niece and himself, and began to drink. He was relaxed, in control, and completely enjoying himself.

He said, "Again, you have no proof, not even a body."

Jace stood. A storm had come up, and the boat began to rock more forcefully. Swaying, Wittman fought to keep his balance. He was also trying to clear his head.

"You killed Celeste?" he shouted at his brother-in-law.

"Of course not. Holmes wants to set us against each other. Mess with our heads. He wants to be let go."

Wittman said, "But that's what we agreed to do. Scare him, get him to back off, and put him back on shore."

"Yes, Jace. Sit back down, rest. I'll crank up the boat in a few minutes, and we'll go to the marina. Promise."

I said, "Jace, he's going to kill me like he murdered Celeste Daniels and Pandora Childs. He may have even poisoned Sue."

Hines charged me and hit me so hard that I fell off the chair. He began to kick me repeatedly. He picked the chair up, held it high and took aim for my head. Wittman crashed into him, knocking him against the glass door.

"Stop it, stop it," shouted Wittman. He was bigger than Hines by four inches and twenty pounds.

Hines let go of the chair. He had his hands on his knees and was breathing heavily. So was Wittman. The two aging, one-time high school athletes were like a couple of old lions fighting over an antelope's carcass.

Jace said, "Holmes, you found the suicide note. We all know Sue killed herself."

My left eye was nearly swollen shut. I struggled to keep consciousness. My brain was shutting down. "What was the secret?" I rasped.

A soft voice spoke. Julie Wittman said, "I am."

Jace charged Bo. A gun fired, and I blacked out.

33

When I woke, my pulse was radiating throughout my body. My head ached with each beat. I took short breaths to get relief from the piercing pain in my chest. The left side of my face was numb. I couldn't hear out of that ear.

I slowly pulled myself up to a sitting position. The storm had passed, and the sea was calm again.

Bo sat across from me, propped up against the glass door with a web of cracks behind his head. Somehow it hadn't shattered.

Bo's eyes were open but had no life. Dark red blood emanated from a hole in his chest and covered his Pensacola Country Club white polo. Blood had puddled under him.

Jace and Julie Wittman held each other on the couch. The father stroked the hair of the sobbing girl. The gun was lying on the floor near their feet.

"How . . . how long have I been out?" I asked.

"Not sure, maybe an hour," said Jace. His bravado had evaporated. He sounded sober.

"Julie shot Bo when I went at him," he said. "She was defending me."

Julie took her head off her father's shoulder. "But I didn't think," she said. "I didn't mean to. I just pulled the trigger, and he fell."

"Hush, angel, you did what you had to do," Wittman said.

But I sensed Julie wanted to talk. No, she needed to talk.

"Julie, what did you mean when you said you were the secret," I asked.

Jace warned, "Holmes, this isn't the time or place for your investigative reporting. Leave her—"

Julie shouted over her father. "I want you to understand."

Jace shut his eyes. He didn't want to hear this but wouldn't stop her.

"At first Uncle Bo was fun to be around," she continued. "He wanted to hear about my day, listened to my stories. Like he didn't cut me off or tune me out. It seemed like he really cared, you know."

I nodded to encourage her to continue talking. I didn't want to interrupt her.

"I really looked forward to seeing him. I loved his hugging me, the smell of his cologne—he was so funny . . ."

Tears ran down Wittman's cheeks.

"Daddy, you were away a lot and Aunt Sue went to sleep early. Uncle Bo would watch movies with me. I stretched out on the sofa, and he sat next to me. Then one night, he turned out the lights, and soon he was lying down behind me."

She talked as if she were describing a scene in a movie. "He put his hand underneath my shirt and began to touch my breasts."

Jace clenched his fists.

"I didn't know what to do," said Julie, who cried softly as she told how her uncle then began visiting her bedroom. She said Hines would talk to her about their "strong connection."

"I was afraid," she said. "But he made me feel important and I really liked him."

"And your aunt found out?" I asked.

She nodded. "I think so."

Julie burrowed into her father's shoulder and started sobbing again.

After a third attempt to get up from the floor, I stood.

Jace asked, "What are we going to do? I can't let my daughter suffer through the humiliation of a trial. I can't."

He was crying, too. "I've been so stupid," he said shaking his head. "Right under my nose."

"Grudges," I whispered to myself.

"What?" asked Jace.

"Nothing. Where's my cell phone?"

He pointed to his windbreaker on the counter near the bar. "It's in my pocket," he said. "What in the hell are you going to do?"

The phone had a signal, but the battery was low. I dialed Gravy.

"Walker, where are you?" he asked. "Childs is dead. Harden has looked for you everywhere."

"I'm on a boat with Jace Wittman and his daughter."

"What?"

"Gravy, be quiet and listen. I've killed Bo Hines."

"Shit."

"It was self-defense," I said and looked at the Wittmans. Jace nodded his head. "Have police and EMS meet us at Palafox Pier."

"Are you hurt?"

My phone died.

"Anyone else have a phone?" I asked, but their phones had lost their charge, too.

"Okay, we need to get back to Pensacola," I said. "But first, Julie, you must scrub your hands with the strongest soap on this boat. We've got to get as much powder residue off as possible."

Jace said, "Won't they still detect it?"

"This isn't CSI," I said. "I'm giving them a better target."

I picked up the gun. It was heavier than I thought. "Jace, go below with Julie. I'll start the engines, but you may still hear a gunshot. It's me putting another bullet in him."

"But I deserve to go to jail," Julie said.

"No one is going to jail. We were having a friendly discussion. Bo became enraged and started beating me. Jace, you tried to stop him, and Bo knocked you unconscious. He pulled the gun. I wrestled with him and the gun fired twice killing him."

Holding his daughter tightly, Jace agreed. "Julie, we can make it work. We've got about a thirty-minute ride. We can get our stories together."

After they had gone below, I started the engine and fired the gun. The glass door behind Hines shattered from the additional force. The motors drowned out the noise. I draped a blanket over Hines' corpse and called for the Wittmans to come back.

I was in no shape to steer the Sundancer. My equilibrium was shot, making it hard to stand.

"You need to lay down," Jace said. "You're bleeding."

Julie was worn out, but she wouldn't leave her father's side. Behind them, the sun began to peek over the horizon.

Jace said, "Let's take you downstairs and put you on one of the beds."

"But we need to get our alibis straight."

"Julie and I will handle our end," Jace said.

They placed me on a bed in the bow of the Sundancer and used pillows to keep me from rolling off. I tried to work out what I would tell the police at the dock, but I only got to "Bo beat the crap out of me . . ." before I passed out.

"Mr. Holmes?"

I opened my right eye and saw a female police officer standing over me.

"Can you get up?"

I shook my head. "I want my attorney."

Her bulletproof vest made her look like one of the Teletubbies, but I couldn't remember there being a blue one. Maybe she was a Care Bear.

She said, "Your attorney is on the dock. The paramedics are going to take you off the boat and check you out."

"I can walk with some help," I said. My voice was hoarse.

"Good thing," I heard a male voice say from the deck. "There's no way in hell we can get a stretcher down there."

Slowly, painfully, they walked me up the curved steps, past Hines' body and helped me off the boat. They lifted me onto a gurney on the Palafox Pier dock.

Gravy appeared at my side. He whispered, "My God, Walker, what happened?"

"Hines attacked me . . . his gun went off," I said.

A crime scene technician stopped the EMTs before they put me in the ambulance.

"We need to swab his hands," she said.

"No," said Gravy. "Not without a warrant."

A thin man in a blue windbreaker came to the technician's aid. "Is there a problem here, counselor?" he asked.

Gravy apparently knew the man. He must have been with either the police or state attorney's office. Gravy said, "Jack, my client needs to get to the hospital. I'm not letting your guys maul him. Clearly he's a victim here, not a suspect."

Jack said, "We have sufficient probable cause to swab Mr. Holmes' hands. You know that, Gravy."

"No, it's fine," I said giving Gravy a slight nod. "Let's get it over with."

He said, "This is over my objection, but he's the client."

I noticed a young, sandy-haired man talking with Jace and Julie Wittman away from the police officers.

"Who's that?" I said nodding in their direction.

Gravy said, "Charlie Wilbrant, an attorney friend. I suspected Wittman might need representation. Don't worry; it helps us."

While the tech swabbed my hands for gun powder residue, Gravy conferred with the head EMT, police investigator, and Clark Spencer. I hadn't noticed him earlier.

Gravy returned. "They are taking you to Sacred Heart Hospital. You need to be fully checked out. They will keep you overnight."

"Just get me home," I said.

"Listen. The police and state attorney's office will leave you alone while you're under the care of a doctor at the hospital," said Gravy. "I've agreed to have you at the state attorney's office at 10:00 a.m. on Monday."

"It was self-defense—" I started to say.

"Stop, no more talking," he interrupted. "Tell the doctors and nurses about your injuries, but say nothing else. You understand?"

I nodded.

"I'll see you at the hospital," he said as they hoisted me into the ambulance. "Don't say a fucking word."

The next eighteen hours were a blur of x-rays, shots, and stitches. I threatened to strangle a male nurse when he tried to insert a catheter. I won that battle.

I remember seeing a different person sitting in my room reading the same copy of *People* magazine every time I opened my eyes. Gravy, Mal, Summer, Jeremy, Theodore, Bree, and even Tiny took turns in the chair. The only ones from the *Insider* missing were Big Boy and Yoste, who had taken time off to work as deckhand on a charter boat in Destin and was oblivious to my status. Summer told me that Dare was taking care of the dog.

"She visited you once while you were sleeping but couldn't stand to see how badly you were injured," said Summer. "Watching over Big Boy is her contribution to your recovery."

I dreamed Mari visited me. She sat in the chair with her legs folded under her. Her long brown hair draped over her shoulders and a red Hotty Toddy T-shirt. I could smell her. She smiled.

Oddly I wasn't shocked that she was visiting me. Mari was never far away, always waiting to reappear and make me face my past. I tried to keep the guilt in a box in the corner of my mind, but my memory refused to be restrained.

The police never found her killer. Campus security discovered her nude body in the woods behind the Tad Smith Coliseum near fraternity row. They first questioned me, but I had plenty of witnesses that verified where I was. Later forensics found the attacker had red hair, which kept me off their suspect list permanently.

I cried and sat with the Gaudet family at her funeral. I almost dropped out of Ole Miss. Everywhere I went on campus and in Oxford reminded me of Mari. I contemplated suicide. Dare stood by me and refused to let me give up.

But I knew that Mari's death was my fault. I should have been at the crisis center to pick her up. The damn story wasn't more important than her. It was my dark secret, something I never said aloud or admitted to anyone—not to Dare, Mari's parents, or my priest.

I became a journalist to prove, in some weird way, that Mari's death wasn't in vain. I pushed myself hard, did the dangerous, impossible investigative pieces to show her I was a great writer and could save the world, even though I couldn't save her.

My editors speculated I had a death wish. Maybe they were right. No, that sounded nobler than it was. I had a dark secret that drove me to expose evil and corruption so I could find redemption.

I said, "Mari, I am so sorry."

She said, "I know. Walker . . ."

A shadow blocked my view of her. She was about to say something else. A nurse stood over me to take my temperature and pulse. When she left, Mari was gone.

34

Before I checked out of the hospital early Sunday afternoon, Gravy brought me the Sunday edition of the *Herald*. The headline read, "Holmes Kills Hines."

"We are going to sue the shit out of them for this," he said. Gravy was angry.

I laughed. "Well, it's true, sort of."

"I'm demanding a retraction," he said. "Dare has already threatened to pull all her advertising from them."

"No, we will demand the same placement when I'm cleared," I said.

"Why are you laughing?"

I said, "I don't know. Get me out of here and to a bar so we can talk."

At the End o' the Alley Bar in the Seville Quarter complex, we sat in the courtyard. We found a low, black cast iron table in the shade and got the waitress to turn a fan in our direction. Gravy had vodka and soda. Though I refused any pain medication that morning because I knew I would be sitting in a bar by the end of the day, I chose to ease myself back into drinking and ordered soda water with a lime.

I wore my Dodgers cap to hide my bandaged scalp and Ray-Bans to cover my black eye. I gave Gravy most of the story but decided not to mention Julie firing the gun. If I had to tell him, I would, but not yet.

Gravy said, "Wilbrant has advised his clients not to make a statement to police. The Wittmans aren't going to talk."

"Shit," I said. "I'll be arrested for murder."

Gravy took a sip of his drink and shook his head. "No, Charlie is doing exactly what I expected him to do. You will be free to tell your side of what happened without worrying about them contradicting you."

"What if the state attorney doesn't believe me?"

Gravy asked, "Have you seen yourself in a mirror? You're lucky you can walk."

He waved for the waitress to bring us some snack mix. Gravy continued, "The only bruises on Hines were on his fists from punching you. He had your blood on his shoes from the kicks he delivered to your ribs and back. He owned the gun. It doesn't take Jessica Fletcher or Hercule Poirot to solve this case."

He handed over the mix. It hurt to chew, but at least the nuts tasted better than green jello.

Leaning back in his chair, he said, "Spencer isn't going to push charging you."

"How can you be so sure?"

Gravy smiled, "Well, for one thing, Hines had the cell phone of the recently deceased Pandora Childs in his back pocket. The woman was found dead in his condo. If he ever had any doubts, our boy Spencer now knows that Bo ain't no hero."

The fog was lifting from my brain. I thought of dozens of holes in whatever story I gave the state attorney's office. I asked Gravy, "Isn't Spencer going to want to know how I got on the boat? About these rope burns on my wrists?" I pointed to the stitches on my cheek. "This was caused by Jace's ring."

The attorney shook his head and sighed. "I forget sometimes that you aren't from here. Pensacola likes neat, Walker. Always has, always will. Spencer doesn't want to run down a lot of rabbit trails. His boss will tell him to close the case and not cause Hines' grandparents any more pain."

"What about Frost?" I asked. "Couldn't he try to take over the investigation?"

"The *Herald's* headline calling you a murderer is all he wanted. Any investigation would only clear you." He took a sip of his beer. "No, the good sheriff thinks he has what he needs to dry up your advertising."

"So I'm worse off than before the shooting," I noted.

Gravy said, "Not so sure. You took a tremendous beating and walked away alive. Most people are impressed, and the old guard is a little scared of you. Not a bad combination for an alt-weekly publisher. The *Insider* won over many more supporters than Frost and Peck can pull away from you. Your next issue will fly off the stands, and advertisers will be begging to be in the newspaper."

He ordered another drink and looked at my injuries. "Damn, you must have driven him mad."

I didn't respond and looked off in the distance. The muscular bartender was reading the *Herald*. He looked in my direction. Recognizing me, he gave me a thumbs up.

I said, "So what do I say Monday?"

"Nothing until we get a use immunity agreement."

The pretty green-eyed waitress with long, blonde curly hair brought more beer to the table. "This Jack and coke is on Barry," she said motioning towards the bartender. "He said he's a fan. Are you someone famous?"

Gravy said, "Yes, he's an MMA fighter."

"Could I have your autograph?" she asked me.

I showed her my heavily-bandaged right hand. "Maybe another time."

Disappointed, she headed back to the bar. I heard Barry's laugh when she shared what had happened.

"What does 'use immunity' mean?"

"You can tell your story, and they can't use any of your words against you in court," said Gravy.

I said, "And they will believe it was self-defense."

"Yes."

Dare walked up as we were finishing. She had Big Boy with her. Wearing a yellow sundress and matching sandals, she sat down in between us. The dog licked my bandaged hand and sat down under the table next to my feet. His wagging tail tapped on my legs.

"I figured we would find you two in a bar," she said smiling. She asked the waitress to bring her a glass of Chardonnay and a bowl of water for Big Boy. I figured Gravy must have texted her our location.

"I'm heading out," Gravy said as he got up. "I'll have the bar keep the tab open for you."

He kissed Dare on the cheek and turned to me, "I'll pick you up for breakfast at eight and then take you to Spencer's office."

Dare asked Gravy, "Is he okay?"

"He's about as okay as Walker Holmes can ever be," he said.

Dare looked at me a long time before she said anything. "Take those sunglasses off," she said. "I want to see your eyes."

She winced when I dropped my disguise. "Oh, Walker, Bo did this to you?"

I nodded and looked away. The waitress was reading the *Herald* article. She played with her curls, and her lips moved as she scanned each word.

"Why?" asked Dare.

I lied to her, something I swore I would never do. I would tell part of the truth, but not all.

"Bo stole the money from the Arts Council. When he learned Childs might talk to me, he killed her and lured me on his boat," I said.

Dare was owed answers. It was my turn to be interrogated.

She said, "I don't understand why Jace and Julie were on the boat if Bo planned to kill you."

I said, "Hines had convinced his brother-in-law that they could negotiate with me and get me to back off."

"They should have known better," said Dare. "Why Julie?"

I lied, "I don't know. Too busy dodging fists."

She said, "And you killed Bo in self-defense."

"Yes, he waved the gun at me. I grabbed it, and it fired twice," I said. "It's a little hazy. The doctor says I have a concussion."

Dare nodded her head. She wanted more details but wouldn't get them from me.

"Bo was a murderer, Dare," I said. "I think he killed Celeste Daniels and Pandora Childs and would have killed me if he could have gotten Jace and Julie drunk enough to pass out."

She said, "Celeste Daniels? The cold case you wrote about on your blog?"

I nodded. "He all but admitted the girl's murder because she had dumped him, and his screwed-up ego couldn't handle rejection. As far as Childs, Gravy said the police found her cell phone on Hines' body. Plus, she died in his condo."

She asked, "Will all this come out?"

"Probably not, no evidence on the Daniels' murder and not enough to conclusively pin Childs' death on Hines."

She said, "Jace heard Bo. He could testify on your behalf."

"On the advice of legal counsel, the Wittmans aren't making statements." I really wanted to take a sip of the Jack and coke, but I finished off the last of my water instead. I tried to calculate in my head when I had taken my last pain pill and if it was too soon to drink alcohol.

"So, it's only your word on what happened," Dare said. She played with the snack mix, looking for almonds.

"Gravy told me that Pensacola likes neat."

Dare said, "This is a weird place, but I guess it's no different than most Southern towns."

We sat alone with our thoughts for several minutes. I tossed Big Boy a peanut.

"Some in this town will always see you as a killer, even if it's declared self-defense," said Dare. "They won't ever forgive you."

"Probably not," I said. The pain was a dull, distant roar.

The waitress didn't quite know how to deal with me, but she smiled when she brought us more snack mix.

"I read the newspaper. You killed a man, but Barry says they got it wrong that you're some kind of hero," she said, nodding towards the bartender.

"I'm not a hero," I said, reaching out my left hand. "I'm Walker Holmes, publisher of the *Insider*."

"I'm Heather," she said, shaking my hand.

After she left, Dare said, "You still have your fans."

I smiled, "Well, I'm kind of a big deal."

We laughed. Damn it felt good to laugh again.

Dare hesitated to ask her most important question. I didn't rush her.

She asked a different question instead. "Have you heard what Jace told the media?"

My stomach sank. Should I have trusted an enemy?

"No, what did Mr. Wittman say?" I asked.

"He refused to talk about the incident on the boat but announced that he and his daughter would be moving to Mobile, Alabama, as soon as the investigation was closed. He plans to enroll Julie in a preparatory school there," Dare said.

"And Save Our Pensacola and the referendum?"

"The television station found some old codger who said they would continue the fight," she said. "But without Jace's leadership and charisma and Bo's money the petition drive will fail."

A minor victory for me.

Dare still tried to gather the nerve to ask her question. She set her jaw and looked at me.

"What about Sue?" she asked.

"Though I can't prove it, I think Bo poisoned her," I said. "He stole the money and cheated on her with Childs. Sue probably found out and was going to leave him, so Hines arranged for her to overdose on her meds, most likely by mixing pills into her food."

Dare asked, "Did he tell you that?"

"Not directly, but when I called him out for it, he became even more enraged and pulled the gun on me."

She nodded her head several times, accepting my conclusion as she absentmindedly touched each of the pearls around her neck.

"Thank you," she said, wiping away a tear. "I'd hug you, but I would hurt you."

I smiled and reached out to touch her hand. "Thank you for believing in me."

"Do you need a ride?" she asked as she stood to leave.

"No, I'm going to sit here for a few minutes," I said. "The loft is only a block away. Big Boy will get me home."

"If not, please call me," Dare said as she kissed my right cheek, the one without stitches.

I put on my Ray-Bans and enjoyed the afternoon sun. In my head, I started to compose my cover story about the demise of Save Our Pensacola. Wittman would hardly be mentioned.

My phone vibrated. Bree texted, "How are you?"

I replied, "Alive."

"Where are you?"

"EOA."

"Want company?"

I finally took a sip of my drink and replied, "Oh, yeah."

ABOUT THE AUTHOR

photo by Barrett McClean, Barrett McClean Photography

RICK OUTZEN is the publisher and owner of *Pensacola Inweekly*, an alt-weekly newspaper that published its first issue on July 1, 1999. Six years later, he launched his blog, aptly named "Rick's Blog," that quickly became one of the most influential blogs in the state of Florida.

His reporting for the Daily Beast on the Billings murders, a double-homicide that garnered national attention, caught the attention of the *New York Times* that then profiled him and his blog. He was also featured on Dateline NBC's segment on the murders, "No Safe Place."

Rick also covered the BP oil spill for The Daily Beast, earning international attention for unraveling the oil company's spin on the disaster. He was interviewed by MSNBC, CNN, CBC-TV, and Al Jazeera English.

He was a finalist for the Sunshine State Awards for investigative reporting for his coverage of the failed turnaround effort of a middle school in the Escambia County Public School District.

Since 2003 Rick has been a regular contributor to *Ring of Fire Radio*, a show created by Robert Kennedy, Jr., and Mike Papantonio. The radio show was originally broadcast on Air America and is currently nationally syndicated.

In 2014 he self-published a digital book on his "Outtakes" columns: *I'm That Guy: Collected Columns of a Southern Journalist.*

Rick grew up in the Mississippi Delta and graduated magna cum laude from the University of Mississippi.

He and his family have lived in the Pensacola, Florida, area since 1982.